PRAISE FOR *THE VANISHING SKY*

"A poignant, sad, beautifully told new novel, a tale in which time and place shape a life and a family." —WBAI Radio (NYC)

"Written in purposefully even prose that is nonetheless harrowing, it's an intimate tragedy that's all the more powerful for refusing the ending we fervently hope for." —*The Daily Mail* (UK)

"The narration . . . deliver[s] the details of privation and fear as well surprising moments of kinship and generosity with an unforgettable grace . . . The future is unimaginable, Binder writes—and yet, somehow, those who are left will find a way to carry on. A masterful story of war, horror, and love." —*Kirkus Reviews*

"*The Vanishing Sky* reveals the German home front as I've never seen it in fiction . . . Binder tells her story patiently, like an artist placing tiny pieces into a mosaic; this literary novel isn't one to race through. But I find it gripping, powerful, and a brave narrative, unsparing in its honesty." —*Historical Novels Review*

"*The Vanishing Sky* reminded me a great deal of *All Quiet on the Western Front*. It isn't an easy book to read, but it's magnificent all the same." —*Seattle Book Review*

"This is a story—in all its rich layers—that dazzles, breaks your heart, clutches you, and gets you back up again." —Paul Yoon, author of *Run Me to Earth*

"[Binder] uses Etta Huber, a hausfrau in a rural village, as a means of feeling her way back into the past, channeling the anguish and uncertainty of the final months of the fighting." —*The New York Times Book Review*, Summer Reading Guide

"A moving tale of a family destroyed by war . . . Binder unfolds a harrowing tale in limpid, expressive prose." —*The Sunday Times* (UK)

"Eloquent, and painfully human." —*The Irish Examiner*

"An empathic portrayal of the human cost of war . . . Binder's etched prose, her unwillingness to whitewash complicity, and the focus on Etta, a mother trying to hold her family together as madness and horror descend, offers a genuinely tragic vision." —*The Sydney Morning Herald*

"There is not one false note. *The Vanishing Sky* is fully controlled storytelling that avoids cliché, even as its winter turns into spring, even as it recounts the final days of a war still being fought by those who barely understand why." —*The Anniston Star*

"Heartwarming and exciting . . . This book, along with movies such as *Hitler's SS, A Portrait of Evil*, and *Jojo Rabbit*, explains how the strands of hatred reached out and entrapped whole families in a web of evil." —*The Jerusalem Post*

"Binder's debut explores familiar territory from a fresh perspective. The result is an engrossing novel peopled by believable and sympathetic characters." —*The Sunday Mail*

"The novel has an unfussy, understated feel—reflected in Binder's calm prose—that belies its powerful impact. It's alternately subtle and striking, quiet, and then, suddenly, deafeningly loud." —*Country and Town House*

"There is a gentle melancholy throughout this novel, as if the author wished she could write something else, something happier, but was compelled to write this story. We should all be glad she did." —*Good Reading Magazine*

"*The Vanishing Sky* tells a tragic story, but it also serves as a meditation on tragedy and the everyday cruelty by which tragedy is so often begotten . . . A moving and worthwhile read . . . particularly relevant today." —*The Washington Independent Review of Books*

"Binder creates a believable, lost world with Etta and Georg. The ending is inevitable, and we are left with an overriding—and poignant—sense of loss." —*BookPage*

"A haunting portrait of a nation slowly collapsing." —*The New York Journal of Books*

"Unpretentious, poetic, and resonant storytelling . . . I loved this book." —Kassie Rose, book critic at WOSU Radio and the Longest Chapter

"Achingly beautiful . . . Binder's work is subtle and compassionate yet also clear and devastating in its depiction of a nation—and its people— suffocating under the weight of an insidious and inhuman ideology, one that ultimately devastates those who believe its illusions. Enduringly relevant." —*The Advertiser* (Australia)

# The Vanishing Sky

ALSO BY L. ANNETTE BINDER

*Rise*

# The Vanishing Sky

## A Novel

### L. Annette Binder

BLOOMSBURY PUBLISHING

NEW YORK · LONDON · OXFORD · NEW DELHI · SYDNEY

BLOOMSBURY PUBLISHING
Bloomsbury Publishing Inc.
1385 Broadway, New York, NY 10018, USA

BLOOMSBURY, BLOOMSBURY PUBLISHING, and the Diana logo are trademarks
of Bloomsbury Publishing Plc

First published in the United States 2020
This edition published 2021

ISBN: HB: 978-1-63557-467-8; PB: 978-1-63557-704-4; eBook: 978-1-63557-468-5

LIBRARY OF CONGRESS CATALOGING-IN-PUBLICATION DATA

Names: Binder, L. Annette, 1967– author.
Title: The vanishing sky / L. Annette Binder.
Description: New York : Bloomsbury Publishing, 2020.
Identifiers: LCCN 2019046034 | ISBN 9781635574678 (hardcover) |
ISBN 9781635574685 (ebook)
Subjects: LCSH: World War, 1939–1945—Germany—Fiction. |
GSAFD: Historical fiction.
Classification: LCC PS3602.I5245 V36 2020 | DDC 813/.6—dc23
LC record available at https://lccn.loc.gov/2019046034

2 4 6 8 10 9 7 5 3 1

Typeset by Westchester Publishing Services
Printed and bound in the U.S.A. by Berryville Graphics Inc., Berryville, Virginia

To find out more about our authors and books visit www.bloomsbury.com and
sign up for our newsletters.

Bloomsbury books may be purchased for business or promotional use.
For information on bulk purchases please contact Macmillan Corporate and
Premium Sales Department at specialmarkets@macmillan.com.

*In memory of my father*

*For my mother*
*and for David and Georgia Lee, the two brightest stars in my sky*

*Your country is desolate, your cities burned with fire.*

—ISAIAH 1:7

# 1

It was worry that made her fat. It made her fat even as it made other mothers thin. Etta shifted her weight, lifting first one foot and then the other. They had never bothered her before, but now they ached whenever she stood too long. Nothing to eat but cabbage and potatoes and soggy bread. No butter most weeks and no meat and the milk ran thin like water, and still she managed to gain weight. Josef hadn't said anything to her, not even when her finger outgrew her wedding ring and she began to wear the cherished gold band on a cord around her neck, but she caught him yesterday watching her during breakfast as she unfastened the top button of her skirt. She had turned away from him then, angry at herself for giving in to discomfort and at him, too, for noticing.

She turned the spigot. It was warm in the kitchen, and the windows ran rivulets from the steam. She washed the potatoes and peeled them, stopping every now and again to wipe her forehead. It had been two years since they'd all been together at the table. Two years since Max had left for the front, and now Georg was at the Hitler School, and there was no noise in the house and no laughter. Housework was her tonic. It was her company those afternoons when Josef went to drink his beer. She cleaned more now than she had when both her boys were home and making messes in their rooms. She washed their sheets every week and scrubbed their floors and took their feather comforters outside to pound them in the air. If work were prayer, then she was the most devout woman in Heidenfeld. Her house was cleaner than all the others, and she raked the leaves from her garden twice each day.

She brought the cabbage pot from its place in the cellar, down by the plums and the apples and the jelly jars. She'd braised the cabbage with peppercorns and apple slices and a dash of wine. The juniper berries had gone soft, and all the juices ran sweet. Just three more hours now, and Max would be back home. He'd sit down with them at the table, and she wouldn't press him to talk. She wouldn't ask him anything because boys needed rest when they came back. They needed time to get their bearings. Josef had grumbled when she brought him the letter. He'd lifted it high to the light and set it back down. "It makes no sense," he said, "it doesn't sound right," but she shushed him. "Don't ask why. Be glad," she told him, "be thankful he's coming home." She had washed Max's shirts already and ironed his pants with vinegar, and just this morning she'd scrubbed his window again so he could see the river from his chair. The house was almost ready. She hummed while she worked. She rattled the pot lids and took out the plates.

"Du, Etta," Josef called over the sound of the radio. "Stop your singing."

He was prickly today, but she paid him no mind. Mornings were hardest for him. He missed his classroom and his chalkboards and the students sitting at their desks. They had been nice enough about it, though everyone knew that he had started to forget things, basic things a teacher needed to know, and had taken to rapping the chalkboard with his walking stick. They had a party for him when he left and gave him a hammered silver crucifix, and the mayor came and spoke. The students were polite. They stood for him and clapped, and a few stayed late to help him pack. He didn't talk to her when he came home that day. He carried the boxes to his workshop and stacked them by the wall, and he labeled each one in his fine script. She stood by the door, and when he was done they walked together to the kitchen. The new teacher was less strict than Josef, Etta had heard, and even laughed in class, and the students loved her already. They didn't know about his forgetfulness and the fear it brought. They didn't understand, she thought, how could they?

He came without her calling. More than twenty-five years away from the army, and still he kept to his schedule. Lunch at twelve and dinner at six and to bed by half past nine. He looked at the stewpot when he sat down. The meat was from their friend Ilse, whose daughter had a farm up in the hills. "You take too much from her," he'd told her once when she came back with a package from Ilse. "We eat just fine with the tickets you get. Rationing hasn't hurt you any," and she sucked in her belly then. She tried to make herself small.

"It's for later," Etta told him, bringing him his plate with cabbage and blutwurst. The stew meat was for Max, who needed a good meal when he came home and not just blutwurst. Awful stuff, blutwurst, all blood and no sausage. She clasped her hands together. "Thank you, God," she said. "Thank you for our food and drink," and he began before she had finished. He emptied his plate and filled it again.

"It's almost time," Etta said. He'd spent the morning in Würzburg with the cousins. They lived in a flat on Semmelstrasse with a refrigerator and a telephone. They'd called the school secretary, who came running to let Etta know when he'd be coming. "God bless your boy," she'd told Etta, "I'm coming with good news," and now he was on the afternoon train and he was almost home.

"No need for us both to go." He dipped his bread in the sausage juices, working in circles around the plate.

"We'll walk together," she said. "It won't take but an hour." It was no good staying mad. It raised the bile. It was bad for his liver, but he wouldn't listen.

Josef stood up from the table. He hooked his thumbs beneath his waistband and hoisted up his pants. A moment later the radio came on in the living room, as high as it would go. It crackled and cleared, and the song began. They played the same songs one day after the next. Funny tunes that mocked the Amis and the British, and songs for the wives at home and marches, too, to speed things up. "*When the night mists churn*," Josef sang, "*to that lantern I'll return, to you, my Lili Marlene.*" He hit the low notes, and his voice quavered like a violin. He had a fine singing voice, and all those years smoking his pipe and breathing in chalk dust from his boards had only made it richer. They played "Lili Marlene" twice each morning and again in the evening. She knew that song and every mournful note, and when it began all the shadows lengthened in the house and her movements slowed.

Josef coughed when the song was done. He cleared his throat. The announcers came back on. She recognized their voices and the fine German they spoke, and she didn't want to listen. Soldiers were dying in the East and it was the younger boys who were being called now. They were leaving for towns and islands that she'd never heard of before. Novgorod and Viipuri and Szeged, Izyum and Tilsit and Vilna and others that were stranger still, and who knew what kind of names these were and what kind of places. The announcers stammered sometimes with the words. They struggled mightily. One of the generals came on next. He talked about East Prussia, how the Soviets had made it inside but not for long. No, the Germans were waiting for the right moment to push them back, and it was always a general who spoke or a government minister and never the Führer.

Josef was taking out his notebook now. He was reaching for his pen. She brought him apple juice and emptied his ashtray, and he didn't look up. He sat straight as a soldier in his favorite chair and wrote down what the general said. "What idiots. They're doing it all wrong." He wagged his finger at the radio as if it were one of his students.

For years he'd written in his journal, and even now he used a few sheets every day. He'd written about his brothers when they died, each of them in turn, with details of their memorial services and the condolence letters from their comrades and their friends, and when the war was done and he was the only child left to his parents, he wrote about the prices as they rose. In March of 1920, a bread roll weighed eighty grams and cost fifteen pfennig. He'd set the roll on Etta's kitchen scale just to be sure the baker was right. In August 1922, the same roll cost twenty marks, and by October the following year, the roll, a single roll, weighed only fifty grams and cost half a million marks. People carried their money in barrows and buckets and in burlap bags, hauling all those pounds of paper over the cobblestones and to the store. Might as well have burned the money and used it to warm the house, Etta thought then, might as well have tossed it into the river and watched it float away, but her Josef wrote the numbers down, and when she asked him why, he just shook his head. "Otherwise we'll forget," he told her. "Someone has to keep the prices." He wrote now while he listened to the radio. All those places where the fighting was, those faraway rivers and towns, and Josef sat there with his pen as if it were a tether and without it he'd be lost.

THE PEARLS WERE tight around Etta's neck, and still she put them on. Mutti had worn them every day, even when she worked in the garden or did the wash, and they'd gone yellow from sweat and her perfume.

She took them off early one morning, just took them off and set them in Etta's hand. "Take them," she said, "wear them and enjoy them." Etta should have been pleased at the gift, but something in Mutti's voice unsettled her. Etta gave her extra food after that, spreading the butter thick on her bread and dropping egg yolks and fructose into her wine.

"It's not too late," she told Josef. "Go get your jacket."

He ignored her. He set his hands on his knees and waited for the music to begin, and so she put on her coat and left alone. Let him sit there. Let him listen to the radio and work in his shop, she'd have no words of comfort for him later. More than two years since Max was gone and how many months since the last letter came, five, almost six, and Josef couldn't be bothered for a walk to the station. He'd go to the gasthaus and not to the station, not to say goodbye and not to greet them either when they came back. She shut the door too hard and scared away the crows that had gathered on her stoop. They hopped by her herb beds and bobbed their shiny heads, and they were back in their places before she'd even latched the gate. They brought cold weather, those birds; they brought storms. The ladies all knew. Winter's coming early, they told each other at the milk stand and down by the bridge. Better bring in the logs. Cover the herbs before it comes and cut back the roses.

She took the long way. She went along Lengfurter Strasse, past the old Nagel bakery, closed since their last boy died. He had died on an island and that's where he was buried, a Finnish island and nobody knew how to say its name. She passed the butcher shop and the Weinsteins' old shoe store, which was shuttered now and boarded shut. There were boats down by the dock, and men in rain gear worked the decks. Women ran by with their pitchers and their shopping bags. They took shelter in doorways and under store awnings, stomping their feet and closing their collars against the chill, but the wind blew the rain slantwise and soaked them where they stood.

The steps to the bridge were slick. She slipped twice and caught herself. She slowed a little. The houses across the river came into view, with their beams and their round chimneys. She stopped midway, between the third and the fourth arches. The river below foamed on its banks as if it were a living thing, and wisps of mist rose from it and disappeared into the rain. An umbrella was no use, not with the wind starting to pick up, and she set hers aside and held the rough stone railing with both her hands. She had seen the river every day of her life, and yet how beautiful it was, how beautiful the rain falling against that still surface.

She looked down at her hands, red now from the cold, and thought for a moment that the hands there were not her own, no, they were her mother's hands, chapped from work and crisscrossed with veins. How her mother, God rest her, had scolded her on rainy days. *Come on inside*, she'd say, *your feet are wet. You'll catch a cold this time, you'll catch a chill for sure*, but Etta didn't listen. She didn't listen to her mother and her boys didn't listen to her, and one day their children might give them trouble, too, and she'd laugh then.

A girl came skipping toward her from the other end of the bridge, her dark hair plastered against her head in snaky waves. She wore a red wool dress, and her legs were bare. The front of the girl's shoes had been cut open, leaving her toes to hang out on the pavement. Poor thing, Etta thought, not even a pair of knee socks to keep her warm. But the child didn't look sad, no, she looked the way Etta felt, happy to be walking alone in the rain. And though Etta had no idea why, she curtsied to the girl as she passed. The girl shot her a funny look, then smiled and curtsied back with that effortless grace only young girls have. "Good day, ma'am," she said. She kept walking as she spoke, going the way Etta had come, a red spot in the mist. Etta reached for her umbrella. There was much to be thankful for, even now.


THE LOHR TRAIN came early. It turned the corner at twenty past, and she leaned over the railing to see. She looked in all the windows. The soldiers came out first. One of them wore a sling around his arm, and his right eye was swollen shut. They weren't tall enough to be her Max, and their hair was blond and not dark, but she watched them anyway. She looked at every man who wore a uniform, afraid that she might not know him anymore. She might not know his face. The injured soldier went to his wife and son. The mother pushed her little boy by the shoulder, but he wailed at the stranger standing there. He looked at that swollen face and cried. She crouched low in her heels to clean his tear-streaked cheeks. "Come, my little man, say hello to your papa," she told him, but he would have none of it and latched his arms around her waist.

The old men came next, and a few schoolgirls from the gymnasium in Lohr who carried their books in satchels. The reunions were quick and quiet, muted hugs and handshakes and somber words of welcome and then the migration in clusters toward the door. Still no sign. She rubbed her hands together and stomped her feet. She was cold now that she wasn't moving. Her feet were wet from the walk, and water dripped from her scarf and the hem of her skirt. Josef should have come. When Georg came home, they'd both be at the station, and she wouldn't give him any peace if he tried to refuse. She'd follow him all through the house.

Max was the last passenger to come through the doors. He stepped down from the train and sheltered his eyes with his free hand. She dropped her umbrella, but she didn't reach for it. She pushed through the gate and went to him. He wore his dark hair longer than she remembered, and his coat hung loose from his shoulders. He's tired from the trip, she thought. He needs a meal at our table. He needs to sleep in his bed with clean pillows and his blanket and all the books he loves.

"Thank God," she said. "Thank God you're home." They'd sent him back to her when other boys were leaving, and she didn't need to know the reason. It was enough to see his face again. She drew him to her, and he didn't resist but he didn't embrace her either. He swayed a little in her arms. She pulled back and kissed both his cheeks. "You're warm," she said. She set her hand against his forehead. "I think you've got a fever."

He straightened, and for a moment his face went slack, unmoored, as if his skin had come loose from the muscles beneath. She saw it as she bent to lift his bag, that strange shadow that crossed his face, and it stopped her midmotion.

"I'm thirsty," he said. He looked at her with eyes she knew better than her own, or Josef's even, and he smiled.

"IT'S THE SAME," Max kept saying when they came to the house. "Everything's just the same." He went straight to the kitchen without taking off his shoes or his coat. He looked all around the room, at the wall bench with its faded green cushions and the pewter candlesticks and the wooden fork and spoon that hung on the wall. He turned the hourglass she kept by the counter and watched the sands fall through.

She knelt to check on the briquette. "Of course it's the same." She turned the knobs to raise the flame. He'd eat a warm meal tonight. They'd sit around the table, and he could have as much as he wanted, and she'd let him lick his plate for once. She wouldn't complain. He did it to rile her, even now that he was grown.

"Where's Tolly?" He was at the window. He pulled aside the curtain and looked out to the beds. "I don't see her."

Her hand slipped from the knob. She turned around to see him better. "You buried her, Max." Tolly had been their dog, a sweet lumbering shepherd who dug holes in the garden and ate all Etta's bulbs. "She's out under the trees."

"She's gone, is she?"

Etta pulled herself up. She took his coat and hung it to dry. She knelt by his feet and took off one shoe and then the other. He had always made odd jokes when he was tired. He was prone to fits of laughter. Josef would get impatient with him. "What's wrong with him?" he'd say. "Why can't he just be quiet, there's nothing funny here." Max laughed even harder at that, until his whole body shook and he gasped for air. And then his laughter ended abruptly, like the hiccups or a sneezing fit, and he wiped his eyes and his face turned serious. He was the same, she thought, just the same.

"And what about our little cadet?" He reached for his chair. All this time it had been empty, and he pulled it out again and sat down. "Is he still running circles at the school?"

"Three months and not a single letter," Etta said. "They must be working him hard out there."

"He's as bad as me then," he said. He rubbed his cheek and smiled. "I'm ashamed for us both." He looked toward the door. He must be wondering where Josef was, but he didn't ask. She brought him a glass of cool water and he drank it all at once and he ignored the napkin she'd set out for him and wiped his mouth with his sleeve.

She sat beside him and refilled his glass and he emptied it again, drinking with an almost urgent haste, and when he was done she touched his cheek with her fingertips. How good to see him sitting at her table, to see those eyes again and how they shone.

She waited ten minutes, then twenty, and Josef didn't come inside. Each time the hourglass was done, Max turned it back around. She drummed her fingers and tried to ignore the ticking of the hallway clock, but her impatience was stronger than her anger, and she went out back. He was behind his bench, filing down a piece of butternut wood. His shop was neat as a doctor's office, with every file and blade in its place and his jars of nails and screws stacked by size along the shelves. He didn't look up when she knocked. He held the wood up to the light, angling it so he could see.

"How is he?" He ran his thumb over the carving. He had a gentle touch with the wood. She'd asked him more than once to make her something nice, some candlesticks or a tray for the dining table or a box for her silver, anything, she told him, anything at all, but he didn't listen. He carved flowers and vines and birds of every sort and grape clusters and elk and strange scowling faces, some so real that she expected them to move beneath her fingertips, and he piled them in his workshop and left them there to warp and crack. Firewood, he called his carvings. The prettiest firewood in Heidenfeld.

"Why don't you come inside and see?"

"In a bit." He picked a chisel and began to work the wood again, pushing with his chest against the handle. He carved with his body and not just his hands. The rain fell against the shingles, and drops fell through the open doorway, but he didn't seem to mind.

She waited a while longer by the door. She was always waiting for him. He didn't know how to make things easy, not for her and not for himself. She left him with his chisels and went back to the kitchen. Their main meal was at lunchtime and not at dinner. They ate only sandwiches at dinner and pickles and radishes, but today they would have stew instead and they would eat in the dining room and not at the kitchen table. She took out the good glasses and found fresh tapers for her candleholders. She set a briquette in the living room oven, wrapping it in paper to make it last because they were expensive, those briquettes, and it was early still and winter was long by the river and damp.

Josef came in just before six. He came in when he always did. He stopped by the door and looked at Max as if he were a visitor and not his son. Max rose from the bench. He stepped toward his father, and Josef looked so small beside him. She could think of nothing to say to bring them together, and so she stayed quiet.

Josef's face was wet from the rain. "You should have written," he said. He folded his arms across his chest. "Your mother was worried." He turned away then, as if regretting that he had been the first to speak. She recognized the expression on his face. It was the look of a man who had carried his anger for too long, who had grown tired from the weight of it and wanted a way now to let it go.

Max went to his father and set his arms around him. Josef's arms hung loose by his sides at first, and then he gave in. He hugged Max and patted him on his back. Max said something to him. She couldn't hear. Josef nodded. *Yes*, he said, *yes*, and he looked away from Max and toward the window instead.

Josef washed up first, and then Max went into the bathroom and latched the door. She set the table for three, with her finest china, the Hutschenreuther set her mother had given them on their wedding day. The girly dishes, Max had called them when he was little, wrinkling up his nose at the border of intertwined pink roses. She wiped each plate with a towel. She loved the blossoms and the fineness of the porcelain and how it went translucent when she held it up to the light. She took it out of the cupboard only on special occasions, to celebrate Max's graduation or Georg's birthday or to have the ladies over for a klatsch. How good it felt to need that third plate, and when Georg came home she'd be taking out another and all four of them would sit together at the table.

Josef went to the basket while she was at the sink. He took a slice of bread, but she saw and threw him a sour look. He set the bread back in its spot, dissatisfied. It was after six, this is how he thought. It was late and they weren't at the table yet and there was no order in the house. He stood by the counter, his hands low in his pockets. He walked to the door and to the window and back again. He sat down and tapped his fingers on the table.

The water ran in the bathroom and went off again. Max came out and stopped at the kitchen doorway. He stood there for a moment, though it seemed much longer, and swayed back and forth, unsteady on his feet. He fell to his knees, as if someone had pushed him down by the crown of his head, and then he rocked from side to side without speaking, his face marked by an anguish that she had never seen before and could not comprehend.

Josef sat on the bench, his mouth hanging open, speechless at Max's movements. Etta stepped toward Max. The plate she'd been holding fell from her hands and shattered against the edge of the counter, sending broken pieces of porcelain into the sink.

"What's wrong?" She knelt by his side and put her arms around him to stop his rocking. "What can I do?"

He began to moan, an animal sound from low in his throat, a sound so horrible that it brought tears to her eyes. He did not stop rocking, and so she rocked with him, holding him tight in her arms, until he grew tired. She led him to bed then. She poured a glass of water and fumbled for a few aspirin tablets. He took the pills from her hand, swallowed them without water, and fell back against his pillow. When she came back to check on him, he was still awake, lying just as she had left him, his eyes open wide but strangely unfocused.

## 2

They walked single file, and the youngest boys were in the back, kicking up leaves. Georg cupped his hands over his ears. The wind blew hard across the lake, churning its waters and bringing up whitecaps. It was time for their winter uniforms. Time for the ski caps and the long woolen pants. Fall came fast in the valley. It came fast and was gone, and the winter would last until April, but the others didn't mind. They shot their rifles and climbed on their bellies in the mud, until their skin went pink and then red from the cold and sweat ran down their foreheads and into their eyes. They chopped wood, too, and fixed fences and worked like farmers because it was good for young men to work in the countryside, especially for the city boys in the group who had never milked a cow before or wrung a chicken's neck. Drafted into the Jungvolk at ten and the Hitler Jugend at fourteen and they were almost soldiers now. Just one more winter and their papers would come.

Who knew why they'd wanted him at the Hitler School. His eyes were brown and not blue. He was fat even before he came, and he'd gotten fatter still because the food was good. They fed their cadets fresh meat and thick slices of bread, and there was butter at the table and sometimes even chocolate. They taught no math and no languages at the academy, no painting or poetry, because they needed soldiers and not scholars. The instructors talked about the Slavs in class and how primitive their faces were and how to use the Panzerfaust, they talked about the Jews and how they had to be rooted out from German soil, and nothing they said made sense. There weren't any Jews here and not in his class back home either. He wasn't sure how long it had been since they'd gone away. Helga Weinstein with her pale eyes and the Stern brothers who lived in the finest house in Heidenfeld and went to Würzburg every week to study violin, they'd stopped coming to school from one day to the next. They'd gone to their cousins in the hills, some people said. They'd gone to America, and Georg was jealous at the thought. He looked at the maps on the wall instead of listening to the lectures. He measured how far he was from home, how far from Mutti and his room. Not even two hundred kilometers if you went straight, but Heidenfeld was as far away as the moon, Heidenfeld and the schoolhouse there and all the things he'd learned, all his Latin and his Greek.

He walked now behind Little Graf, who swung his arms by his sides. The wind blew down leaves, and they fell slow as confetti. He stopped to catch his breath, and the others passed him in the line. "Come on, old man," someone said, "you're almost there," and a few laughed. Georg laughed with them. He knew humiliation. He knew all their jokes. They teased him because he was fat around the belly and his shoulders sloped. They teased him because he lingered over his old magazines. *Youth and Homeland* and *Der Pimpf* and *The Young Fellowship*, he had them all and knew the pages with the best photographs. The boys were perfect in those pictures, caught in a perfect moment when the light fell soft across their skin. They threw javelins. They jumped and ran and shot their bows. They looked beyond the camera, toward the finish line, toward the sky, and they were graceful as cats the way they moved. "Those old things again," someone would say when he pulled them out, "why not look at something new." They shook their heads because he was a hopeless case, and sometimes they didn't let it pass. There was a strange tone to their teasing then, but he pretended not to notice, and once Müller had come in and sat with him. "Give me one," he said, and they read together, and the others went quiet and left them both alone.

The boys came to the schoolhouse and found their spots by the long table. The classroom was empty and the teachers were gone for the day, and it was time for cleaning. All their rifles lay in a line, their bronze brushes and rags and jars of oil. Georg dipped his patch in the bottle. He loved the smell of the solvent, thick as liquor and sweet. He was scrubbing out the bore when the droning began. It was distant at first, and no one looked up. They were accustomed to the sound. Every afternoon they heard it. They had gone to the shelter the first few times, huddling close in the cellar under the town's only hotel, but it was worse in the shelter than it was outside. The old folks gasped for air down there and fanned themselves with pieces of cardboard. Babies cried, and mothers shoved one another to find a place. They stopped going after a while, a few at first and then more and more still, until they all stayed in their rooms and worked right through the noise. "Damn wasps," one of them said, "that's all it is." They measured the sound in wasps, saying that wasn't too bad. It's three wasps at most or maybe four. But they were nervous even as they laughed, and the sound worked its way through them until they quivered like tuning forks.

Georg took a fresh patch from the pile. He reached across the table for the solvent. "Something's different," someone said, "they sound different this time." There was a moment of perfect stillness in the room, and all the air went heavy. Before anyone could rise from the table, the walls shook, and the windows shattered. The glass came down onto the worktable, and it fell in pieces against their heads. Some of the boys were cut, and the blood matted their hair and ran down their cheeks. They knelt together in the center of the room and waited for the rumbling to stop, and when it did, they went outside and looked to the sky. Smoke rose in pillars from the town center. It drifted lazily toward the hills.

They walked together toward the smoke. The youngest boys ran, and even the ones who were bleeding came. Ash floated in the air and fell soft as powder on the buildings and the streetlights. Townspeople stood on the curbs and gathered around the buildings that were hit. Men were high on the piles already, pulling out bricks and planks and tossing them down. Old women fetched buckets and shovels and barrows. They ran fast along the streets, those gray women. They were accustomed to cleaning up. A girl sat at the side of the road and held her head in her hands. Two friends spoke to her and stroked her hair, but she began to wail anyway and the sound carried all along the piles.

The older boys climbed on first and pulled the young ones up. They scaled the rubble as if they were going for a hike on a hill and not climbing over bricks and wood and broken glass. They passed the debris piece by piece down the side of the pile until it reached the bottom, where it was sorted and put in barrows and carted away. It was hot on the pile. Georg could feel the heat through the soles of his shoes. He'd have blisters for certain when he was done. All the air smelled of metal, and even when he drank from his bottle the ash burned in his throat. Little Graf worked just below him and took his bucket when it was full. He gave it to the next boy, who passed it down the line.

"What a mess," Little Graf was saying. "What a waste." He looked around for someone to agree, but nobody listened. He was compact like a gymnast, and his voice hadn't changed yet. It was high as a choirboy's, and so the boys all called him Little Graf, because *Graf* means "count" and they thought that was funny, having a Little Count in school with them. "Next best thing to a Little Prince," they'd say, "just about as good."

Georg pulled shingles from the pile and jagged stones, and farther down he found coins and leather purses and envelopes that crumbled

between his fingers. He worked, and the pile revealed itself. It yielded
all its treasures. He dropped a shoe into his bucket. It looked like one
of Mutti's walking shoes, built of stiff brown leather and thick laces that
she pulled tight around her ankles. The heel had broken off clean.
Where was she, this lady? Where had she gone? He reached inside the
rubble. She might be watching barefoot from the street below where
the children and the injured had gathered and the ladies with their
coal shovels. She might be waiting inside her house or pushing barrows
with the other ladies. But he knew. He knew where she was, this lady
who wore brown boots. She lay inside, deep below where the wood and
the stones had fallen first. He was standing over her. The piles were like
the pyramids, and people were buried inside with all their things. They
were buried and could find no air. The boys went quiet as they worked.
They were stepping on graves, and it wasn't right to shout.

His eyes burned and stung. He rubbed them but it did no good. He
wanted to be done with the digging. He wanted to pull away all the
things and throw them to the street, and still he was scared to see what
lay beneath. Max had told him once that people woke up inside their
coffins. It was a scientific fact. A poor woman in Köln was buried alive,
he said, she was buried in her coffin, and no one knew. His eyes shone
in the telling. Her name was Bischof and she was young, and a pair of
grave robbers saw the marks she'd left. All the papers talked about it
and the radio, too, how she'd scratched at the sides of the box and her
fingers were raw with splinters. Imagine how many more there might
be—Max had laughed then—imagine how many more and no one will
ever know. He could tell that Georg was scared at the thought, he could
always tell, and so he laughed again and told him not to worry, there
were special coffins with telephones and alarm bells just in case. That's
what you'll have, he said, only the best for you. He had a way of saying
things, his brother. He made his own trouble.

Georg knelt by the pile like a parishioner. He filled his bucket, and Graf grunted below him, and their faces went shiny from the heat. The girls were setting up the lunch truck on the street. They were bringing out the soup pots and slicing loaves of bread.

He pulled a plank from the pile and slid it down the side. When he turned back, he saw a hand curled like a crab where the plank had been. He looked at it for a good while. It was real as his own hands and would not be denied. He turned around and waved. "I've got someone," he shouted down the pile, "I've got someone here," and all the nearest boys climbed to his spot. They pulled out wood and piping and broken bricks and threw them down the side, forgetting the buckets and the people below. They followed the hand to the wrist and then to the elbow.

One of the young boys didn't want to wait. He took hold of the wrist and tugged. No one paid any attention. He tugged again and fell backward. He let out a shriek, holding it up like some terrible trophy, that arm that ended in nothing and was connected to nothing, and he ran down the side of the pile. He held tight to the hand, resisting when two older boys tried to take it from him. "Don't touch it," he said, "let me go," and he was shouting still when they led him away. After that Georg didn't look at what he found. He set things in buckets and didn't look. They worked until dark, and when they left, the ladies were still sweeping the streets with their long twig brooms.

They didn't talk about the piles that night. They didn't pull out their decks or magazines, and when the lights went out, they turned to the wall and slept. Graf was crying again. Every few days he cried, but he didn't remember when he woke, and if somebody mentioned it he walked away angry and didn't listen. Georg waited. He set his hands behind his head, and his fingers were sore from working the piles. He knew the sounds the other boys made. He knew Müller and how he breathed and how Schneider cracked his knuckles, and farther along the wall, the Heller brothers rolled and twisted in their blankets. He knew all their nighttime sounds and feared that they knew his.

He went to his rucksack once the last of them were asleep. He rolled to his side and reached for it like a friend. He had three sausages tonight, a slice of buttered rye bread, and a single spotty pear. He ate the bread first and then the pear. Schneider talked in his sleep two beds over. He laughed and spoke low in his dream language, and Georg understood none of it. He ate the sausages one after the next. His cheeks bulged big as a trumpeter's, and he was ashamed and contented both. He thought of home when he ate. He thought of home and how the kitchen smelled. The pork fat was soft against his tongue, and though he was thirsty from the salt he lay back down when he was finished and belched under the sheets. He kicked his blanket and rolled around to find his spot. His sleep was uneasy. It always was when his belly was full. His dreams were strange and fleeting, and he sweated from the heat of all that food, and when he awoke he was hungry again. He was first in line for breakfast, and at breakfast, he thought of lunch, and so it went. It was a beast, his belly, and it had to be fed.

THEY LIKED TO sit around the table after dinner. "Who's prettier," someone would say, "Brigitte Horney or Zarah Leander?" and they'd lean in close to bicker. *She's too dark*, or *she's too pale, she's klotzig, that one, and her bones are big*. They wagged their spoons and elbowed each other to make their points. Actresses and boxers and planes and battle tactics and Churchill who was fat like a turnip. Spartans against the Romans, who would win if they fought? And what about the Vikings? The Vikings would beat them both. They argued about all these things, and they shouted sometimes and laughed. They were alien to Georg as moon men. They were fifteen years old, just like him. He'd left them in the dining hall and gone back to their room.

He knelt by his headboard and reached between the mattress and the metal frame. The pouch was where he'd left it. Its leather was soft and had gone dark around the edges from wear. He unwound the string, and the ladies tumbled into his hand. Five perfect Lady Liberty half dollars, gifts from his uncle Fritz, who had left Germany years before and settled in Milwaukee. He'd written and told them about his travels, about the Indians he saw and enormous red rocks and San Francisco where the sun shone even in December and all the pavement sparkled. "It's the quartz," he told them, "there's quartz in the streets and everything shines in the city." Georg and Max fought over his letters, reading them and rereading them until the paper went soft.

Of all the gifts his uncle had sent, Georg loved the coins best. He loved the smell of them and their feel against his skin, and the look of the ladies, all vertical lines and fabric draped across lithe bodies that walked toward the setting sun, their arms held high as if making an offering. Max had taken them first, of course. "Respect your elders," he said when he took them. He kept them in his pouch, and he turned down all the things Georg offered him in trade. I don't want your stamps, he'd say, and I'm too old for marbles, and what would you do with them anyway, these shiny new coins, but just before he left he gave them all to Georg. "Take them," he said, "take them for luck," and he tossed the pouch and laughed when Georg missed the catch.

Georg took the honey he'd filched in a napkin from the dining hall and worked a little into his palms. The school had real honey and not the *kunsthonig* the soldiers had to eat. Mutti would shake her head if she knew. What a waste of good honey, what a shame it was. He rubbed his hands together until they were warm. He had good hands for magic, fingers plump as sausages and straight, with no windows between them that might betray the workings of his trick. He palmed the coins to warm up, and when he was ready, he took a deep breath. He looked straight ahead.

"This is an old trick," he said. "Kalanag did it years ago." He raised one eyebrow for emphasis. It had taken months before a mirror to get the eyebrow right. He'd never met the great Kalanag, of course, and besides Kalanag was a big-tricks magician. Entire cars vanished from his stage, and ladies dressed in satin, and once he'd even levitated a locomotive and all the audience gasped. It was just patter. It was what he said to give the trick its rhythm. Only the coins mattered and the crowd he imagined there in the room with him. They were watching him with eyes wide because that's how good he was, and all the men and all the boys were jealous of the way he worked his ladies.

He set his left hand over the coins and his right hand flat on the desk. He shut his eyes and exhaled. When he lifted both his hands, a coin had moved to the right side. He held his hands over the coins again, like a healer or a holy man, and when he lifted them, another had jumped across. The trick grew harder for him here. The third coin always fell from his palm no matter how hard he squeezed his muscles together.

Someone rattled the door and pounded hard against the frame. Georg jumped up from the desk. They were coming back early today. He dropped the coins into his pouch and pushed it down his shirt, but the drawstrings trailed behind and caught on his collar buttons. He opened the door and stepped aside.

"Why'd you lock it?" Müller looked all around the room and at the desk especially. They were bright and impenetrable as church windows, those strange gray eyes he had, and he fixed them on Georg.

Georg stepped back. He moved toward the desk and thought hard of what he should say. He set his hands inside his pockets, and just then he felt the ladies start to move, down his shirt and under his loosened belt and straight down his right pant leg. He reached for his knee. He tried to stop their fall, but it was no use, and they landed on the shiny linoleum floor with a musical sound, four of them, four of his ladies, faceup in the light from the window.

This was not a good development, no, not at all, he knew this already, but all he could think of as he stood there was how strange it was that they had landed faceup like that. What were the odds of that? Surely less than one in four, no, it would have to be one-half multiplied by one-half four times over, or one in sixteen, but that didn't sound right either. He had paid no attention when they learned probabilities in school. He doodled in his notebook instead and looked out to the treetops. They were a strange thing anyway, probabilities, with their permutations and combinations, as if things could be figured in that way when everyone knew that there was no pattern to things, none at all, and that things happened all the time for no reason. No, the probability that the ladies would fall faceup was one hundred percent. It was as inevitable as Müller coming back early from dinner and finding him there in the room.

Müller knelt down and picked one up, holding it between his thumb and his index finger. "An Ami coin," he said, "you've got an Ami coin." He stood up straight.

Boys were in the hallway, opening doors and closing them, and somewhere someone laughed and said "Idiot, you're an idiot." The others would be back soon from dinner. They'd be coming to the room, arguing still and pushing their way through the door. Georg wanted to reach for his ladies and put them back in their pouch. He wanted to leave Müller and the rest of them and walk down by the trees. He knew where the barn owls were, all their secret places, and he wanted to go see them. They perched by the fence posts behind the track and sometimes by the well. He pushed his hands deep in his pockets and stayed just where he was.

Müller was looking at the coin in his hand and Georg was looking at Müller, and the fifth lady slipped from the pouch and fell between his feet.

"Are there more?"

Georg shook his head. "That's the last of them."

Müller picked the fifth coin up. He was solemn as a choirboy, the way he set them on the desk. The silence from Müller was a terrible thing. The news traveled through it, Georg could feel it rippling outward through the school. The administrators would come running and the Bannführer with his badges. There'd be consequences. They'd send him home. They'd send him east, because that's where the punishment posts were, and he'd have only himself to blame. He should have brought his aluminum coins. He should have brought his pfennig pieces, but he had left them home on his desk and taken the ladies instead because they were beautiful. "I need them," he said at last. Müller was still looking at him, and he had to say something. "I need them for my vanishing tricks."

Müller considered this. Georg looked for surprise in his face but found none. "Show me something," Müller said, folding his arms.

"I'm out of practice."

"Show me something easy then."

The sun set in the window. Its rays came across the desk and lit up the ladies as if they were on a stage and all the lights shone down on them. Georg took one in his hand and pressed her tight against a fold in his pant leg. He yanked the fabric over her. He lifted his hands, and she was gone. The trick was a simple one and meant for small children, but Müller smiled.

Georg took the ladies and set them back in their pouch. People usually wanted to know how the illusion worked. They wanted to see the mechanics of it, the inner workings, and they pestered him when he said no. *Do it again*, they'd say, *right now, not later, do it slow this time*, and sometimes they were angry because it was an insult to see something and not to understand. He held the pouch by the strings and waited, but Müller was looking at where the coins had been.

"You're funny," he said. He reached for Georg's wrist and squeezed it hard. He was the best boxer in the class, and he could grapple, too, wrapping those legs tight around his opponents. He knew how to choke them out, knew it from instinct and not from the lessons they took together, and the poor kids who fought him went down on the mat and twisted round themselves like carnival pretzels. Their eyes bulged, and their faces went red, and all the others leaned in to watch. He came so close that Georg could see the blond whiskers that grew along his jaw. "No wonder they give you trouble." He let go of Georg's wrist all at once.

Georg put them to bed when Müller left. He slid the pouch back under the mattress. He went through all Müller's words and his inflections and found hidden meanings in them, and though he should have been scared that Müller knew about the coins, he felt relief instead. He was unburdened.

It took days for the bruise to fade to green, those five circles that Müller's fingertips had left when he'd grabbed Georg by his wrist. The next time he took the ladies out, Müller sat with him and watched, and though Georg knew the tricks and had done them all a hundred times before, his hands shook anyway.

MUTTI HAD GIVEN him the book when he was ten, going on eleven, and sick with a lung infection that kept him in bed all summer and into fall. She kept the curtains drawn to keep out the heat and the bugs, but the flies still came inside and she ran after them with her swatter. She brought him tea and apples and thin butter cookies. She sat with him and her fingers were cool against his wrist, but he didn't move under his blankets. He didn't answer when she spoke. The breeze from his window was heavy with the smells of summer, of soap and sweat and the linden trees in bloom. Outside boys shouted. They played ball in the street and climbed the apple trees that grew between the houses, and he slept through all their noise, the laughter and the shouts, the feuds and the reconciliations that followed. He slept, and the sounds fell away. He was hungry for sleep that summer. It was better than food to him, and the more he slept, the more he wanted to sleep, resisting Mutti when she leaned in to check on him. "Wake up, Georg," she'd say, "have some tea and talk to me," and he'd close his eyes all the tighter and try to get back to that dream place where the flies didn't buzz and the air was cool.

She didn't give up so easily, his mutti. She brought him books and left them open on his table. He fought her at first, but then she began to read to him, and he was caught. Who knew where she had found them; she must have taken the train to Wertheim to buy the stories he loved, or maybe she asked Max to bring them when he took the train back from Lohr. *Distant Worlds, The Tunnel, The Hands of Orlac, The Amazon Queen,* she read them each in her steady voice that never rose or fell, with all the solemnity of a priest giving a sermon. She sat so straight in the oak chair by his bed and read to him of spaceships and water tunnels, of platforms floating in the sea. Her voice wound like ivy through his dreams. He was with Professor Schulze and Captain Münchhausen, who was fatter even than Georg, and Lord Flitmore and all the rest of the crew aboard the spaceship *Sannah*. He was with them on Mars, and they walked along its craters. They saw legless beetles there and flying snails. They saw the glowworms that lived under its snows. She read to him, and there was no resisting her or the stories she told. He opened his eyes. He sat up against his feather pillows and listened, roped in by her voice, which pulled him through those dark days of summer.

When he was strong enough to come down to the kitchen for his meals, she brought out a package and set it by his plate. He could tell it was another book. He undid the twine and tore away the paper and let it fall to the kitchen floor. *Conjuring Made Easy*, the cover promised, *A Magic Book for Everyone, by Ernst Firnholzer*. There were photos inside, dozens of them, and detailed explanations of every sort of trick, not just the regular ones but strange ones, too, that required silk string and doves, apples and sugar cubes. He pushed his plate aside and thumbed through the pages. "It'll take forever to learn all these," he said.

"The good things take work." She wiped her hands dry on her apron. "They're a sharpening stone." She made no sense sometimes, the way she said things, but he was used to it. They all were. They ate and let her talk, and they nodded sometimes to show that they were listening. *Yes*, they'd say, *yes*, and they'd reach for the ladle or the bread basket.

Mutti left him and went out to the garden, and he sat with his book. It must have taken old Firnholzer years to pull the tricks together. He went through the pages and imagined the author and just how he was. He was old, Georg could tell from the way he wrote, and he probably lived high on a hill. Moonvine grew in his garden and primrose and angel's trumpet, and all the flowers opened up at night because that's when he worked, that's when the coins and the cards moved best beneath his hands. What a sweet life he had, old Firnholzer. What a sweet life to make things vanish.

He kept the book in his room. He tried the tricks, but he was lazy about it and undisciplined. He left his coins where he had dropped them. "Something's wrong with them," he'd say, "they're too big and these ones here are too thin and they slip between my fingers." He went peevish at the coins and cursed them, and he set the book aside and went back to his stories.

When the carnival came in October, Mutti took him because he loved the games there and the hawkers with their fresh pretzels and their bouncing balls. She gave him a few coins and left him by the gate. He walked tall through the crowd. His legs were shaky from all that time in bed, but still it was good to feel the sun shining on his head. An old man was there that day, stooped low over his accordion, and though Georg wanted to play darts and buy a goldfish in a bowl, there was something in the old man's face that stopped him. His eyes were shut tight, as if he were sleeping in his chair. He played a mournful song, a song that didn't belong at any carnival, and the accordion wailed and quavered and beat like a heart between his palms. The old man was communing with the angels, Georg could see it in his face. A strange power was working its way through him and pulling all the people toward the sound. Georg wondered how it would be to stop people like that, to stop them where they were and make them listen.

He left the carnival with the coins still in his pocket. He didn't want goldfish anymore or caramels. He picked up old Firnholzer's magic book when he came home and read it from the first page to the last, and when he was done, he read it again. He set aside part of his room as his studio, and Mutti found him a little folding table and a piece of black velvet. She brought him whatever Firnholzer called for, sugar cubes and extra-soft pencils and silk thread spun fine as a spiderweb. She found it all. She let out a sigh when he asked her for a bird, but then she gave in and brought him a yellow parakeet. She'd gone three towns over to find the bird, and all the people had looked at her when she carried it back on the train. He'd wanted a fat gray dove and not a parakeet, but he was happy all the same, and when he practiced there in his room, with Kaspar whistling and pecking in his cage, time stopped for him, and he was content.

He took his coins everywhere he went, even to school, and as he walked he held them tight in the fold of muscle between his thumb and his palm, so tight that he could swing his arms from side to side and wave at old Frau Fader as she swept her stoop and the coins would not come loose. He checked the tricks off as he learned them, and each time he'd call Mutti to his room. "Come see," he'd say, "come quick," and she sat in his chair. He'd clear off his table and smooth out the coverlet and rub his hands together to warm them up. He watched Mutti as he worked, to see whether she was looking in the right places. He could tell from her eyes just how the trick had gone. He worked early in the morning before he left for school and after dinner and on weekends, too, and all the pages came loose and fell across his floor.

The day he left for the academy, when his trunk had been packed and she'd walked with him to the station, Mutti set the book in his hands. She'd repaired it with binding tape, page by page, a job that must have taken hours. She'd cupped his face in her hands and gave him a kiss on each cheek, and she was waving still as his train pulled out and rounded the corner.

GRAF WAS WET from the lake. He shivered in his chair at the mess table, and Georg handed him a napkin to dry his face. They staged their boat fights even when it rained. They fought for fun when their classwork was done. They wrestled for a spot on the boats. *What's the cold to us*, they said, *what's the cold to soldiers*, and they puffed their chests. They rowed together toward the center, shivering until the work raised their blood. Their hair was damp and stuck to their foreheads, and their breath rose gray as smoke. Georg watched from the shore usually, unless he was feeling brave. He stood by the reeds and the grasses, and the only sounds he heard were the eagle owls high in the trees and the oars slicing through. When the boats came together, the leaders in the front touched oar blades. They were gladiators then. They fought like old Romans. Boys reached across and grabbed arms and oars and sometimes hair. They nudged the other boat and tried to turn it over. They were mostly quiet while they worked, but sometimes one shouted as he went in, and the sound rose from the water and was gone.

The others came to the table. They looked at Graf, who sat dripping in his chair, and they teased him and jabbed him with their fingers, but it was a gentle teasing and left no marks. "We've got a mermaid at our table," they said. "A pretty little fish." Graf rolled his eyes and laughed with them, and he raised his soup bowl and drank from it.

They set their elbows on the table. They leaned in close to talk, and a few went back to refill their plates. When the table went quiet, Schneider pulled out the book. *The World's Great Beauties*, it was called, and he kept it in his bag. "Not that old chestnut," someone said. "It's older than Methuselah, that book, and the ladies are, too." But they turned the pages anyway and looked at all the photographs because they were beautiful, all those ladies from Finland and Austria and France. There were exotic ones, too, from India and China, from Argentina and islands in the Pacific, and they had smoky eyes and waves in their hair, and their lips were shiny as lacquer. The boys knew them all. They gave them names like Liliana and Isabella and Fatima, and they argued the merits of each. *She's horsey, that one, and her eyes are too small, and this one is moon-faced*, and on they went, and Müller laughed the whole while. He laughed at them and leaned back in his chair, and Georg looked at Müller and not the book.

They were leaning in to see when Bannführer Frisch came in. They were all the way to Pomerania and Portugal when he called them to attention. He stood by the front table. He was a tall man and his face was angular, and there were shadows under his cheeks and in the hollow of his throat. He spoke a high German because he was from up north, and his words had none of the softness of the southern dialects. All the boys in the hall sat straighter when he came into the room. Schneider moved quickly. He was deft as a magician, the way he pulled the book under the table and set it back inside his bag.

Frisch was talking, and the whole room was quiet. "It's time to fortify the wall," he said. "Time to shore it up." They'd go west. They needed to repair the Westwall to keep the Amis and the British out. Six hundred and thirty kilometers of ditches and pillboxes and cement to keep out the enemy tanks, and they needed to get them ready. The efforts were already under way in places, but there was much more to be done. The work wouldn't be easy. Long hours digging and hauling dirt and rocks and laying down wire, but they weren't little boys in knee socks anymore. No, they were soldiers now, and their country needed them. They'd be in towns near Karlsruhe mainly, and a few would go even farther. They'd stay for ninety days at least, depending on how fast the work went, and they'd be paid just like soldiers. They'd get their eighty marks.

Georg looked at Müller and Graf and all the boys across the table. He heard what Frisch was saying. He heard every word, but it wasn't until he saw their faces that he understood. The youngest boys set their hands on the tabletop. They pounded their palms against the wood, and there was a strange light in their eyes. A shout went up in the room, and the boys stood together in a single motion. They rose from their chairs. They threw their arms around each other's shoulders, and someone in the back shouted. "Finally," he said, "we're finally going," and Frisch stepped back and let them celebrate.

# 3

Ilse was waiting at the milk stand the next morning, her eyes ringed in blue. She had grown as sleepless as Etta in recent years. "Look how old we are," she would say, and they laughed at how true it was. Etta stood behind her and watched the stragglers come. They had finished their breakfast dishes and were coming with their pitchers and their shopping bags. Maria Keller was there and old Frau Schiller and Hansi Bollinger and Hilde Zeister, who'd never married because no one had asked her. They all stood around like soldiers and waited for their milk.

Ilse took Etta by the elbow. "How is Max? God bless your boy. I hope he's well."

"He's sleeping," Etta told her. "He's been sleeping since yesterday evening, and I don't want to wake him."

Ilse nodded. "Let him rest. Sleep is better than food for him."

A few other ladies stopped to say hello, to pat Etta on the shoulder and congratulate her because her boy was home. Our best to Max, they told her. Thank God in heaven he's back. Bring him by, bring him by so we can see him, and they were happy for her and sad for themselves and they went back to their places in line.

"They took the Hillen boy." Ilse spoke in a whisper, and Etta had to lean in closer so she could hear. "At four in the morning they came and took him from his bed." Nobody knew where he was now. Poor Ushi, poor Ushi who cried for her boy all morning on her steps. Why take Jürgen, why take him, with his sweet face, and Etta just shook her head.

A group of six German League girls passed by just then. They wore crisp blouses and dark blue skirts and the lucky ones had climbing jackets nipped tight at the waist. Ilse stopped talking when she saw them.

"It's turning," Etta said, watching the girls. "It smells like more rain."

"It's come early this year," Ilse agreed. "I could tell from the crows, how they gathered on my tree."

"The earwigs came in August this year and not in October," Regina Schiller said from the front of the line. Her hands shook, but not from the cold. She had the shaking disease just like her mother. "It'll be stormy this winter. There'll be no place to put all the snow." She shuffled toward the stand.

The German League girls cut through the line, and they were worse than the HJ boys, how they behaved. They pushed their way through without apology, and one of them stepped hard on Etta's foot. They walked in a bubble. They laughed and nudged each other, and their legs were pink from the chill. They should be in school. They should be learning their lessons, but they wore uniforms instead and walked along the streets. They were organized into squadrons and groups and battalions. Disciplined as cadets. They cleared fields and ran around the track and went to the depot to sort through donations, the old coats and scarves and silverware and all the wool the ladies had made from unraveling socks and sweaters. They had a shine in their eyes, those girls, and they walked past the old women and gave them no greeting. "You've got no manners," Etta said. She said it in a low voice so nobody else could hear. "Your mother didn't raise you right."

Ilse was at the barrel now. She set her pitcher on the table, and Etta stood behind her. Farther back the ladies had begun to barter. Eggs exchanged for a single square of chocolate, fresh churned butter for tea bags, sausage links for colored wool. Deprivation made them hard. They'd saved and skimped and worked for years, and all they had now was ration coupons and runny milk and what they could get from their families up in the hills. All their frugality had come to nothing. They should have married farmers. They'd be eating then and their pantries would be full, and still they contented themselves. Things could be worse. Thank God they weren't in the city, thank him twice over, because that's where the bombs fell. Emmerich was gone and thousands dead, Emmerich and Kleve, and these cities were far away but what difference did a few hundred kilometers make when the enemies flew their planes across the country from one side to the other.

Etta tapped Ilse on the shoulder. "I want to have a klatsch." There were more reasons to mourn than to celebrate, but she wanted the ladies around her table again. There had to be at least two cakes for the table in better days. Two cakes and coffee and real black tea and, once the cakes were gone, a bottle of bocksbeutel wine or fruit liquor to keep the conversation going. The good tablecloth came out and the silver serving pieces, and all the ladies sat together and drank from dainty cups. They knew whose husbands drank or chased the cleaning girls in town, whose boys had brought home unsuitable girls or no girls at all. They knew which houses were messy and which ones loveless and which ones strapped for cash, and still they drank their coffee and talked of other things.

Ilse turned around. She looked at the line behind Etta. They were all the way to the butcher market already, and soon they'd be turning the corner. They stood in their walking boots and their thick stockings, and all around them the air went damp and the first drops began to fall.

"All the ladies can come," Etta said.

"I don't know." Ilse squinted. "People might talk." The old woman filled Ilse's pitcher, careful not to spill. She brought it back to the table and took Ilse's green rationing ticket and her money, and her hands shook the whole while.

"Let them talk." Etta set her empty pitcher down. There wasn't anything wrong with having a klatsch even now when food was scarce. It was the company and not the pastries that mattered. It was having the ladies round her table. "I'll make my cake."

Ilse tilted her head. She was tempted now, Etta could tell. Ilse was quick with the serving knife. All bones and no meat, and still she ate more than the other ladies, and when it came time to bring the sweet liquor out from its cabinet, she jumped from her chair to fetch the bottle. *What a sweet drop*, she'd say, setting her hands across her belly. "People might talk," Ilse said again now, but her voice had turned doubtful, and Etta smiled then because she knew.

MAX WAS RESTLESS as a puppy when he finally woke. He walked with Etta along the streets, and people nodded at Etta and stopped to shake his hand and to wish him well. *He's back*, they said, *God bless you both*, and she thanked them, but when she stayed to talk, Max tugged at her arm. They were on their way to church, but he wanted to see the river first. He wanted to sit by the bank. He walked fast, setting his hands inside his pockets. A few times he stopped and turned around to see. He looked at the butcher-shop window and the ironwork balconies with their flowerpots, at the fountain and the old linden tree where the boys went in summer to play. It was all just the same. The church steeples and the pharmacy with its polished countertop and the water-spout down by the square. He looked at all these things, and he reached out to the sandstone walls and smiled.

He had slept for almost forty-two hours. He awoke once or twice and waved to Etta from his bed and then fell fast asleep again. He slept even when the floorboards creaked and the clock chimed by his door. Josef had grown impatient when Max didn't wake up. He went fussy. He paced around the kitchen, then out to his workshop, once, twice, three times, and finally to town, to drink at the gasthaus with the other men who were too old to fight but could talk of little else. There was not enough soap or butter or wool, there hadn't been in years, but there was plenty of watery beer in town, and the few men left did their best to drink it. They sat at their table and bickered, and after a while old Herr Scherber brought out his deck, and then they didn't leave until dinnertime.

Max tugged at her hand and they passed the steps that led to the bridge, following the path by the bank where the reeds grew and the river grasses. Farther along the ferryman sat waiting on his boat. Even on Sunday he worked. Ten pfennig to cross, seven for the pretty girls, and he talked while he rowed and whistled through the gap in his teeth. "Faster than the bridge," he'd say, "much faster, and you get my singing, too." The air was soft and buttery, warm as April and not October. The sky had cleared, and the sun shone on the water. A few fishermen tended to their barrels, and tomorrow the ladies would come and haggle, pointing to one fish and then another before reaching for their purses. Farther down little boys ran along the bank, jackets open because there wouldn't be many days like this, a few more and then the damp would come and the river would run to gray.

They came to the benches and sat together. A boat came by. It was a big one this time, and it sounded its horn when it came close. Men were uncoiling ropes in the front and the back. They shouted and waved their arms. Just last year a crowd had come and looted all the ships. She knew the old men who did it. Nimble as boys they jumped aboard and threw down what they found. It was only ribbon in the crates. Bolts of seam binding in yellow and purple and cornflower blue, strange bright colors that were nothing like the clothes that people wore, especially now, when fabric and dye were scarce. How strange it was, men on canes and little boys and women holding babies to their chest, all shouting and shoving each other to catch the ribbon as it fell. A pair of old women fought over a red bolt, their lips pulled back from their teeth, and they looked like wolves and not women, wolves fighting over a bloodied piece of meat. They kept pulling even after the ribbon had come undone between them and they'd stomped it into the mud. Girls wore dresses made from the binding afterward. Their mothers had split the ribbon lengthwise and knit with it, and they pretended the yarn was theirs. *All this time it's been in my cupboard*, they said. *I remembered it just now.* They should have been ashamed for stealing. They should have hung their heads, but people didn't feel shame anymore. They lied and after a while they believed the lies they told, and this is how it went.

"How often do the headaches come?" Etta set her arm around his shoulders. She could see the fine blue veins in his temples, and she wanted to lay her fingers over them to feel the beat of his blood. "Are you better now that you've slept?"

He looked toward the water and the bend where he'd gone swimming when he was little, where the vines grew around the trees and the bravest boys swung like monkeys from the branches. He always made a mess when he came home. "Just look at the mud you brought inside," she'd say, "look at all the water," and he left his shoes by the door and walked barefoot through the house.

"I haven't seen any planes yet," he said. "Not a single one."

"It's early still." The planes came in the evening. They flew low sometimes, and once they dropped bombs over the fields and scared the
women who'd gone digging for potatoes. *God help us, they're coming.*
They jumped into ditches and covered their heads. *God help us, we're
dead for an apronful of potatoes.* And not the good potatoes either, but
the small ones the farmers threw aside.

She took his hand. Good that he was sitting outside. His skin was
translucent, the color of invalids and angel heads and the ivory church
saints, and he needed sunshine to bring the pink back to his face. She
set his hand between both of hers and squeezed.

"I'm worried about Georg," she said. They'd taken him from her
once already. They took him to the school and the next time they took
him they'd send him to fight, and who knew when he'd come home
then. He wasn't even shaving yet. No whiskers on his cheeks, and they
were making him into a soldier.

"I can hear them." Max watched the boat come to dock. A few old
men onshore were lining up to help with the crates. They were bringing
carts and straps.

"It's quiet today. It's only the boats you hear." She shifted on the
bench and thought about what to say to him and what to ask.

"They're coming over the hills," he said. "Any moment they'll be
coming and then we'll burn to ashes." He pulled his hand from hers.


THEY WALKED TOGETHER up Obertorstrasse just as the bells began to
ring. They rang at St. Laurentius in the center of town and then at the
smaller evangelical church on Friedenstrasse where the Protestants
went. When he was done in Heidenfeld the ringer rode his bicycle up
to Rothenfels and climbed the towers there. He rang them to mark the

hours and before confession and evening mass, and when people died he rang them extra slow, those passing bells, and everyone stopped to listen. Not even thirty yet, and he was deafer than a grandfather. The bells were his salvation. He stayed home when all the other boys left to fight.

Max flinched a little at the sound. "It's another sour milk day," he said.

"The milk's not sour." She pointed to the shuttered stand. "It's closed today. We won't have more until next week." It was strange the way he talked. It made her uneasy. She didn't let her milk spoil. Her food was fresh and her kitchen clean, and he wasn't making any sense. She wished Josef were there with them, but he had stopped going to services years before, except for obligatory visits on Easter and Christmas Eve, and even then he griped about the priest. "That fat old mule," Josef said, "he'll choke on a sausage, God willing, and then we'll have some peace." She scolded him when he started in. Pfarrer Büchner was a fine speaker. And Josef would be fat, too, if people brought him the best cutlets and wine by the case. He'd be round like a barrel.

A few ladies came up to say hello, but Max looked right past them. He tilted his head and smiled.

"He's tired still," Etta said. "He's tired from the train."

Max stepped back from the crowd and looked up at the dome. She stepped back with him. It was fat and round as an onion and it didn't reach for the sky like the grand spires did in the city. All its beauty was hidden inside. Masons had worked for years on the arches that ran to the altar, all those hands working the stone, and it was spun fine as sugar.

He almost forgot to dip his fingers when he came inside. She took his hand and set it over the water, and he remembered then and crossed himself. They took a pew near the center. She sat there every time she came. All the people had their regular places, women on the left and men on the right, but the rules had loosened with the war, and so she sat beside Max now and nobody minded. She sat in the middle and Ilse was up front, and some of the ladies came twice each day and they sat closest to the back so they could see who came late and who didn't come at all. They were the scorekeepers. They shook their heads because people weren't devout the way they should be. The boys and girls in town hardly ever came to services because the HJ and the German League took up all their time, and the adults weren't much better. Ilse was inside already, just beneath the stained glass window of Kilian the missionary giving food to the poor, who looked more confused than grateful for his help. Etta could see her gray kerchief pulled tight around her head. They would see each other afterward. They'd walk together to the cemetery and tend to the stones.

Pfarrer Büchner and the servers stood by the altar steps. He'd gotten even fatter now, and his robe was big as a curtain around his belly. "Introibo ad altare Dei," he said, his words clipped, hard as hail hitting a roof the way he said the *t*'s and the *d*'s, still foreign to her ear after a lifetime of Sunday services. Max had learned Latin in the gymnasium, and Greek, too, and he could understand the priest's words, and Georg was better still the way he learned his languages. He memorized the conjugations and the constructions, all the details the others complained about were the things he loved best, and he wrote out the grammar exercises though he'd already done them all at least twice before. He took languages apart the way others dismantled an engine or a clock. And when she asked him why—why dead languages and not something living—he was serious when he answered. "Because they give me no cause to talk to anyone," that's what he said, and he went back to his books. If only he were home now, too, the house would be complete.

Büchner began to confess. "Confiteor Deo omnipotenti," he said, and she understood none of it. She squeezed Max's hand. His skin was smooth, soft as the hand of a child and not a soldier's hand, not the hand of someone who had marched in the cold and the dark, who carried a gun and knew how to shoot. She wondered for a moment what those hands had done. What he had seen so far away and why the officers had sent him home. All the other boys were leaving, even ones who were young like Georg and hadn't finished school yet. They were leaving and Max was coming home and the letter never said why. The priest kissed the altar and then stood straight, his back to the people. The servers knelt on the steps leading to the altar. "Kyrie, eleison," the priest said, "Christe, eleison."

A few people coughed or shifted on the hard wooden stands. Etta looked over at Max. He was wide awake, his eyes still focused on the stained glass window, as if he were in a movie house and not in church. She had seen that look before, the time they had gone together to the big planetarium in München and they sat close together in that dark room. He laughed when he saw the stars come into focus. *Mutti, look how close they are*, he'd said. *The sky's come down, it's come into my hand.* He was quiet that night on the train. He sat with his back to the window and closed his eyes, and he looked so young while he slept. Another year and he was gone. They sent him east, and when Etta saw the stars at night she wondered where he was and if he saw them, too.

"Gloria tibi, Domine," said the priest. Someone near the front of the church sneezed violently, paused, and sneezed again. She looked to Max, suppressing a smile, but something wasn't right. His lips were moving. He began to speak, quietly at first and then louder, so the people beside him could hear. He was speaking in Latin, in Greek, in all the dead languages they'd taught him in school. People turned to see. They turned around and looked at Max, and old Herr Gerberich's mouth was open wide because no one had interrupted mass before, not even when Henriette Mayer the diabetic had gone into sugar shock. She fell back against the pew and her head hit the wood, but she fell quietly, with decorum. Men carried her out like an old plank. They hoisted her up and carried her, and old Büchner went on with his sermon and didn't stop once to look.

"Maxima culpa," Max called out. He stood up and pointed to the altar.

"Be quiet, Max. Be still and sit with me." She reached for him. People were staring. Even Büchner had turned to look at them, tilting his head at the disruption.

Max looked up at the window and started to laugh, his mouth open wide. His eyes were clear like water. They were too pale to be human eyes. No, they were angel eyes, lit from within. "Mea maxima culpa," he called out, reaching up with his hands. She didn't recognize his laughter, it was not her son's laughter, not the way her boy laughed, had ever laughed.

"Max, what are you doing?" She spoke low. This was madness, it wasn't happening, and all the people looked at her. They'd take him if he acted this way. They'd take him away like they took Jürgen Hillen and nothing and no one could help then, not even his father and all the people he knew. She led him by the arm. He did not resist her touch. He went with her. She took him down the aisle, and when he refused to turn away from the window she pulled him backward, through the doorway and out to the steps.

## 4

Georg was in the middle of the line. It wasn't even six in the morning and they were marching already. They carried shovels over their shoulders and marched like soldiers to the pit. Every day they dug trenches at the Vorfeldzone of the wall. The boys at the front held a banner, and the people stopped to watch. This new town was nothing like Heidenfeld. There were no fine houses here, no carvings above the doors and no stone bridge. Not even the doctors had cars. People walked and rode rusty bicycles and pushed buggies, and their manure piles reached to the roofs. It had been two weeks and two days since he had come to the wall. Two weeks, two days, and fourteen hours. The numbers gave him no comfort.

They came to the pit and started to dig without anyone telling them what to do. Georg shoveled dirt into his bucket. Boys stood along the trench walls, their faces pinched from the cold. Behind the trench there was barbed wire and an old concrete pillbox to protect the soldiers inside against enemy fire. The boys worked one next to the other, clinging like mountaineers to the sides of the hole. He felt the first drops across the tops of his hands. It was a relief when it started. All the heaviness was gone from the air. The drops rolled down their faces and under their collars, and their undershirts stuck to their skin. By midmorning the water was up to their calves. It flowed down the sides of the trench, bringing that smooth dirt down and foaming like a river in the channel at the bottom. The soil was heavy by the trench. It was thick as clay and black, and still they worked their shovels. They leaned in close and dug.

He filled his bucket and swung it to the boy above him, who gave it to Müller, who was manning the barrow. The wind began to blow and the rain fell harder, needling his face. It was hard work lifting his feet from the muck, which held on tight and released them only reluctantly, with a sucking noise. He lost count of how many buckets he'd filled. The sameness of the motion deceived him. He counted some twice and missed others, but he counted anyway. The numbers gave rhythm to his work. He wiped the mud from his eyes and took another bucket from the stack. Where did it come from, this endless supply of dirt? They could break themselves against it, and when they were done, the trench would absorb it all, their digging and their hauling, their buckets and barrows, and would fill itself again, unmarked.

He set his shovel aside and funneled the dirt with his hands. His neck hurt from leaning, but he didn't slow his pace. Fear kept him working. Every now and again the sergeant walked along the trench, looking for slackers. He was old and his arm was wrecked, and he always wore a sling. He called them out when they slowed down. "Give me twenty," he'd say, or fifty sometimes if he was cranky, right there in the dirt, for all the others to see. "Best be ready," he told them, "the Amis are coming. The British, too. I can hear them already."

"Du, Huber." A voice called from the top of the trench. "Come up here."

Georg squinted into the rain. He shielded his face with his hands and looked.

The voice called him again, and in a friendly tone. "Come on up," it said. "I'll trade with you."

Müller stood overhead, his arms on his hips. He was working the barrow today. It was the job that all the others wanted. He could stand up straight and sneak a cigarette, and when the lunch girls came he ate first and didn't have to wait. He waved at Georg and slid down the side. He smiled easy as a beachgoer as he went. It was summertime, this was how he acted, it was June and the sun was shining on the water, and there was no rain for him and no cold. Georg looked at him and wondered how someone like Müller could sleep in the same room with the others and eat at their tables.

"Get up there, Huber." Müller reached for the shovel. "Get going before the sergeant comes back. Hurry, hurry or I'll change my mind." He laughed then and pushed Georg toward the wall.

The rain stopped and started and stopped again, and the sun began to shine. Georg emptied the buckets as they came. He stood beside a bare apple tree and stretched his arms, and when the barrow was full, he pushed it across the road and tipped it. It was easy work, and a few times he sat under the tree and closed his eyes. He ate two bowls of soup when lunchtime came, finishing before the others had even climbed up, and when he tried to fill his bowl again, the girl took the ladle from him and gave him only broth. He took a piece of bread when she wasn't looking. He set it in his pocket, careful to wrap it so it wouldn't get too soggy.

The boys came up from below. Their muscles twitched from bending over the buckets. They stretched and leaned against the tree trunks. Müller stood with them while he ate. The dirt had dried on his face and cracked like leather. "It's easy work," he told Georg, setting down his empty bowl. "It's not so bad." He climbed back down with a wave.

Georg stopped at the edge and watched him work the shovel. There was no explaining Müller, why he chose Georg and not someone else, what strange charity moved him. He was god of the dormitory. He acted with a random benevolence.

Georg waited for Müller when the shift was done. He tried to thank him, but Müller shook his head. "We'll miss the digging when we're gone from here," he said. There'd be rain for weeks and then snow. The water would freeze in the trench, and all the dirt would be hard like stone and no pick and no shovel could break it, and still they'd miss it. "Things will only get worse when we leave. We'll miss the hole then and all our shovels," Müller told him. "We'll miss the rain and the sergeant, too." It wasn't true what he said. They wouldn't miss the sergeant and his puckered face, but Georg laughed anyway.

The boys left for dinner in small groups. They didn't march at night, and they carried no banners. They hobbled like old men. They swung their arms and turned their heads around and their faces were caked with mud. Georg and Müller stayed behind. They let the others go ahead. "We'll finish here," Müller said. "See you at dinner," and they stacked all the buckets and turned the barrows over and leaned the shovels against the walls.

When they were done Müller reached over and took Georg's hand again, but he didn't look at Georg's face. He looked at the ground instead. "It's late," he said.

Georg pulled his hand free. He reached up and touched Müller's dirty cheek, and he was surprised even then at how bold he was and how unafraid. It came easy as breathing, touching Müller.

They walked together, and Müller lit a cigarette. He looked like a wolf, the way he pulled on his cigarette. He smoked Zubans, No. 6 if he could find them, but he smoked Junos, too, and Africaines. He wasn't picky. "I've got chocolate for your cigarettes," he'd say to the older boys, and he was quick to make his deals. He kept his packs hidden because the Unterbannführer was a stickler when it came to tobacco.

They were just by the trees when Georg heard a whistle. He stopped and turned around to look. The last boys had climbed up, two tall ones and a stocky one with bowed legs. He hadn't seen them down below. They must have hidden against the wall and waited. They reached the top and stood together, and then they walked toward the valley that lay beyond the trench. They looked behind them and all around. Maybe they smelled Müller's cigarette. They walked slowly at first, then faster and faster until they were running, heads low and arms pumping like pistons at their sides. Georg and Müller stood under the trees and watched them go. They stood like that for a good while, and Georg breathed hard at the strangeness of what he'd seen. They'd be sorry if they were caught. They'd swing from the trees. They'd be sent east, and the snow would cover them. Twelve hours is all they had before the commanders would find them missing, maybe less if someone saw their empty beds before the lights went out. Twelve hours running through the trees, twelve hours in the dark, and still he was jealous.

Müller dropped his cigarette. He ground it down with his heel, and they began to walk again. They stopped just before the path turned and looked back, but Georg saw only the hills against the sky, only shadows in the field and the first pale stars.

THE NOTIFICATIONS CAME in no particular order. Boys left the wall without regard to their surnames or month of birth or the training they'd done. The commander called them to his office, and they were gone within a day or maybe two. Most were glad to go. *It's about time*, they said, *I've been playing long enough in the sandbox*. But a few knew how to fly, and they were angry when their orders came. They weren't infantrymen, not with all the tests they'd passed and all their glider flights. What a waste it was. What a waste of good pilots, and they kept the wing patches on their shirts anyway just so people would know. Georg shook their hands when they left. He told them there might be planes where they were going, you never could tell. He waved from the curb, and he was glad the Unterbannführer had called their names and not his and not Müller's either.

It wasn't easy to sit around the table anymore. They didn't joke anymore or tell funny stories now that the orders were coming. They talked about who might leave next and what had happened to the ones who'd gone already, the ones who went up north. He tried not to listen but he heard the news anyway. Schiemann had gone to the forest, and he was there still, and Reidel was shot, and a truck had run over both Baumgartner's feet and he was home now and all his toes and his ankles and the arches of his feet were ruined. They knew who had died. They said their names in low voices, with reverence, and they talked about towns as if they were people, as if they, too, fell dead on the field. They talked about Nimwegen and Arnhem and Oosterbeek, and what about Aachen, what would become of it. The Amis were coming and the English, too, and they were pushing toward the wall.

They sat around the tables and talked like generals. Surrendering was worse than dying, they said. Better to bleed out. Curse the Jews because this was their doing. Curse the Ivans, too, and Georg was lonely when he sat with them. He was lonely even with Müller two chairs down. They listened to the radio and jabbed each other, and sometimes when there was no news from the field they reminisced instead. They remembered the biggest rallies they'd seen and all the high officers they'd met and they called Müller out then, they called him dais boy and a pretty blond thing. Müller blushed at that. His ears went red, and he waved the talk aside, and when they didn't stop, he left the table.

Georg must have seen him there at the rally. He must have looked straight at him and never known. He'd taken the train that year. He was one of a dozen boys from Heidenfeld who went all the way to Nürnberg when they were only nine. They weren't old enough for the HJ yet, but they wore their Deutsches Jungvolk uniforms with their special belt buckles and that was almost as good. He went because his father was head teacher and not because of any gifts of his own, but he was proud anyway. He set his fingertips to the glass and watched the fields and trees. Mutti had been worried when he left. She packed plenty of chocolate in his bags. "You'll be sharing a tent with older boys," she told him, "who knows what food they'll have there and what hours you'll keep." She would have been happier if Max had come, too, but Max was on crutches that September with a sprained foot and so Georg went without him.

The boys jostled each other on the train and talked without stopping, not even to eat. "There'll be lights," one of them said, "and rockets, too, and we'll have to shade our eyes." *Yes*, they said, *yes, there'll be rockets for certain*. They spoke of banners and marching bands and regiments called to order, of tanks and horses and officers in boots. At each stop more boys came aboard, until all the seats were taken and boys stood in the aisles. They wore short pants and pressed shirts, with ribbons and patches and shoulder braids showing their order and their rank. There were banner boys and band members and cavalry boys without their horses, glider trainees in blue and a solitary HJ sailor with his square collar and his navy cap. They were rolling toward the city, those boys, rolling in from every direction, and Georg was certain the city could not contain them all. It would flood and its buildings crack, and more still would come.

They changed trains in Würzburg, and hundreds more joined them there, city boys who stood taller somehow because they lived on busy streets and could go to the movie house whenever they wanted and their fathers drove cars. They passed through Kitzingen and Erlangen and Fürth, and they were getting close now. They pressed their faces against the glass to see.

When the train doors opened and they stepped out, even the oldest boys went quiet. It was a city built of canvas and not of stone. There were thousands of white tents, entire fields set in rows that extended outward like star rays. There were bands, too, on every corner. The city was filled with the sound of trumpets and drums. The group from Heidenfeld marched between the tents. They blinked in wonder. Boys from other towns and other provinces walked with them. The groups flowed together as they went, and all the streets were like rivers. They wore the same uniforms, those northern boys with their blond hair and the dark-eyed ones from Bavaria and the ones from Berlin and still farther east, who were sharp-faced and had a funny way of talking. All Georg could see was boys, boys in every direction, and still there was order in the city.

They slept on cots and ate at long tables. It was September, but it felt like June, and it was warm even at night. They marched to the plaza, and women in sundresses waved at them and threw flowers. A few ran to the older boys and gave them kisses, leaving coral and scarlet gashes across their cheeks. The sun shone the whole day long. The city was golden in its light and smelled of roses. This is how he remembered it still. Gentle light and smiling women and roses underfoot. Boys sat on the platform during the introductions, under the banners and the flags. That's where Müller was. That's where they put him. He was one of those golden heads. The others stood in rows. They listened to one speaker after the next. Tall men in uniforms who talked about work and the joy it brings, who talked about destiny and keeping Germany pure. The Führer whose voice rose and fell like a teacher's, who promised them that the works of the Reich would endure forever. We make art for ourselves, he told them, for Germans and no one else because we are all blood relatives. Every one of them was united by German blood and they would work together to create something beautiful, something for the ages. Georg listened for hours, he stood all day with the other boys in the arena but they weren't tired, and when the sun set at last and the sky went to purple and then to black, the lights came on. They came on together and shot pillars into the sky.

"God," Georg said then. He'd forgotten all his languages. *God* was the only word he knew, and he said it again and again. They were in a cathedral. It was made of silver and light, and he wept at the sight of it and shouted with the others until his voice cracked and broke. He expected angels to come down and join them there inside those pillars. Not angels with ringlets and lyres; no, they'd be angry angels with sky-colored eyes, who carried swords and daggers, and they knew no tenderness and no mercy. He didn't sleep that night or the next. None of them slept. They were restless and dreamy, and their thoughts went round in circles.

The effects lingered for weeks. He was absentminded when he sat with Mutti at the table, and when she asked him about his time in the city, he looked over her shoulder and toward the window. "It was something," he'd say. "It was all right." She asked him again, but it was no use, and so she cleared his plate and left him. He paid no attention in school either, drawing pictures instead of pillars and lightning bolts and angels with slanted eyes. His father called him up and whipped his hands with green reeds, and he woke for just a moment, he woke to feel the sting, but he went dreamy again before he'd reached his desk. When they teased him now for being the fattest in the group or running knock-kneed as a girl, he could muster no anger. They'd been there, too. They'd seen those lights in the sky, and Müller had sat high above them.

SCHNEIDER CAME RUNNING to the trench with the news. His boots were both untied, and it took him a while to catch his breath. "They got them," is what he said. He coughed and fanned his face. "They brought them back already."

Georg kept stacking the buckets. He didn't want to stop. He didn't want to listen, but he could hear Schneider and everything he said. They'd gone only eight kilometers before the border police found them. Eight kilometers in three days because they went in circles once they were in the forest. He'd heard it from Graf who overheard the nurses talking by the infirmary, and so it had to be true. They walked around the same trees and couldn't find their way, and on the third day they lay down beside a beech tree and went to sleep. That's how the police found them, sleeping by a stream.

He saw them the next morning when he marched to the hole. They were strung from two of the linden trees in front of the church. They swung like lanterns, and the littlest one had reached around the rope and his fingers froze like that, they clenched tight by his throat. All day Georg thought of them and how they swung. He stopped by again that afternoon. He stayed late at the trench so he could walk back alone and visit them. Idiots, the way they did it. They should have planned it better. They should have brought maps with them and a compass and warm clothes because the weather was turning already and soon the snow would start and what would they do then, what would they do in their shorts and their thin socks. They could have asked him. He would have gone. He and Müller both, and the five of them would be far from the trench and the mattresses and the linden trees. They might even be home already. He tried to feel sorrow for them, but only anger came. He wanted to bring them back so he could shout at them and tell them all the things they'd done wrong. He wanted to shake them by the shoulders. He stood below the branches instead and looked at their muddy shoes.

The next morning someone had lettered a sign by the base of each tree where they hung. *Look at me*, the signs said, *look how far I ran*. They hung for four days, and then they were gone and the signs were gone, too, but he could still see the marks the strap had left on the branches.

## 5

E tta waited until Max had left before she went into his room. He was out walking again. He left every morning after breakfast. He came home for lunch, but he left again right afterward and was gone until dark. Who knew where he went or what he did outside. When he came back at night he paced around his room, and she heard him knocking sometimes against the walls. The sound kept her from sleeping.

"This one's a roamer," her mutti had always said when Max was just a baby. "I can tell from the light in his eyes." He followed the tracks when he got older, all the way to Hafenlohr and farther on to Rothenfels. He was restless, so different from Georg, who stayed inside his room even on sunny days. Max climbed trees and dug around the muddy banks, and he brought home frogs and worms and river snakes. He hid them in secret places, but she found them anyway. "This is a house," she'd say, "a house and not a zoo," and she'd march him back to the river. "You have to put them back in their spots. You have to bring them home." He hid them and she found them, even the snails in their sour brown water. *What a mess you've made, what a stink*, and though she aired his room and mopped his floors with vinegar, the smell lingered. She scolded him then. She shook her finger in his face, but he looked at her with those pale eyes, crestfallen that his three snails had died neglected in their jar, and she gave up.

His room was messier now than it had been when he was little. She took off the sheets and pillowcases and dusted all his books. An old almanac and Bernhardt Otto's *Natural History of Birds* and the complete works of Lucretius and books in Greek and English and French. His room looked more like the library in Würzburg than a bedroom. She left the books open so he wouldn't lose his place. He had underlined some passages in pen and marked the margins with strange scribblings, with stars and numbers and arrows that pointed to nothing. They taught him strange things in the army. He hadn't written in his books before, not even with a pencil.

She opened his window to bring fresh air inside. A lone black bird flew in circles above the trees. She caught a motion below. It was Josef out there in the garden, hopping on one foot. She leaned on the sill to get a better look. There he was, jumping up and down first on one foot and then the other, his face flushed from the damp air. He stopped his hopping and started to run in place. Puffs of steam came from his mouth as he exhaled. He was exercising, and in the cold. It was no good, these strange exertions. Every day he became more peculiar. Sometimes he sat in his chair and rubbed his chin and she wondered who he was, this old man with his pen and paper, and what he'd done with her Josef.

She went down the stairs and out the back door. "Josef," she said, "stop for a while and come inside." She reached out to touch his arm, but he kept running. "It's too cold out here. You'll catch a chill. You'll get a lung infection."

"I'm getting ready," he said. His nose dripped, but he didn't stop to wipe it.

She sniffed but could smell no beer on his breath. "Tell me what you're doing." She reached for his arm again and caught it.

"They need me." He licked his lips. He was tired from running and began to slow his pace.

"Come inside for a while," she said again. So he'd seen the posters and wanted to join. She knew he'd see them when he went into town. They were everywhere, by the waterspout and the bank and outside the beer hall, calling for old men and boys to sign up and fight. *Come and join the Volkssturm*, they said. *We'll all do our part. For freedom and survival.* Men were joining in all the towns and cities, old men and the injured and veterans with bandages. Soon there would be only women left in Heidenfeld, old women and the bell ringer and the priest to bless the dead.

Josef squinted at her but didn't resist. They went to the kitchen together, and she pulled his damp jacket from his arms. Drops of sweat rolled down his forehead and into his eyes. "I don't have much time," he said, and he rubbed his eyes with his knuckles.

"Have some soup, and then you can go back outside."

"We meet next week." His hand shook a little as he lifted his spoon. "We're all going together."

She set a spot for Max in case he came back early. Josef dipped his bread and drank from his bowl, but he stood up from the table as soon as he had finished. He went back outside, and she watched him from the window. He ran between her beds, where the chamomile grew and the peppermint. He stopped every little while and bent at the waist. She shook her head. All those old men training like soldiers. They were an army of grandfathers, and it was a sorry thing to see. He pumped his arms. His hair was wet and lay flat on his head, and as he hopped she saw his bare ankles under the cuffs of his pants. He'd forgotten to put on his socks again. She noticed this only now. She'd set them out for him, and still he forgot. He'd get blisters in those stiff leather shoes, but she didn't go to him.

HOW GOOD IT felt to move in the damp air. How good to get the heart pumping instead of sitting by the radio waiting for more news. He had another half hour before the announcers came back on. Every day the battle was coming closer. Every day another place was lost, and they'd have to work together to push the Bolsheviks back, every boy and every man from nine to ninety. Age didn't matter when duty called. It was almost two years since Stalingrad was lost, two years falling back, and it wasn't any better to the west. The Amis were pushing hard against Aachen and Metz, but none of the sacrifices were in vain, the announcers were certain. Every battle lost was a prelude to the victory that would come, and so he ran around Etta's rosebushes and the low herb beds. He slipped on the wet stones and went down to his knee like a suitor asking a girl to dance. His wool pants were torn. His knee throbbed. It would swell and turn blue, but he didn't care. He looked up toward the kitchen window to make sure Etta hadn't seen, and then he pushed himself back up and kept on with his running.

He was as fit now as he was at forty, even Etta would have to agree. All those years he rode his fine Hercules bicycle around the country-side, and even now his muscles remembered how to move. He rode when he was free for summer or when the schoolhouse was closed for measles. It's better than the train, he'd told Etta, much better because you can see things as you go. He'd put on his fine wool knickers and his cap or his rain cape, and off he'd go, pedaling fast as a boy. Max was still in elementary school back then, and Georg was a baby who wailed through the night and found no comfort when Etta held him against her breast. While Etta stayed home with the boys, Josef toured with the other teachers in the group and he joined the ice-skating group, too, and a choir. He loved his groups, he did, he loved their politics and their administrative duties and all the meetings and discussions necessary to keep their affairs in order. They'd meet in the beer hall, sitting at their regular table and holding their glasses close to their chest, usually the house beer but on special occasions they'd have a glass of fine Kulmbacher beer, too, and he missed those afternoons when the work was done and they sat together playing skat in groups of three. The men were old now and some were dead already, and his bicycle was long gone, too, and he didn't remember what happened to it, but his body was still strong and for that he was grateful.

ETTA TOOK OUT the tablecloth she'd made years before and centered it on the table. She'd tatted the border and embroidered all the roses, and it didn't have a single stain. The china came out and the candlesticks and what silver she had left. She'd traded away all the serving pieces, one by one they went or sometimes in pairs. She traded them for knitting wool, for black tea and smoked ribs and cases of writing paper for Josef. The teapot was gone and the sugar tongs and her creamer, but she had eight forks still and eight spoons, and she stayed in the kitchen while she polished them because it smelled so sweet there by the oven. Ilse had given her butter, just enough for one of her cakes. Butter was how heaven smelled, she was sure of it, butter cookies and butter cakes and thin veal cutlets fried in buttery pans.

The ladies came just before two, wearing hats and their best shoes. She opened the door and took the *mitbringsels* they brought. They gave her marmalade and dried fruit, and Regina Schiller gave her a piece of perfumed soap wrapped in silk, so old that the scent was gone and the silk had faded at the edges. Ilse was the last to knock. Her eyes were shiny as a cat's when she came inside, and all the ladies looked at the bowl she brought, heaped high with whipped cream.

Regina sat beside Etta and then came Maria and old Hansi the spinster and then Ilse, who sat on Etta's other side and was closest to the platter. Etta cut the cake and ladled out the cream, and they were impatient and fingered their plates. They tried to eat slowly, all of them, putting their forks down from time to time and sipping *mucke-fuck*, chicory coffee, from their cups. Ilse finished first and cut herself another slice. *Thin as a knitting needle, and look how she eats.* Etta uncrossed her legs. Her skirt was tight already, and she wanted to unbutton it.

"How is Max?" Maria set her cup on its saucer. She was wearing rouge today and her perfume was strong and smelled of gardenias. "He looks busy when I see him."

"He's fine," Etta said. She cleared her throat. "Every day he's better."

"Of course he's better," Ilse said, with a sidelong glance at Maria. "I saw him just yesterday walking the bridge. He's fatter already and not so pale." Nothing better than being home again and walking in the air. Georg would be home soon, too, and then Etta would have both her boys.

The ladies went quiet. They raised and lowered their cups. They reached for the sugar and smoothed their skirts, and Maria cleared her throat and tried again. "Frieda Richter's off to the old people's home," she said. She leaned over the table, and her voice dropped low. "To a shared room." They shook their heads. What a shame how those girls treated their mother. They were tight with the money, and her youngest lived just two towns over and still she couldn't spare the time to help with the move.

Maria sat back in her chair and folded her hands across her lap. She was finding her rhythm, and they all leaned in to hear. She knew things. She heard things at the beauty shop and in the milk line and down by the bridge. Young Fischer was back. He'd lost his hand. He wouldn't be playing the piano anymore, but at least he was safe. Dr. Kleissner was making his rounds again. He was going on visits all over town. He went to see the Schneidermanns about their boy, their soft-cheeked Franz whose voice had never changed and he was almost sixteen but he didn't know his numbers or his letters and he sat beside his mother while she worked and clapped his hands and sang. Dr. Kleissner with his shiny leather satchel, and Etta's chest went tight at his name. He had a new office down on Marienstrasse, and who knew what he did all day because he birthed no babies and stitched no cuts. He came from the city and he had no family in Heidenfeld and no wife or children either.

And what about Trudi Helmner, Maria was asking. She was big enough for twins, the way she waddled, and she'd dropped already and was carrying them low. What a scandal. What a shame for the family and her mother especially, who acted like the bump wasn't there. It was best to agree with the poor woman. Something might come unstrung inside her head if they didn't all agree. Yes, they said, it's a pity, the men are all gone and the girls are having babies. Godless times we live in. Strange godless times, and two more boys were dead and buried. The Gabler brothers from Rothenfels, and Etta blinked hard to keep from crying. The radio announcers spoke of battles in distant cities and how things would turn around once their boys were closer to home and fighting on their own land. Victory was inevitable, they said, victory was a given, but the ladies knew better. Their boys went away, every day they left and they didn't come back or they came back broken and what use was victory then when everything was lost.

Etta brought the wine jar when the coffee was done. She filled their glasses, and the windows steamed from the heat of the stove. The rain came down against the panes and the garden was empty and the street beyond, and all the world was gray. "You make a sweet drop," Regina said. "Honey-sweet." The stove clicked and popped, and they all nodded, yes, it was sweet as peaches. Etta knew just how to soak the berries. Not so long ago their boys would play outside while the ladies chatted. Even in wintertime they played, Maria's boys and Regina's and Max and sometimes even Georg when he was willing to set aside his books. They ran around her garden and the neighborhood boys would come, too, and bring their soccer ball, and their shouts and their laughter came through the window. Etta would warn them if they got too rowdy. "Careful with my roses," she'd say, "don't climb up on my shed," and she'd shake her finger and smile because they were boys and wild and she left them to their running.

Regina went to the piano when the talk began to slow. She played classical pieces and a few popular ones, too, sentimental songs that the ladies all knew. They sat around the table and drank their wine and listened to Regina, whose eyes were closed. Her hands stopped shaking when she worked the keys. It was better than any medicine, and that's why she still played the organ at services, even in wintertime when it was cold inside the church and everyone else wore mittens.

"One more," Ilse said when Regina stopped. "Just a quick one." Ilse's eyes were soft from the wine. She didn't want to go home just yet. The other ladies clapped. "Just one more," they said, "it's early still. It's not even dark outside." This was the nicest time, when the wine jar sat on the table and the candles burned low and cast a sweet light around the room. Their houses were empty and their stoves cold, and they didn't want to leave. "One more," they said again. There was time for another song. Etta went around the table and filled their glasses, but only halfway this time. She still knew how to make them happy. Even now she threw a fine klatsch and kept them in their chairs.

Regina sat back down. She took a breath and played something she had never played for them before. It started slow, sped up and slowed down again, lingering in unexpected places. It was mournful, the way she played it. She moved her head to the music, and Etta was certain Regina was with her boys, with her three boys who were buried where the ground was always frozen and no flowers bloomed. She looked around the table at all the ladies. Their springtime had long passed, and their summer, too, and they were deep into winter now. Bare as the branches of the trees.

Nobody spoke when the song was done. It was time to go. They walked with Etta to the door and thanked her. Regina leaned in to give Etta a peck on the cheek, and she squeezed Etta's hand. "He goes to the cemetery. Every morning I see him there." She pulled Etta closer. "Keep him home if you can. He shouldn't be out walking."


IN THE MORNING Etta gathered pine branches for her mother. The weather had started to turn, and it was time to cover her. She tended to the grave as she would a garden, planting roses there and pansies, and tulips for the springtime. In winter she set pine branches over the mound to protect the bulbs, and she set the prettiest branches in the urns and tied them with ribbons. "Winter will pass," she said, "it will pass and all the flowers will bloom for you." Her mother had hated the snow and the gray days of winter. She had loved spring best and summer and the warm evenings when she could stand outside in her garden. The light went soft then, and people fanned themselves and talked until late. All these things were lost now. Her mutti was gone, and she'd taken them with her. Etta laid the branches down. She sat on the bench and waited.

Max came through the iron gate just as Regina had said he would. He came through at half past ten. He tapped the cisterns as he passed and dipped his hand inside, but they were empty already, drained for winter. He walked past the stone building that held the dead for burial. He stepped off the path and onto the grass. Etta rose so she could see him better. He stopped beside a gravestone and held out his arms, as if beckoning someone to come. He hadn't shaved and his hair was too long and he looked like a conjurer and not her boy. He looked like a gypsy.

She walked toward him. He gave no sign that he heard her steps. He raised his arms toward the sky and threw back his head. She was afraid for a moment that he was not there in the yard, that it was someone else standing there, some stranger casting spells over the stones. She came closer, and then she heard his voice, her boy's voice, speaking, cajoling the headstone, "Loud," he said, "you're being too loud, and I can't hear."

She touched his shoulder. He gave her his hand as if he'd been expecting her, and they went together to the nearest bench. He put his hands in his lap and rocked a little. "I'll sit for a while," he said, "just a little while, and then I've got to go."

"Come home with me," she said.

He looked at the gravestones. "All their clocks have stopped." He tapped his chest. "Mine should have stopped, too. I don't know why it keeps on going."

The first flakes began to fall. They wouldn't stick. The snow would turn to rain again, but they fell now, fat flakes that melted against her cheeks. He had always loved snowy days. He stayed outside for hours when he was little, pretending not to hear her call. He skated on the pond, tracing circles in the ice, asking to stay just a little longer, *Come on, Mutti, just a little longer*, and his face was pink from the wind. She squeezed his hand. The first ladies were coming through the gates. They descended like crows, those ladies in black, and huddled low on the mounds.

Even when he was little Max had a way of fixing his eyes on her and asking questions that had no easy answers or no answers at all. "Mutti," he'd asked her once when he was only six, "where do birds go to die? I see birds every day and never a dead one. Where do they go then?" and Etta could only shake her head at her boy, who thought of such things. "They go someplace nice," she told him, "where it's quiet and the cats won't find them and the wolves and foxes neither. That's why we don't see them. They go to bird heaven." He looked at her a long while and then he nodded, satisfied with her response. It made sense that birds could find their way to heaven. They flew beneath it every day. It would take only a breeze to bear them up and through the gates, only a breeze and they were gone.

She took him by his arm and stood up from the bench. "It's time," she said. "It's time to go home and rest," and there were red marks on his wrists like scratches from a cat. "What happened to your skin?" She tried to look. She bent close and reached for his sleeve, but he pulled his arm away.


SOMEONE WAS KNOCKING at the front door, but Etta stayed on her step stool. She had no need for company. Max had left the house early again. She'd tried to hold him back. She took him by the elbow because people would be watching him now. His outburst at the mass had drawn their attention. They'd be looking for more signs, but he shook himself free and he left without shutting the door behind him. She wiped each of the crystal drops on her entry chandelier. She used a white cotton cloth and she worked her way around its arches. She had been cleaning for hours. She had started with the bedrooms, stripping the sheets and reaching under each of the beds with her feather duster. She used a fine brush for the baseboards and the sills, and she'd wash all the windows next, even though it looked like rain. Everywhere she looked she saw dirt and dust and smudges. It was a wonder anyone could live in the house. The visitor knocked again, more loudly this time. She sighed and climbed down.

She looked out to her stoop from the hallway window. Dr. Kleissner stood on the steps, holding the banister with his left hand and his satchel in his right. He wasn't her doctor and not Josef's either, but she had to open the door. He'd seen her behind the lace curtain. He'd caught her eye and waved.

"Guten Tag, Frau Huber." He took off his hat and held it against his chest. His pale eyes watered from the wind. "Winter has come early, hasn't it. There's no going back now."

Etta nodded. "Guten Tag, Herr Doktor." She opened the door wider, but she didn't move aside to let him in. "How nice to see you."

"I'm frozen through." He stepped around her and into the hall without waiting for an invitation. He set his hat on the credenza. "It's the wind and not the cold. No jacket is warm enough when it blows."

Etta didn't move toward the dining room or offer him a seat. "I'm afraid there's been some mistake, Herr Doktor. We haven't called for you. You walked all this way, and on a day like this."

"Is your husband home?" He looked past Etta into the kitchen, where she had a pot of chicory coffee brewing for Josef. His hair stood up in wisps from his head, but he didn't try to smooth them.

"He's doing his exercises." Etta pointed toward the back of the house. "Every day he goes out there even in this cold."

The doctor nodded. He set his satchel down beside his hat. "It's good to see our older men working on their fitness. Your coffee smells good, Frau Huber. Might I have a cup?"

Etta set a place for him on the dining table. She brought out her good Rosenthal cups and peeled and sliced an apple and fanned the slices on a saucer. Josef was jumping now, she could see him through the window. He hopped in place on the rock path between their garden beds. Up down, up down, like a boy and not an old man, up down, and he stretched his arms out and bent at the waist and touched his shoes.

"What about your son?" The doctor ate the apple slices one after the next, and his hands were delicate and plump as any woman's. He dabbed his watering eyes with his napkin. "Is he home?" the doctor was asking. "Is he home today?"

"I have two boys." Etta turned from the window. "I have two and they're gone the both of them." She set her hand to her throat to make sure her pearls were still there. "Georg is at the academy, and Max is outside walking."

"He likes to walk, does he? The whole family is very fit then. It's a good thing to see. Fit in the body, fit in the mind." The doctor reached for the last apple slice.

"He likes the cold air, my Max. He goes down by the river." She found herself talking without meaning to. The doctor said nothing. He sat there with his coffee cup, and the silence in the room weighed on her. She talked just to fill the empty air. "He's always been an athlete. He's like a fish how he swims."

Just then Josef pushed the kitchen door open and let it close behind him with a slam. "Du, Etta," he said. "Where are my good socks? These socks here are much too thin." His cheeks were red from the wind.

The doctor stood up when Josef came into the dining room. "Herr Hauptlehrer," he said though Josef wasn't a teacher anymore. He extended his hand across the table. "It's an honor to meet you. I've heard so many things about your family."

Josef's chest puffed at the doctor's words. He stood a little straighter and he gripped the doctor's hand with a crisp nod. "I've heard about you, too, Herr Doktor. Forgive my hand. It's a cold one today. Cold as January the way the wind blows."

"It's nice and warm in here," the doctor told him. "Come join us. I've been chatting with your wife. She's told me about your boys."

Josef sat down and waited for Etta to bring him his coffee. She didn't want to leave them alone together, but she went to the kitchen and came back out with another cup and saucer.

"I might come see you," Josef was saying as Etta came to the table. He set his hands together, and they were chapped from the cold. "I might need to bring you a form," and the doctor nodded, but he was watching Etta as she poured the coffee. Her hand was shaking and she rattled the pot as she set it down. "I'm almost sixty and they might need a signature before they can sign me up."

Dr. Kleissner nodded again. "Not a problem." He watched Etta as she lifted the cup, but Josef didn't notice. "You look perfectly fit." He checked his wristwatch. "He stays out for a long time, doesn't he, your Max? He must have many things to do."

The doctor sat there like somebody on vacation. He looked at Max's medals on the wall and at the window to the garden where Etta had cut back her roses and covered her raised beds. The apple trees were full with crows. The wind bent the bare branches, but the crows stayed where they were. "It's a nice house you have here. A very nice piece of land. It must be lovely in summer when the roses are blooming."

"We grow vegetables, too," Etta told him. "We grow more than we can eat."

"That's good to hear. I've got other houses to visit, but I'll come again. I'll come when Max is here. It's a formality, nothing more. It's for the records office. I'll come by in the morning sometime and drink more of your good coffee."

Josef pointed to the doctor's empty cup. "Pour him another," he told Etta, but the doctor shook his head.

"Another day," he said. "Another time when I come back," and Josef walked him to the door. They stood together at the top of the steps for a long moment, just two gray shadows against the rain-gray sky, before Josef came back inside and closed the door.

## 6

The planes hovered in the air, and everything was still. Only the bombs were moving. They fell from the sky. Georg saw them fall, slowly, slowly, saw them glint for a moment and pick up speed. The thunderclap came next, a rumbling that seemed to start in his belly, the sound of rocks rolling down a hill. Boys jumped into ditches. They lay on their stomachs and covered their faces. Four trucks lifted from the road and their fuel canisters popped. The debris blew out in all directions and hit the boys who'd been walking closest. Their jackets fluttered like birds and fell to the ground. Things arced and pirouetted and shot flames. They moved with a strange grace.

Georg held his hands against his ears. He lay under the trees, and Graf was there beside him, but he didn't know where Müller was. He hadn't seen him since the early afternoon. When the sky was quiet again they ran to the road. They found Schneider first, and two younger boys beside him. They were black from the heat, and their eyes were flat and had no shine. Dull as fish the way they looked toward the branches, not even surprise in their faces. Georg touched Schneider's wrist. He held it and set it back down.

Graf didn't look at Schneider. He was on his knees, spitting into the mud. Farther up boys shouted and wept. A lieutenant came and gave them shots for pain and pinned the empty syrettes to their belts, and they went quiet. Their skin was blistered and hung from their legs in strips. It was an awful thing to see, and still Georg was jealous. They'd be home soon, where they could lie in bed all day, and their mothers would bring them all their meals and sit with them and read them stories while they rested.

Georg pulled Graf to his feet. He shook him by the shoulders. What was wrong with him, falling down like that and crying. He wanted to slap him, to pull him by his ear. "Get going," he said, "we need blankets," but all the focus was gone from Graf's eyes. "Blink," Georg said, "look at me," but it was no use, and so he walked the road alone. Some younger boys brought blankets, and Georg helped cover the dead. A few lay where they'd been walking, and one had gone upward into the branches. Two boys were up already in the tree, shaking the pieces loose.

Georg looked at each of the bodies before he covered them. He breathed deep and looked. He saw a boy who was burned and blistered, and his hands reached up toward the sky. He saw another boy he knew. His knew his face but not his name, and he looked so peaceful there, as if taking a rest from the buckets, just a rest and then he'd be back and filling them with his shovel. His face had no marks. He wasn't burned or cut. Who knew what strange trajectory had brought him to the sharp rocks and not the dirt and the pine needles that might have cushioned him.

Georg walked up and down both shoulders of the road, and then he went between the trees because there was no telling where the boys might be. His legs were shaky. He took off his jacket and tied it around his waist. He was a doctor. He was a hunter and a surgeon and a scientist. He felt nothing when he saw them. This is what he told himself. All those Saturdays hunting with his father and Max had taught him about blood. "Be brave," the old man said. "Blood washes clean." He looked at the boys the way he looked at the bucks his father shot. They were reduced to their elements, reduced to bone and muscle and skin, and he felt no sorrow, not even a twinge. He was angry when the others wept. "Be quiet," he wanted to say, "stop your crying," but his right eye began to twitch and his knees didn't stop their shaking, not even when he went to bed.

Müller came in just before the lights were out. He took his spot and he closed his eyes before Georg could talk to him. Georg cried then. The tears came because Müller was alive and not lying beside the road, and what grace there was in the world, what perfection, was safe for a little while longer. It was there in the room with him, three mattresses over.

TRUCKS CAME THE next day and took away the bodies. Georg and Müller helped with the birch crosses. Georg held the planks, and Müller nailed them together. "We'll need more," Müller said. "Ten isn't nearly enough." The rain began to fall while they hammered them into the ground where the boys had fallen. The wood turned black from the water.

A captain came especially from Karlsruhe to speak. He said their names and how old they were, would always be, and the names of their parents and their towns. Abt, Adler, Bader, Durr, Eichel, Fränkel, Gersten, Meissner, Schreiber, Vogt. He said these names as if casting a spell, as if saying them aloud raised the dead from their boxes. "They were brave," the captain said, "they were all brave," and Georg wanted to correct him. They weren't brave, he wanted to say, they were unlucky. They were walking back to camp when they died. They were thinking about dinner.

Georg held his cap against his chest. He bowed his head. The boys stood in rows, and the youngest ones were at the front and Graf was with them and not with his group. Something was strange about him,

Georg could tell. Something wasn't right. Graf looked at the road and not at the captain, and when it came time to sing, he stayed quiet. The boys knew all the words. "*I had a comrade once,*" the song went, "*none better could you find,*" and Graf stood perfectly still and looked at those black crosses.

MÜLLER LIT A cigarette. They had been granted leave, only for a day, but still it was a day away from the buckets, and it felt like freedom. They climbed together after lunch. They were at the summit by half past two, and the mist rolled below them and made islands of all the hilltops. Müller smiled at him with a thievish detachment. Georg was close enough to see how pointed his teeth were and how yellow from the smoke. "Give me one," Georg said, though he was no smoker and it burned in his throat and made him cough and spit. Müller laughed then and shook his head. Georg laughed with him, embarrassed but happy, too, because they were alone there under the trees. The others were too lazy to climb. They napped on their straw mattresses or walked the streets and waited for the café to open. Müller was the only one who came along when Georg had asked at breakfast. "Why not," he said, "I'm sick of beer already. I'm sick of this sorry town." They climbed without stopping to rest, and their breath went raspy before they reached the top. The valley and the supply road and the trench, they were gone in the mist, and only Müller was left, only Müller and his cigarette.

Georg sat against a tree. He drew his knees up and hugged them. A few times the mist blew clear, and he could see the steeple and the trucks below and the schoolhouse where they slept. He squinted. He tried to make out who was walking the road and who was talking to the girls by the gate, but everyone looked the same from where he was.

"Baumgartner's out of the hospital," Georg said. "He's at home already and walking with a cane."

"I heard that, too." Müller pushed back his sleeves. He tapped his cigarette pack against his palm. He set it in his pocket and took it back out. He was fidgety today, and his hands were never still.

"There's more papers coming," Georg said. "Any time now they're coming."

Müller shrugged. He closed his eyes and opened them again. "Bring any coins?"

Georg shook his head. It had been weeks since he'd taken them out. He didn't have time to sit by himself anymore. The doors were always open, and he never knew when the others would come. "I've forgotten all my moves."

"Then you should practice more," Müller said. He reached for Georg's hand and held it up high.

"Not until I leave this place," Georg said. He wanted to run like the three who went into the forest. Müller would come and they'd leave the trench and the buckets and the crosses on the hills. Müller's grip was loosening on his hand, and so Georg pulled him closer. He reached again for Müller's face.

The kiss tasted of onions. It tasted of onions and tobacco smoke and salt from the climb. Georg closed his eyes. He should have been afraid because they'd hang if anybody saw. He was fat and had no grace and Müller could see his belly and how it hung over his belt. He should have been embarrassed, but he felt only wonder.

The wind began to blow, but they didn't climb back down. They talked about where they'd go once the fighting was done. They talked about school and finding rooms in the city, small rooms that were close to campus, and they'd walk together to their classes. They'd be

engineers. They'd study languages, and Georg would remember his
Latin and his Greek.

"Leave with me," Georg said. "Let's leave before our papers come."
Müller smiled at that and reached for his cigarettes.


GRAF CAME TO Georg at dinner. He sat down at the table and waited
until the others had left. "I need to show you something," he said. He
looked at Georg, as if gauging his worthiness. He tapped his fingers
while Georg finished. It was distracting to have someone watching, and
so he didn't take any food from the table. He'd be hungry tonight, and
it was Graf's fault.

They went to the basement together and down a long hallway. Graf
took him to a supply room that nobody used. It smelled of urine and
mothballs inside. There were two windows high on the wall, with
narrow panes of rippled glass, and one of them was cracked and let the
cold air in.

Georg saw the blankets first and then the pink ears, giant as bat ears
and pointy, with skin stretched so tight the capillaries showed. The
thing yawned and stretched one paw straight in front of it. It was a red
cat, no longer a kitten but tiny still. Graf rubbed its chin. Its fur was
paler there, the color of apricots and honey.

"Where'd you find him?"

"Out by the barrows." Graf reached into his pocket and pulled out
a stained napkin. "She'll eat anything, this one will." He fed her stew
beef from lunch, long stringy pieces, and she reached for them with her
paw.

Georg leaned in to see. He took a piece and fed her himself, and she
bared her little teeth at him.

"Will you feed her when I go?"

"Why me?"

Graf gave him a sly look. "You're good at taking food." He folded the empty napkin and put it back inside his pocket. "She'll be nice and fat with all you bring her."

Georg ignored that last remark. "They won't take you just yet." He watched the cat lick her paws and circle around before finding her place. She stretched and then lay down, looking at them through half-closed eyes. "You'll be the last one here," he said. He knelt by the blankets and stroked the cat's belly. He could feel her heart beating through her fur, and he wondered how it could pump so fast even as she rested, how it could go on like that for years, when it was only a little knot of muscle and blood.

"I'll be seventeen next month." Graf sat back against the wall.

Georg looked over at him. How could Graf be almost seventeen? He looked twelve, the way his jacket hung from his shoulders. "What's her name?"

"Maus."

"That's no name for a cat."

"Too late now." Graf stood up. He set one of the blankets over her, and only her nose showed and her white whiskers.

He didn't go into the room again with Graf, and neither one spoke about the cat, but Graf looked relieved regardless. He sat at the table with the others, and when they talked about who was leaving and when the next set of papers was coming in, he went quiet and looked down at his plate.

IT WAS THE middle of October when Graf slipped at the trench. He slipped and drove a pickaxe clean through his foot. The ground was slick, and all the boys slid and stumbled in their leather boots, but some talked anyway about how Graf fell. They gave each other knowing looks. He screamed the whole way back to camp, Georg heard. He screamed worse than a girl, and no medicine and no shots quieted him. They put him on a truck the next morning. Georg was there to wave goodbye, and for a moment Graf met his eye, and then he was gone. Georg fed Maus after that, sometimes more than once a day, and he spoke to her like a friend. Müller came along when he could, and it was their secret, this room in the basement and the cat inside, and they sat together against the blankets and watched the windows go dark.

## 7

M ax held his head when the pain started. He stayed in bed instead of racing along the streets. His eyes lost their focus, and Etta gave him aspirin and set a cool washcloth across his forehead. She rubbed ointment into the scratches on his arms. She needed him to get better, to come back to himself. When the aspirin didn't help, she went to the forest to pick feverfew for his tea. She knew where the best bushes grew. She had gone since she was a girl, pulling branches with her mother and picking rosehips and berries. *Come along*, she'd tell her boys when they were little, *come with me and help*, but they had no patience for picking. They longed for the sea instead, for the salty water. Who knew why, when the sea offered so little, no mushrooms and no berries, no shade under the branches, nothing but cold water and cold wind and a shore that stretched ahead, unchanging. Might as well long for the moon.

She took the paring knife from her basket and cut the fattest leaves. She tasted one out of habit and spit it out, puckering her mouth at the bitter taste. It was stronger than chamomile and aspirin and peppermint, stronger than any medicine. When the basket was full, she pushed herself up and brushed the bark and the needles from her skirt. A brown owl called from high in the branches. It turned its head around and its eyes shone bright as lanterns. People said owls bring bad luck, especially in the daytime, but the bird was beautiful and she was happy to see it. Etta took her basket and her walking stick and went back along the path.

She made tea for Max when she came home. She brewed those bitter leaves. She added honey and sliced him an apple, and he was still tapping his fingers when she brought him the tray. His books were stacked unevenly on the table, another one and the whole tower would fall. He was fixing the dictionaries, is what he told her. The languages weren't right. They were missing words, and he was filling them back in. He emptied his cup and didn't complain, but his eyes stayed cloudy. The pain came and went of its own accord.

THE NEXT TIME Max left the house, she went with him. He was going to walk the six kilometers to Rothenfels, and though she knew he wanted no company, she buttoned her coat anyway and came along. She wanted to see him when he was outside, away from his books and his bed. They walked beside the tracks, and it wasn't easy keeping up with him. "Slow down," she told him, "my legs are shorter than yours," but he didn't listen. The train passed them by, puffing steam as it rounded the corner toward Hafenlohr. The trees grew thick over the track in places. She had played in them when she was little. She sat high in their branches and waited for the train, and when it came she couldn't see her hands anymore or her friends or the tracks below. Everything fell away, and the air smelled of sulfur and milk.

She gave Max her hand. They were at the old furniture factory and Rothenfels proper, with its stone houses and its steeple, and they climbed the steps that went to Bergrothenfels high on the hill. The old castle was up there, and it housed German refugees from the East who'd lost their homes and all their things the year before when the

Soviets pushed their way through. The sandstone was slick from the rain. Max went first, and she held on to the railing. She should have pulled a pair of socks over her shoes, the way the ladies did in wintertime to keep from slipping. They passed the Kreuzschlepper, Christ carrying his cross up the steps, and they came to the top and sat together on the bench the way they did in better days when both her boys were home. A dog barked somewhere below.

"Do you know what the Greeks do?" Max found a small pebble on the wall and cupped it in his hand. "They dig up their dead. They wait a year and they dig them out of the ground and polish all the bones." He let the pebble fall and found another.

"You're making things up," she said.

"They polish them like furniture and set them into piles." He smiled a little. "It must reach the sky by now." He looked around for another pebble, and she gave him one.

"You should rest more," Etta said. "All this talk about graves will give you strange dreams."

"I found plenty of bones," he said. "I gathered them up." He spoke slowly, with the measured rhythm of a teacher or a priest. He spoke more than he had in all the weeks that he'd been home. They'd been fighting outside Stalingrad, along the Volga River. The city was burning. He hadn't seen the sky in weeks. The nights were hot as the days, and the smell of the dead and of gasoline and burnt powder and ash was so thick that it caught in the men's throats and made them gag. So much ash, and who knew where it came from. It fell like snow on the men. They tried to spit it up, tried to clear their throats and breathe, but the dust was deep inside their chests and could not be dislodged. Worse still was the noise, of screams and grenades and the tanks rolling over the dead and the dying and crushing their bones into the dirt. The ground was covered with a paste made from men.

Blunt died there and Steinmüller and Henrichs and both the Schmidt brothers. He said their names, and he lingered on Blunt because it was sad how it went with him. Blunt took a shell and bled out, and his face was sweet just then, as if he'd seen something strange and beautiful above the branches. A wife and a baby son, and he didn't say anything when he died, though Max leaned in close to hear. Fischer was there, his classmate from the gymnasium, and it was good to have someone from home even if they didn't know each other well. He didn't sleep at night. None of them did. The wind and the smoke made it hard, and the clouds were orange from the flames. Dogs howled and ran to the water. Who knew where they came from, those white dogs, but there was no crossing the river. Their heads bobbed in the eddies and were gone. "Saddest thing I saw," he told her. "The saddest thing. I've been other places, too. They dug their own graves and nobody tried to run. We shot them where they stood. Partisans, the lieutenant called them, but they looked like ordinary people." He rubbed his eyes, and it seemed for a moment that he wanted to say more, and then he turned away.

She touched his cheek. "Let me cut your hair," she said. He'd feel better without all that weight. He needed to stay home with her until he started acting like himself. He needed to stay inside so people wouldn't talk. "Come home with me. We'll take the train back together. I'm too old for all this walking."

He sat still for her when they came home and let Etta shave his beard. She was gentle with the razor, scraping it lightly against his skin. He hummed while she worked, a strange atonal buzzing that sounded like an engine or a wasp, and he opened his eyes only once, to look at the birdcage she had set in the hall. It was warmer there than in Georg's room, where she kept the door shut and lit no briquettes.

"I don't like that bird," Max said. "He's dirty."

Etta wiped the razor. "His cage is cleaner than a kitchen, the way I scrub it."

Max didn't answer. He closed his eyes and let her work. When she was done with the razor, she cut his hair, too, that beautiful hair of his that was so soft and curled around her fingers. He'd been born with all that hair, and people had all told her they'd never seen a baby like her Max, with his dark ringlets and those eyes blue as cornflowers and always watching.

"You look like yourself again," she said. She rinsed the razor and dried it. When she turned around to see him, he was gone already from the kitchen, and it was almost midnight before he came back home.

JOSEF WALKED ALONE to the schoolhouse. Kids taught the classes, no older than sixteen from the looks of them, and they showed him no respect when they talked. They called him old man and not Herr Lehrer, which was how they should address a teacher, and he could feel the blood pound in his temples at the insult. They pulled out rifles, taking them apart and cleaning them and explaining how things worked and who would do what. He listened to them and concentrated on the instructions until sweat drops rolled down his brow, but the words jumbled one into the next. They ran like water through his fingers. He let them go, the words, and listened like a foreigner to their rhythms and their strange harmonies.

Things were better when it was time for their exercises. He focused on the motion, arms bent at his sides, breathing in, breathing out, swallowing that damp air. He was good at training. The instructors had always singled him out when he was young. "Look at Huber," they said, "that's how it's done." It had gotten harder for him once he was in the field, where none of the exercises mattered anymore, where there was no pattern to things, no set time to sleep or to eat or talk things through, no order at all. Faces came close in the trenches and went again, and all the food tasted sour, and still he wanted to go back.

He felt a hand against his arm. She was always stopping him from his exercises, talking nonsense about the chill in the air or trying to feed him. He ignored her touch, but the hand did not let go, and he turned around to look. It was a boy, the youngest of them, no older than Georg. He was saying something, frowning at Josef and shaking his head. The sounds were muffled, as if the boy were underwater, and Josef caught a glimpse of a bubble as it rose from his lips and floated over their heads. He concentrated on the words.

"Time to stop," the boy said. "You're holding up our lunch." Time to stop and come inside. The others were all watching him. They waited by the door.

He went in where the food was. His eyes watered from the warmth in the room. He had wanted to tell them something, something important, but the words didn't come. The room smelled of soup and cooked blood sausage. He waited in line for his bowl. This was his room. He knew all the desks and where the troublemakers sat. He'd rap his walking stick against the floor when he saw a mistake, and they all jumped a little at the sound, and if they were unruly, he'd bring out his willow branches and snap them hard across their hands, right where the skin was the thinnest and the veins showed. He cut his branches down by the bank where the river ran slow. That's where the best ones grew. His students didn't complain when he took out his sticks, though the welts came up quick and their eyes brimmed. Even Georg had been brave when he held out his hands. How sweet to be back and how strange it was. The room should have folded itself up when he left. It should have disappeared, but everything was in its place, and the light still came through the windowpanes and the desks were just the same.

"My knees hurt," Schiff said. "I don't like all this hopping." He looked around for sympathy, but no one was listening. The men sat at the desks and ate their soup, and it was quiet in the room.

"Wipe your nose," Josef told him. "It's dripping again." Almost sixty, and Schiff still whined like a schoolboy. Josef dipped his bread. He looked around at all the men. He saw them in the beer hall every week and listened to their nonsense, and he'd taught their children and their children's children. Most of them he knew from earlier still, when they were little and walked to school together, and in summertime they raced their toy boats and ran along the bank to see, but the boats were always faster and outstripped them and shrank from view, until they were just a few colored dots in the water and then were lost to the ripples and the sun. How hard it was to look at them now, all those gray heads leaning over their bowls and the spotted hands with their enormous knuckles, shaking, shaking as they held the spoons. They'd been soldiers once and strong. He straightened in his chair. They needed discipline, not soup. Time to go back outside and work the muscles.

They cleaned their guns when the meal was done. The barrels would foul from the primer if the men weren't quick to clean them. They worked in the courtyard and by the gate. The lucky ones sat on benches, and others knelt on the stones. Josef knelt apart from the group. The solvent soaked into his skin and under his nails, and his fingers went stiff from the cold. The sun was going down. He stopped for a moment to watch it drop. It hung just above the hills before it went, throwing colors on the clouds. The men looked at their guns and not at the sky, and they didn't see.

"Look at that," he said. "Look at it fall away." He rubbed his eyes with his knuckles. He'd caught a fish once, unlike any carp or river eel, and it turned colors on the hook, thrashing from blue to violet to red and finally to gold. He wanted to show his boys. He packed up all his gear and went home fast, but the fish had gone dark by the time he reached the door. They wouldn't have believed him anyway because fish don't change colors when they choke on air. He closed his solvent jar and gathered up his patches.

They called them up one at a time and gave them their bands. The tallest boy, the one who'd called him an old man, handed them out as if they were a trifle and meant nothing. When Josef went up, he stood extra straight, to show them how a soldier stands, and he took his armband, red and white and black, and put it on his arm. It had two eagles on it, their wings stretched wide. The old men had no uniforms. They had only their rucksacks and their garrison caps. Etta had found his old steel helmet, too, and he held it against his chest. He waited until the distribution was done, and he gave them a crisp salute. He felt young as a boy, and it didn't matter that the wind was blowing harder now and the others had turned to leave.

It was late and she'd be waiting, but he went down by the river when the ceremony was done. He walked fast toward the bank, where the dirt was wet. He cut a few branches with his folding knife, feeling them with his fingertips to make sure they were smooth and had just the right amount of spring. They had to be green enough to bend and snap against the skin. He didn't use the branches they had at school, which were too brown and brittle and would break sometimes before he was done. He looked to his left and his right, but he was alone there on the bank. He tucked the best branches into his satchel before walking back home.

IT HAD BEEN hot the day he came back home to her all those years ago. Even now he could feel the heat and the bumping from the train. He had slept for most of the trip, turning first one way and then the other against the hard bench, his satchel wedged like a pillow under his head.

He awoke just as the train left Wertheim, and he blinked the sleep from his eyes and watched through the window. Women were working barelegged in the fields. The hills were still green, and the river looked just the same. Farmers were plowing as if nothing were wrong, as if there were no fighting just beyond the horizon, no fires and no gas that came in clouds and smelled of rotting hay. He pressed his fingers against the glass and thought of Etta's face. Her voice had faded from his memory during his time in the trenches, but her face remained, and her eyes, he could see them even now, how they turned up when she smiled, so dark, black almost, and shiny as cherries.

They had sent him home because he was sick, trench fever, they called it, and it sapped him dry, leaving him cold and shaking even in the summer heat. He ignored the signs at first, the headaches and the chills, but then his legs grew stiff in his boots and the visions came, strange devilish dreams that unspooled inside his head and kept him from sleeping and from waking, too, until he couldn't remember where he was. He began to make mistakes, sending out the shells too early or when the winds were wrong, and the gases made his own men fall to their knees from the burning in their eyes. They knew it then and sent him to the infirmary, where he made a quick recovery, and he went back to the trenches. But the fever returned and went away and returned again, and they gave up and sent him home.

He saw her right away, standing there so straight. He stood on the platform and she pulled him close, and though he tried not to weep, the tears came. She sang for him that night so he could sleep. She sponged his face with cool water.

For months afterward he dreamed of mud and parapets. On rainy days when the air smelled fresh like dirt and the river rose on its banks he went peevish and couldn't sit still in his chair. He didn't want to sit with his mother or drink coffee from fine cups. He didn't want to pray

in church. The smell of the mud was what he wanted. Cold coffee and
sour water and all the men squeezed in close. They didn't let him go
back. He petitioned twice and filed his papers, and they didn't even
reply.

His brothers had gone to the Kriegsakademie in München and they
were promoted to first lieutenant, all three of them in turn, and
they received the Iron Cross, Second Class and then First Class, and
his mother was proud and clipped the announcements from the paper.
She kept their death notices, too, as they came. Their comrades wrote
later with the details, and she kept those letters, too, but she read them
only once and didn't look at them again. She was angry when Josef
found them. She took them from his hand. Erich had taken a shell to
the neck and bled out on the field. It was quick the way he went. He
closed his eyes and slept. Oskar brought three men to safety before
succumbing to the fumes. And Richard, her youngest, the one who
looked most like her husband, God rest him, had only a sore on his foot
when he went to the infirmary. It festered for weeks, and no matter how
much they cut, the gangrene was faster than the surgeons.

After Richard died she went into her room and didn't come out, not
even for the memorial service, which was held at ten in the morning in
the old Heidenfeld church. Hundreds of relatives and parishioners
came, and the church choir sang the requiem in voices so clear and
beautiful they raised the hairs on his neck.

She wasn't the same afterward, his mother. She threw out her furniture for no reason. "Out with it," she'd say, "out with it all because it has
the woodworm and there's no fixing it." She tossed the pewter, too,
because it had tin pest and was starting to dissolve. He checked and
told her it was fine, but she didn't listen. On All Saints' Day she'd take
out pictures of her three boys. "Who's going to tend to their graves,"

she'd ask, "with them so far away?" She hung their medals in a box on the dining room wall, and when he looked at them, he saw only the reflection of his own face in the glass.

ETTA SAT IN Ilse's kitchen drinking coffee, and before their cups were empty Ilse went to the cupboard. "Let's drink something better," she said. "We'll have just a little glass." They should be at the cemetery preparing the mounds. In another day it would be All Saints' Day, and they needed to get the graves ready, but the wind was blowing and they sat inside instead. Ilse brought the jars to the table. She poured the liquor, careful not to spill, and it was dark like wine. She picked elderberries right after the first frost, when they were sweet from the cold. She had a gift for steeping, and not just with elderberries. She picked rhubarb and plums and apples, and one summer she steeped a handful of rose petals, but the ladies had wrinkled their noses at that. "It smells like perfume," they said, "you've made perfume and not schnapps."

Etta drank slowly. It burned a little in her chest, and it worked its way through her like medicine, loosening all her joints. "Something's not right with Max." She didn't mean to say it, but the words came anyway. "He doesn't listen to me or to Josef either. He pounds the walls at night."

Ilse nodded. "I see it when he walks."

"Are people talking?"

"They always talk. Tomorrow they'll talk about something else."

"Nothing helps with his headaches," Etta said. All the herbs she brewed and all the tablets, and nothing eased his pain. They'd take him away if they knew how bad it was. They'd take him just like they took the young Hillen boy, and nobody knew where he went.

"I'll go to Dr. Ackermann." Ilse finished her cup and poured herself another. "I'll talk to him tomorrow." If anyone could help Max, it was Dr. Ackermann. There was no better man in Heidenfeld, Ilse was saying. "Poor man. He hasn't heard from his boy in months. Every Sunday I bring him a warm meal, but I don't let him inside my house. He doesn't eat from my table." Her Walther might see. He'd be angry if another man sat at his spot. He'd been gone for twenty years now, but sometimes his chair still rocked and the curtains fluttered even when her windows were all closed. "He's just saying hello," she'd told Etta more than once, "he's just letting me know he's here." Spirit roaming, she called it, he's spirit roaming today, and so the doctor came only as far as her door.

"It's good to have somebody." Etta set her glass down.

"Keep him inside in the meanwhile," Ilse said. "Keep him away from the windows so people can't see."

"What are they saying?"

Ilse shook her head. "Keep him inside even if he wants to leave." She looked at Etta for the longest while, and there was something strange about the set of her face. She was lonely, Etta thought. It was the wine that brought it out. All the scrubbing and the washing, the mopping twice a day, and time passed so slowly, especially now. It was probably easier in the summer when she could work her beds. She grew herbs of every sort and beets and turnips, and for a short while she kept bees, which yielded a strange honey that was pale and tasted of clover. She had the heart of a farmer, Ilse, but none of the greed. She poured Etta another glass, and though she wanted no more liquor, Etta drank it.

Ilse took Etta to the cellar when it was time to go. She took her down the stairs, past the straw beds where she kept her apples and her plums, and lifted her oil lamp high. Etta blinked and her eyes adjusted, and she stepped back at what she saw. There were silver candleholders and serving platters and fine inlaid tables. Clocks ticked in the silence of that room, porcelain mantel clocks and larger wall clocks propped up one against the other. A grandfather clock stood improbably in the corner, and she wondered who had brought it around the house and down those narrow stairs. There were tea sets and goblets and dressing combs, cigarette cases and leather-bound books. Porcelain dolls with fine painted faces sat in a row, their blue eyes open and unblinking. Things were stacked neatly against all three walls—wonderful lustrous things that were the pride of their owners, that belonged on dressers and piano tops and dining room hutches and not in a cellar that was dark and smelled of earth and hay.

"By God," Etta said, "it's a museum you've got here."

"They're not mine." Ilse drew her hand across a blue silk dress. "I'm watching them."

It had started with old Frau Singer, Ilse told her, who had come for a visit five years before and sat in her kitchen. Ilse looked around the room. Her voice was low when she spoke. She looked at the clock and not at Etta, and her voice shook a little from the liquor. The old lady had been nervous and held her purse against her lap. They drank coffee together and talked of little things, and when the coffee pot was empty, Frau Singer waited a good while longer before asking. Frau Weinstein came next, and then the young Frau Stern, who had the grandest house of all, high on the hill where the tower stood. They came to her and asked for the same favor, and each time Ilse agreed because it didn't seem right to say yes to one and no to another. She waved away their offers to pay. "Keep your money and your gold," she told them, "I'm an old woman and have no need for them." Her cellar became a warehouse of beautiful and cherished things. She came down and dusted the piles every week, and she wound the clocks and polished the silver because it tarnished fast in the damp air.

"When they come back, they'll thank me." Ilse nodded as she spoke. "They'll thank me for taking good care of their things." And even as she said it, they both knew it wasn't true.


MAYBE IT WAS the liquor or maybe the coming rain. The roads looked narrower than usual when Etta walked home. The wind bit through her scarf. She thought of those dolls in their patent shoes and all that fine silver and the clocks ticking in the cellar and Ilse keeping watch, just Ilse and her whiskey jars. How hard to be in that house, alone with all those things. The air must be thick with ghosts. How little she knew about Ilse. More than forty years together and church every week. They drank their coffee and birthed their babies and knelt together at their family graves, and they were mysteries one to the other.

Etta stopped once by the bridge and wound her scarf across her mouth. People were inside already. They were drawing their curtains and snuffing out their lights. They huddled close to their wood-burning stoves, which sent up smoke into the sky, gray on gray. People were born in Heidenfeld and buried there and their children, too, and their children's children. They lived in the same houses, one generation after the next, and went to the same schoolhouse and worshipped at the same churches. The buildings outlasted them all. And still people went away. They went away sometimes, carrying only a satchel or a trunk. She'd seen it herself. The Weinsteins and the Singers and the Sterns who left behind their things. The two sisters who were prone to twitches and to fits, twins who dressed alike and worked side by side for Frau Ebing the seamstress, and they climbed aboard the train one morning and never came back. Young Hillen with his baby face was gone, and the gypsies went somewhere, too. They were gone from one day to the next, and there were no more bonfires by the riverbank then and no more dancing. How easy it was to forget them. Things changed and the mind adjusted, and it was an act of will to remember anything at all.

## 8

Müller left the first day of November, and he died the same week. Somewhere up near Aachen, they said, but Georg didn't listen when the details came. He held his hands to his ears and didn't listen because he knew already how Müller fell. He could see just how it happened. He was leading a charge into the trees when he was hit. He was stepping from his bunker. He was opening the door to the firing chamber. Working the turret with his crew. The scenarios came unbidden. Georg saw the tanks and how they moved and Müller was waiting for them to come closer, waiting, waiting, and then he pulled the cord. He had only nine seconds now, but the tank was covered in concrete and the grenade wouldn't stick. He lay down in the trench and waited some more. Just seven seconds now, just six. Everything was quiet, and he lay alone in the mud. Five seconds and four, and he reached up. The grenade stuck fast to the belly. The tank rolled over him and shuddered and stopped. He heard nothing when it happened, and he felt no heat. It was dark and the ground covered him. He'd been too slow. He needed a few seconds more. This is how it went with Müller. This is how it went with all of them. They died heroes. They died heroically and for no purpose.

Georg stopped eating in his bed when he heard. His rucksack was full to bursting, and he didn't reach for it. He stopped eating at the table, too. He fed Maus and sat with the others, and he didn't listen to their talk. Things ached for no reason. His teeth hurt, and he felt pangs just behind his eyes, and sometimes his vision went blurry and he heard the rushing sound of water. Müller's bed was the same and the chair where he sat at lunch. The books he touched and his boxing gloves and his civilian winter coat were packed in a trunk, and it was a full two weeks before someone carted it away.

Müller had his papers the day they climbed the hill together, Georg learned this only later. The Heller brothers saw him leaving the Unterbannführer's office with his packet, but he hadn't told Georg, not on the hill and not those evenings with Maus in the basement, and it was a double dying, this secret Müller had kept from him. He mourned his boy twice over.

THE RAIN FELL just as Müller had said it would. Some nights it was cold as January and the roads shone with ice. Trucks stuck in the mud and slid from the roads into the ditches below. The drivers cursed and leaned out their windows, and the boys came running. They found branches and pebbles so the wheels had something to grip, and when they were done, their faces were covered in clay and only their eyes were white. Water filled the trench and all the buckets, and even the sergeant shook his head then and sent them back to their rooms.

Mutti wrote him letters, but he didn't open them. Seeing her fine handwriting would only make things harder. The boys gathered around the postman, and they cheered when their names were called. They jostled each other to reach for the bundles. He left the letters from Mutti by his bed, and he didn't write to her either. He was ashamed for not writing. She loved it when letters came. She called Josef to come listen, and she laid them in her Bible when she was done, pressing them like flowers between the pages. He should have written, he knew this even then, but the longer he waited the harder it was and he didn't uncap his pen. He walked around the town instead and looked at all the boys and soldiers. He looked for eyes like Müller's, but there was no finding them.

THE DOCTOR HAD come especially from München just a few months before. They were still at the academy then, and Georg hadn't even spoken yet to Müller. The doctor wore a fine wool suit. He'd called them together and opened a folding box and they waited in line, unsure. This was when Georg first saw Müller, really saw him and how different he was from the others. The line moved slowly up the length of the assembly room and into the hallway. All morning they waited for their turn. The doctor lifted one glass eye after the next to find a match. His touch was tender as a mother's while he held their heads and looked. They held their breath when he leaned in, even the dark-eyed boys like Georg, hoping that he might see something beautiful in them, but he marked their forms and waved them each away.

The doctor frowned when Müller sat down on the stool. "Come here," he said, waving for his assistant. "Come quick." They looked together at those eyes and conferred in hushed voices and looked again, and Müller smiled the whole while. What a waste of time. This is what he must have thought. Grown men playing with marbles. Let the boys have them instead. Throw them high into the trees with slingshots and scare away the birds. Set them into statues. Give sight to all those blind faces from ancient Greece and Rome.

Müller answered the doctor's questions about his parents and their parents and his brothers and uncles and aunts, and the doctor wrote everything down. He scratched his head and adjusted his spectacles and looked at his notes and not at Müller. The boys were getting rest-less. It was time for lunch, and they could smell the sausage cooking and the hot dumplings. The doctor rubbed his chin, and the clock chimed in the tower. He shrugged and picked the blue eye, the lightest of the blues. It wasn't right and it wasn't true, but he checked the box and the next boy came to him. Blue-eyed parents had blue-eyed babies, and so gray eyes are blue because they must be. That's how things worked. Truth was iron bent over the anvil. It needed pounding some-times. It needed the hammer.

Müller had looked at Georg when he stepped down. The doctor was still writing in his journal, and the other boys waited their turn. Müller had put his cap back on, and the light fell slantwise across his face, and he was beautiful. Every time Georg looked at him afterward, he saw only gray in those eyes, only gray and no blue.

THE ROAD BY the wall was busy even when it stormed. Trucks and cars and men on bicycles and horses were all going north, north to where the fighting was. Men walked the road. They walked in the treads and along both shoulders. There were Germans and Poles and Hungarians and a few brown-skinned men in turbans who squatted together and smoked and their eyes were black as inkpots. They looked straight ahead when they walked and some were injured and bandages hung loose from their arms.

The boys went north sometimes, too, to help with the roads and to clear out the pillboxes where the farm ladies kept their birds. Apples on the ledges and chickens inside. The farmers had made coops of all the bunkers, and the sergeant shouted when he saw. He went red in the face. "Clear it out," he said, and the ladies gathered all their fruit and coaxed out their chickens. One old lady was slow to catch her birds, and the sergeant shot them where they were, and she carried them in her apron then and looked at the ground as she passed.

Georg was hauling dirt to the road when the commander signaled for the boys to come. "I need ten of you," he said. For a longer trip, to Saarbrücken this time. It would be two days, at most three, and then they'd come back and rest. He called them by name and gave the list to the driver and before he left he looked once more around the group. He pointed to Georg and a younger boy. "You two go as well." He waved his arm toward the truck, but he didn't bother to add their names to the list. "No harm in having a couple more up there. No harm at all."

Georg took his ladies. He packed his rucksack and wiped his mess kit clean. He tried to fit Firnholzer's book inside his bag but there wasn't any room. He set it under his mattress, with Mutti's letters and his favorite magazines, and smoothed his blanket so nobody could see. He went to visit Maus before he left. He filled her dish and sat with her, and she pushed her wedge-shaped head between his ankles. He brought her stew meat and peeled apples and told her to eat slowly because she'd get no more until he was back. She rolled over and showed him her belly, which was soft as a peach and warm from the blankets.

The road was pocked from the treads and the rocks and the sand they threw in wintertime. The truck was covered only with canvas, and the wind blew through the slits. They couldn't sleep at first with all the bouncing. They closed their eyes anyway, and a few boys covered their heads with blankets. Georg sat near the front and held the canvas open to see. There were men walking alongside the road. They leaned forward into the wind, and a few had fallen and lay on their backs. Farther on, two men knelt in the dirt, their hands held high, and a man stood over them with his rifle. He closed his eyes. They should have left weeks ago. He shouldn't have listened when Müller said no. They'd be far from the buckets now. Müller would be alive still and striking his deals. He always found what he was looking for, cigarettes and chocolate, folding knives and old magazines. He knew just where to look, and if anybody asked how, he set his finger to his lips.

Georg let the canvas drop. He turned first to one side and then to the other and he remembered his bed at home, how soft the mattress was and how cool the pillow felt when he first lay down. The hallway clock ticking outside his door and Kaspar sleeping in his covered cage and Mutti was probably still working in the kitchen. The motion of the truck rocked him to sleep and he saw his house again. The cemetery and the gasthaus and the schoolhouse with its leaded windows, he was flying over them and how small the buildings looked from above, how small the half-timbered houses. Max was there beside him, he was home from school and they were floating together and they rose and rose and they broke through the clouds. "Don't be afraid," his brother told him, and they were freer than they'd ever been or would ever be again.

The sky was clear when Georg awoke. The truck was moving more slowly over the ruts. He looked out through the canvas. There was no moon shining and no lights in the field. The darkness outside was a palpable thing, so real that he could feel it press against his skin like water, and the weight of it made it hard to breathe. He wanted to reach outside and feel the air. He wanted to spread it with his fingers just like Moses spread the sea. The others were still sleeping. They didn't stir when he rose from his spot. He leaned over to look through the opening and to the road below, which was black like a river and promised to pull him down to itself. He touched the pouch inside his shirt and felt the ladies there, giving him luck. He took a breath, a deep breath of that cold dark air, and he jumped.

## 9

Fischer looked earnest as an undertaker when he opened the door. His face was sharp, as if cut from wood and the carpenter had forgotten to smooth its fine planes. Etta took his left hand in both of hers and tried not to look at his empty sleeve. His mother had pinned it just below the elbow. Poor woman. She'd have plenty of sewing to do, stitching all his right sleeves shut so nobody could see. "Mutti isn't here," he said. "She's at the warehouse sorting wool. Every Wednesday she goes."

"I'm sorry I missed her," Etta said. She stepped inside. "You're thin." She took off both her mittens. "You all come home so thin."

She gave him the meringues. She'd used the last of her eggs to make them, and she set a walnut on top of each. The other ladies tried to bake them like hers, but they had no luck. Theirs were too dry or too chewy, and they'd complain then about how their ovens weren't working right or the eggs had been stringy. *It's the eggs that do it*, they'd say, *it's all in the eggs*, but they were jealous because it was such a simple thing making meringues and still it was hard.

They sat at the table and Fischer ate the cookies and his mouth was white with powder. "They're good," he said.

Etta took a cookie. She ate it slowly and thought of how to ask. She looked around the room, anywhere but that pinned sleeve. There were plates on all the walls. Beate had painted them herself, working for hours with brushes so tiny they had only a few bristles. She painted violets and snowdrops and finches, though she was better at flowers than birds. She made the heads too big, and the eyes looked strangely human. "Max says hello," Etta said.

He nodded. "I'm starting to play again." He reached for another cookie. "I've got music already."

"You should come by and see him."

"It was written for the left hand. For the left hand especially." He wiped his mouth with a napkin. "If I run out I'll write my own."

"Does it hurt?" It was rude to ask, but he didn't seem to mind.

"It itches," he said. "And sometimes I can feel my fingers. Where they were." He flexed his left hand and spread his fingers wide. They were long as a surgeon's and fine-boned. She looked down at her own hands. All those Sundays he'd played in church, even when he was just a boy. His mother had set books on the stool those first few years so he could reach the keys. He played for himself and nobody else and he sat so straight, and even Regina shook her head in wonder. "There's nothing I can teach him," she said once, "he knows exactly how to touch the keys." He was remembering, not learning. He was born with the music already in his head.

"Max has been home six weeks already," Etta said. "He talks about bones sometimes. He talks about collecting them."

"Have another, Frau Huber." He pushed the plate toward her.

"What did he do with bones?"

Fischer slumped a little in his chair. The light from the lamp cast shadows on his face, and his eyes were dark as sockets. He looked old. How strange to see a young man grown old like that. The thought made her tired. "He brought them back," he said at last. "He brought them so we could bury them."

She started to speak but changed her mind. Best not to interrupt because he might tell her something that could help. She sat by the table and looked out the window where Frau Fischer saw her finches. It was getting dark already. The branches swayed in the wind.

"They fell faster than he could find them." Fischer tugged at the pins in his sleeve. Max brought the dead back, he told her. He carried them on his shoulders. He pulled them through the dirt and ran with them. It was cold where he was, and when the bodies froze in the dirt and there was no lifting them, he brought something anyway. His hands were never empty. He brought their tags back or their helmets. The dead were buried all together. Sometimes the men gathered flowers and branches and set them on the graves, and all the fields were full with markers. "I was sorry when he left," he said. "The others weren't nearly so good."

"You came home before he did," Etta said. "He didn't leave until October."

Fischer shook his head. "It was June when he left, maybe July. They sent him farther east. They sent him to a punishment post."

She leaned across the table. "What do you mean, a punishment post? Punishment for what?"

"I didn't see anything." Young Fischer smoothed his sleeve. "I wasn't there when he left." People came all day long, he was saying. They came and they went again and most groups had a trembler or maybe even two. All the pounding had rattled something loose inside their heads. It was real as a bone break when it happened. Their eyes went funny, cloudy like milk glass and unfocused. Max didn't tremble, but he laughed when he shouldn't and he said things that made no sense. He disappeared once and nobody could find him. The lieutenant didn't like Max, everybody knew it. He didn't like anyone, the lieutenant. He was always moving his men from one post to another. He made decisions too quickly and changed his mind, and nobody ever knew where they'd go next.

"Did he hurt himself? Did Max hit his head on something?"

Fischer shrugged. "Sometimes people bleed when they're hurt, and sometimes they don't."

Etta tried to think of more questions. She needed to know what was wrong so she could help her boy. She sat with Fischer and looked at that strange face he had, which should have been beautiful with its fine lines but it looked unfinished instead. There was nothing more he could tell her. Her boy collected bones. He brought them back. All his life he'd been carrying things. He'd always been the one who lifted others onto his back. He'd carried Georg once, when they'd been skating together and Georg's blade caught on a twig. His knee had gone one way and his ankle the other, and Max brought him home on his shoulders. Georg wasn't a small boy, not even then, and Max climbed the hill with him and carried both their skates in his hands. He came home smiling. He was gentle like a doctor, the way he set his brother down.

Fischer held the door for Etta when she left. He stood by the steps and waved. "I'm lucky," he said. "If it had been my left, there'd be no music for me now." He promised to come visit. He'd spend some time with Max. They'd go out walking. It wasn't true. He'd stay where he was, they both knew this, but she thanked him anyway and put on her wool mittens.

It started to snow as she walked home. A gust took the scarf from her head and lifted it to the trees. It caught high on a branch. She waited for it to come back to her, but it was stuck fast, and it was there still two days later when she walked by.

JOSEF WALKED FROM the schoolhouse to the church steps and back behind the cemetery, but he couldn't find the buckets and the shovels. This was only his third week working and someone had taken them

when he wasn't looking, he knew this for certain. Someone had
snatched them to make trouble, and he'd spent the whole morning
retracing his steps, looking behind buildings and woodpiles and
digging up fresh snow with his hands because they could be anywhere
and he needed to find them before the lunch bell rang. He was kneeling
in a snowbank when one of the HJ boys came up to him and led him
back to the schoolhouse. They thanked him for his work there and let
him go. Josef told them it was early still, it wasn't even ten, and he had
an idea of where the shovels might be, or at least the buckets, but they
just shook their heads. No, they said, no need to look any further, and
they thanked him again for all he'd done and told him to go home.

     The other men were still clearing snow as he walked past the church.
Even old women were out there in the cold with their shovels and their
picks, throwing ashes and moving the snow before it got too heavy. They
were making a mistake letting him go. They needed him, they needed
every boy and man because the Bolsheviks were coming closer and the
Amis, too. He walked circles around the town without noticing where
he was going. Past the pharmacy and the bank and the post office and
the fire brigade with its red shield, past the shuttered butcher shop and
he was at the old stone bridge now and at the train station and he went
inside and bought himself a ticket. He rode to Wertheim where people
didn't know him and he spent the afternoon in the empty movie house.
He had no interest in movies, but there was a newsreel first and it
showed the Panzers fighting the Bolsheviks in the East, new Panzers
every day rolling over that white landscape, and the SS troops fighting
at the Oder bridgehead, fighting to keep the Bolsheviks out of Europe,
and he could watch the footage all day, the Führer proud as any father
pinning medals on a young airman, the *tuk-tuk* of the artillery and the
rocket launchers rearing back like horses, all the dead Bolsheviks on the
road, the broken buildings and the fires and the planes in the milk-white

sky, the German soldiers in their helmets smiling for the camera. He'd come back tomorrow and the day after that. He'd come again and again and he'd sit there forever if he could and watch those flickering pictures.

HE WENT TO see Dr. Kleissner on his way back home. He needed a paper, only a paper from the doctor, and then they'd take him back and he'd be clearing the roads again and getting ready for the final push. He tapped the stones as he went, and he wished all the ladies well. He asked about their sons, who'd been his students once. He stopped to rest halfway up the hill. He leaned against a lamppost. Look at those students, look at those girls up there and how they walked. They cut off that old woman by the nursing home. They walked around her on both sides and squeezed in tight, and she almost fell. If they were in his classroom now, he'd whip them and not just on the palms. He'd hit their knuckles too and split them open. He took his glasses off and wiped them with his handkerchief. No order to the young and how they acted. They shouted in the classroom. Just last year they'd stopped answering when he called their names, and they laughed when he turned to write on the boards. It only got worse once they were older. All their uniforms and their marching and they were wild underneath. They were uncivilized.

He stepped away from the post. He swung his arms as he walked the steepest part of the hill. He looked for those girls, but they were gone already and the old woman was gone, too, and he was breathing hard by the time he reached the doctor's office. He was sweating in his coat. Dr. Kleissner smiled when Josef came through the door. He held out his hand as if he'd been waiting all day for the visit.

*   *   *

DR. ACKERMANN CAME UP the walk, his head low because the wind was blowing. Etta let him inside. "He's upstairs," she said. "He's resting in his bed. He's tired from all his walking." She took the doctor's hat and coat and hung them on the hook.

"Let's see him." He smiled at Etta, and he looked like his father and his son, all of them doctors, and who knew if there'd be another. She wanted him to hurry, and she wanted him to wait. It was better to know. It was always better to know, and still she went up the stairs more slowly than usual. She hesitated at the door. She hoped for just a moment that Max would be gone when they came inside. That he'd be walking outside, and Ackermann would have to come back some other time. She took a breath. She pulled the lever and turned on the light.

She sat by the window and watched Ackermann work. He took a thermometer from his bag and then a stethoscope, and he listened to the beats of Max's heart. It raced fast as a puppy's, she knew this from sitting beside him and holding his wrist on her lap. It raced even when he rested because he worked at a higher pitch than other people, and she wanted to lay her hand against his chest and calm him. *You'll wear it out. You'll use up all the beats God meant to give you and then there'll be no more.*

She opened the curtains and straightened the coverlet and waited, content in the gentle way the doctor touched her boy. Max was quiet while the doctor worked. He raised no fuss, not even when Ackermann lifted him from the pillow and listened to him breathe. Ackermann shone a light in both his eyes and looked into his mouth and checked his knees and his elbows with a rubber mallet, and Max did everything the doctor told him to. And then Ackermann waved her outside and he stayed with Max for a good while in the room, and Etta heard voices through the door and Max's laughter.

The doctor came into the kitchen when he was done. She poured coffee into his cup and sat with him. He was quiet for a long while, and when he finally spoke, his voice was clipped.

"I can't tell you for certain what's wrong with your son." He held his cup but didn't drink from it. He talked of tumors and diseases with strange names, of schizophrenia and depressive disorder and psychosis. These things can run in families, he told her, they often come just past childhood, in the bloom of youth. Soldiers are susceptible. "I'm no psychiatrist," he told her. "There's not much I can do."

She nodded. *Yes*, she said, *yes*, but he was wrong. Max had no tumor and no brain disease either. The doctors might not know why he was sick, but Etta knew the reason. It was the war that brought it out, that gave Max his strange visions. Max's sickness and Josef's forgetting, they were different one from the other but they led to the same place. She looked at Ackermann's satchel and its engraved clasp. There was nothing inside that could help. All those fine instruments and those vials of powders and pills. They had no reach behind those eyes. And still it was a relief to sit in her kitchen and speak openly about her boy.

She shook his hand when he left. His fingers were chapped as a washwoman's from clearing the roads. "Keep him at home," he told her. "Keep him at home for as long as you can, and don't sign any papers." All his learning, and he told her what she already knew.

SHE DIDN'T MENTION Dr. Ackermann's visit to Josef when he came home that night or when they sat together at the dinner table. He was in a strange mood, and it was better to wait. Max stayed in his room, and it was only the two of them at the dinner table. Josef fidgeted while he ate. He kept looking at the switches he'd brought home a few weeks before. He'd left them leaning by the door. She asked him about his day working on the roads, but the questions made him prickly. He waved her down. They're idiots, the lot of them, he told her, and he turned toward the window though it was dark already and there was nothing outside to see. He was in a forgetting mood, she could see it in his face. He left the table before she'd finished eating and turned on the radio as loud as it would go.

Forgetfulness ran in the Huber family in the way of freckles or knock knees or red hair. Josef's father the head schoolteacher had been absentminded. His students and his drinking buddies had all joked about it. Look at him searching for his pen when it's right there, tucked behind his ear. He's misplaced his wallet again, they'd say, and can't pay for his beer. Even Josef had laughed. But then the old man's eyes went dark, it seemed to happen all at once, and the jokes didn't feel right anymore. He was *verkalkt*, the townspeople said. He shouldn't have eaten all those egg yolks. He smeared too much pork fat onto his bread. "Who are you?" he'd say when Etta came to visit. "What are you doing in my room?" Other times he reached for her hand. "You never come to see me, it's been too long," but he looked at her with frightened eyes because he knew. How lonely it must have been for the old man, who was lost inside his living room.

Josef came along sometimes, if she pestered him enough, but he didn't talk to his father and he didn't reach for him, and when Josef began to forget, she recognized the look in those pale eyes of his. She had never seen the resemblance before, but he looked like his father. He sat just like him in his chair.

"There's no shame in forgetting things," she'd say when the lapses came. Josef drew himself straight then and squared his shoulders, and he seemed to grow taller in his anger. "I remember everything," he told her. "What people said twenty years ago and when they graduated and were married and when they died. Don't talk to me about forgetting."

*Yes*, she'd say then, he remembered things she'd forgotten long before, the names of cousins and colleagues and former students and all the dates from the history books. He remembered all the details and wrote them in his journal. He was absentminded is all it was, just like any good teacher should be. And though he nodded at her words, she knew they were no consolation because it was working its way through him. It wound through the Hubers like a black vein, through Josef's parents and probably his grandparents, too, and up through all the branches of their tree, and it had no name and it had no remedy, this strange forgetting. It was relentless as the sun.

She checked on Josef when she was done with the dishes. He was asleep already in his chair, his journal open in his lap. He'd left his pen on the paper, and the ink bled through the pages. She took it from his hand and capped it.

## 10

M en were on the road the whole night long, and Georg walked
with them. Mountaineers and infantrymen, old men and boys
in sandals. They marched together, and some had no uniforms and
wore only hunting jackets or sweaters. Their backs were rounded from
all their gear. They carried rucksacks and blankets, one or even two if
they were lucky. They carried mess kits and canteens and packs of
cigarettes and a few found sticks in the fields and tapped as they went,
tap-tapping like blind men. They stopped when they were tired. They
sat under the trees. Droplets fell from the branches and rolled under
their collars and they slept anyway, and sometimes they lay down and
didn't get back up. Georg tried not to look, but still he saw them. A man
was dead under a beech tree, and another stopped and pulled the boots
from his feet. "He has no use for them anymore," he said. No point in
letting them go rotten, and his eyes were dark like well water.

The sky went from black to pink to palest yellow. Georg left the road.
He went through a potato field, and none of the men seemed to notice.
He slipped once and sat down hard in the mud, cursing at himself
because his was an advanced form of clumsiness. It could not be taught,
not even to the willing. He wiped his hand across the front of his pants.
He found a rock and sat on it and waited for the rain to start. The
clouds were already beginning to cluster. Snow, rain, snow, rain, every

day the sky was heavy, and he wanted only sun. It bred weakness, this endless succession of gray days. People squinted in the summertime and shielded their faces. They said how nice to see the sky, how blue it was, but they were delicate like ferns and they covered themselves.

He opened his bag. He had one Franconia chocolate bar, three smoked sausages, a tin of sardines, four pieces of dark bread wrapped in a napkin, and butter cookies broken to crumbs. Water was the only thing he didn't need to worry about. Water abounded. He spread his food across his blanket, and he thought of Maus. He saw her room, with its closed windows and its closed door and the bowl half filled with water. He saw the apple slices he'd set beside her blankets. He stood up and sat back down. He shouldn't have shut the door when he left. He should have left it open. He should have told someone where she was. He rubbed his eyes. She'd be all right without him. She'd go mousing in the room. It was a big room, and she'd eat her fill, and he cried because he knew it wasn't true.

All the boys who were gone, all the ones who fell up north and were buried, and he cried now for a cat. Müller was dead and how many others, and he cried for a stray. She'd have died for sure if Graf hadn't found her. She'd have frozen out there by the wall. A fox would have gotten her or the other boys, who were quick to grab their shotguns when rabbits came too close. They'd shot a tree full of starlings once because they were in a killing mood and could find no bigger birds. She'd be long dead by now, but he cried anyway because she was his and he had left her.

IT RAINED THE second night, and Georg rested in a woodshed behind a barley field. The farmers had probably just harvested their summer grains a few weeks before and now the land looked shorn. He lay between the woodpile and a rusted-out barrow, and it felt sweet to have a roof above his head, even if the thatching had gaps and let the water in. He fell asleep though he tried hard not to. He slept and he didn't dream and it was light already when he woke. He ate a piece of his dark bread, listening carefully for any footsteps. He wanted more bread and one of the cookies, but he wrapped his food back up and set it inside his sack. He had just stepped outside to stretch his arms when he felt a dirt clod land against his shoe.

"Get out, you thief." An old man was shouting. He was close, no more than ten meters away and coming closer. He wore a leather apron and a farmer's cap. "Out with you before I get my gun," and he threw a rock this time and it bounced off the dirt and hit Georg in the shin. He reached down for another rock, looking all the while at Georg.

Georg didn't answer and he didn't stop to set his pack over his shoulder. He held it tight against his belly and ran through the field. He didn't stop when he reached a grove of spruce trees. He kept on running until his breath grew raspy and he went down to his knees.


JUST A FEW days of walking and he was far from the soldiers and the paved road. He was coming to the forest, he could smell it already. He knew all the trees and the plants that grew. He knew the fringed leaves of the chamomile bushes and the field lettuce and which mushrooms were good and which ones poison. He learned these things from Mutti, who said the names of the bushes and the berries while she picked. Every week they went together so she could gather beechnuts and boil them into oil. "Poor man's butter," she'd say, "might as well spit into the pan." She was slow to fill the basket, and she picked leaves sometimes and tasted them and spit them out. She scolded him when he fidgeted. She wagged her finger, but she understood, and she bought him a cider afterward at the old gasthaus. They sat under the antlers and the pewter plates, and sometimes she closed her eyes and dozed a little in the chair, and all the lines on her face went smooth.

He found a spot behind a spruce tree and took off both his boots. His feet were swollen from walking. He couldn't feel his ankle bones anymore, and there were blisters along the bottom of his heels. He worked his fingers through the holes in his socks and rubbed his arches. All that training and he was lame from a few days in the field. A deer came to him just as he lay down. It looked at him with eyes so dark and unafraid he was struck still. The only beautiful thing he'd seen in weeks. He was lonely when it left.

The moon was nearly full when he awoke. It shone on the puddles and the rocks in the field. He rolled to his side and pushed himself up. His neck was stiff because he had no pillow. It was too cold to use his jacket, and the leaves were wet and he didn't want to sleep on them. He cut another piece of sausage and set it on his tongue. He broke off a piece of chocolate, just a single square, and he sliced the sausage extra thin because he had only one left and he needed it to last. He hummed a little while he ate. He hadn't heard another voice in days, not since the farmer had shouted at him, and he hummed now just to hear something. He talked nonsense sometimes, too, and snapped his fingers.

He laced his boots again and began to walk. The road rose gently ahead and fell, and rose and fell again. His stomach rumbled while he walked, and his hands were cold. He saw things only in silhouette and in shadow. He saw black branches against a black sky and solitary lights between the trees. Each time the road branched he took the easterly route. He took narrow roads and not the paved ones and footpaths when he could find them. He had no map and no compass, but he knew he wanted to go east because east was away from the wall and the men that walked the road. It led home. It led to Mutti and her kitchen.

Twice he stepped into a puddle and the water soaked through his boots. "Verdammt," he said. He stopped to tighten his laces. He should have paid attention when they went walking. He should have listened to his father and not just Mutti. "Here's a lark's head and a bowline," the old man would say, "here's a half hitch and look how easy it is to tie." How to set traps and find kindling even when it drizzled and how to recognize the constellations and to build a shelter from branches and from snow, he showed Max and Georg all these things, but only Max had listened. Only Max watched and asked questions and remembered what the old man said, and Georg felt all the lonelier then. He walked behind them and didn't answer when they talked.

Planes flew overhead a few times during the night. He stopped to look but there was nothing to see in the sky, and he couldn't tell where the sounds were coming from or which way the planes were going. He counted his steps to pass the time, but quietly, in case someone else was walking. He stopped at random numbers, at one hundred forty-seven and three hundred twenty, and he began again, and his steps were like the buckets by the trench. They needed counting.

He stumbled just before sunrise and dropped his light. A brand-new Daimon torch and it fell against a stone and though it wasn't cracked and nothing rattled when he shook it, it didn't work after that. He sat down on a stump and cupped it in his palm. He'd been saving it for the darkest nights, for when the moon was new and he couldn't see the road, and now it was broken and he didn't know how to fix it. He left it on the ground and walked a little longer before stopping again to sleep.

EVERY SATURDAY HE'D gone hunting with his father, even when it snowed. Max came home from the university when he could and joined them. "This might be the one," he said. He reached for Georg's head and tousled up his hair. "I have a good feeling." He walked beside the old man and turned back occasionally to smile at Georg, who was always a few steps behind. Just a little longer, he was saying, but Georg didn't return his brother's smile. He wanted to be done with these trips. He wanted to bring one home, so the old man wouldn't tease him anymore or push him to come along. He prayed on his tenth birthday and his eleventh that this would be the year. Let me get one, and then I can stay home. Even if it's a baby, or lame from a trap. He carried his rifle over his shoulder, and he didn't listen when his father showed them things. There was never any peace with the old man. Even the forest was a classroom.

Max saw it first. Georg felt the air go sharp, and he looked where Max was pointing. All day they'd been walking and twice they lay for hours in the needles, waiting beside a stream, and still his neck went tight when the moment came. He gripped his rifle by the stock. His thoughts wandered, spiraling outward, tempting him to laugh, to throw down his rifle, to shoot into the air. He wanted a clean resolution, an end to the long arc of disappointment that he felt himself traveling but was powerless to change. He looked down the barrel. He could feel their anticipation, could hear it in their breathing. He waited, he had no idea what for, and the sweat rolled down his neck. His finger shook on the trigger. The old man nudged him. Quick before it goes. It smells us in the air. Be quick now.

The sound of the discharge shook the sparrows from their perches. It was a shoulder shot and clean. The deer lay twitching, its hind legs kicking hard against the ground. He felt pride at the hit and looked to his father. It was only then Georg realized he had felt no recoil from his rifle. The old man stood straight. He brushed the needles from his pants. His rifle was smoking still, and the air smelled of burnt powder. Georg followed him to the deer, staring at his back and wishing he could burn a hole straight through his wool jacket and into his heart. He could have made the shot. He needed more time. Just a little longer. He rubbed his eyes with his knuckles.

He tried to be strong when they gutted it. He tried to be brave. He'd skinned rabbits before. He cut around each back paw and defrocked them easily as pulling off a sweater, but when it came now to dressing the deer he went queasy. It was the smell that did it and the way his father cut upward through the belly. Its insides were shiny. They were coiled like snakes when they fell out.

Max came to help. He reached for Georg's shoulder and pulled him up. They brought it home together. They tied it to a sapling and carried it out. The roughness of the fur surprised him. He had expected it to be soft. He looked at the ground and not at the deer as they walked. "By God, that's a nice one," Mutti said when they came. The house smelled of stew and warm bread that whole week, but he couldn't eat any. He set his spoon on the table and left the bowl untouched. It was only later that he learned the old man had kept the secret. He'd told his friends at the hall that his boy had bagged his first deer. A ten-pointer, he told them, but bigger than any twelver he'd ever seen. The revelation only compounded Georg's shame.

THE TREES WERE growing denser, and the air was clean and smelled of sap. He had only the sardines left in his bag and he didn't want to open them. He knelt along the shoulder instead and drank from his canteen. A figure was moving between the trees. He stood to get a better look. It was a woman in black. She was shooing away the crows, waving her arms and hissing. The birds flew around her head and up to the branches. They flapped their wings and swooped back down, unafraid.

She saw him move by the road. "Come over here," she called to him. "Come and help me." She squinted when he came close. Her left eye was cloudy with cataracts. She lifted two buckets half full with water. When he hesitated, she stopped and threw him a look. "Don't be slow."

"I'm going that way." He pointed back toward the road.

"There's nothing up there," she said. "Town is the other way."

"Which town?"

She threw her head back and laughed. "Which town, he wants to know. Which town. That's Ettlingen up the road. Ettlingen and Gaggenau and then nothing for a good long while."

She turned away. She stepped through the puddles and the clumps like a boy of twelve and not a gray-haired lady in a skirt. She looked over her shoulder again. "I've got stew," she said. "If you want to help an old lady."

## 11

Every weekday morning Josef waved goodbye to Etta and swung his lunch pail in the air as he rounded the corner. He went to the station and took the ten o'clock train to Wertheim and sat in the gasthaus until the theater opened. He sat in the front row and waited for *Die Deutsche Wochenschau* with its opening horns and the eagle silhouetted by the setting sun. Entire American regiments were surrendering near Arnheim, the announcers told him. All those Amis waving the white flag, and the Volkssturm soldiers were gearing up at home because everyone had something to contribute. Josef saw himself in the footage, in all those wrinkled faces waiting for their rifles, and he saw Etta, too, in the women who served them soup, and sometimes she was young again and sewing Wehrmacht uniforms in a factory or she was with the girls in Belgium and in France waving from the rubble as the German troops came through. Every day he saw something different. Sometimes he caught a glimpse of his brothers in the background carrying their rifles, Erich and Richard and Oskar with his round glasses. They were with the wounded soldiers coming off the train and he leaned closer then, he blinked to see them better, but they were gone, they were always gone, and who knew when they'd be back. Look at these faces, the announcer was saying, all those Slavic faces, and the camera lingered on Soviet prisoners waiting for their orders.

This is what awaits us if the Bolsheviks break through, and Josef stayed in the movie house and ate the lunch Etta had packed, the damp rye bread and the blood sausage and one of the wrinkled apples she kept in the cellar. He ate like a thief in the dark and waited for evening, and then he went back home.

THE FISH WERE sluggish in the winter waters. They moved like ghosts down by the slow eddies and in the elbows where the feeder creeks ran to the river. Etta picked the fattest one she saw. The fisherman cut and cleaned it for her and scraped a sucker from its belly. When he was done, he took off his gloves and tipped his cap. She saw then that the middle finger on his cutting hand had been sliced clean through at the second knuckle, ending in a little pucker of skin. She took the package from him, waving away the change because it was Christmas and no easy thing to angle when the wind blew damp over the water.

She walked back quickly along the bank. She passed the spot where old Willi had drowned, but she didn't slow down. It was time to get the oven started. Cooking the fish right wasn't easy. It took extra washing to get the mud out, and even then they tasted cloudy sometimes because they liked the silt at the bottom. They fed on bloodworms down where the water ran slow. Years before she'd seen one dance. It walked on its tail before twisting back down. They lived long as people, that's what her mutti said. They lived to a hundred sometimes, swimming in the same waters all their lives, along the river and up into mountain lakes and back again, their scales going from bronze to gray and then to white.

She caught up with Maria by the bridge. "Your hair looks nice, Maria," she said. "And on a day like this." Maria was the last of the ladies who went to the hairdresser. She went every Wednesday and gave them trouble. *This isn't right*, she'd say, *it's crooked* or *it looks too flat* or *it starts one way and then goes another*, and the poor ladies would run circles around her chair. She could come home bald as a darning egg and her Klaus wouldn't notice. He loved his beer better than he loved her, she said so herself, but still she made the effort.

"It's a wet winter we're having," Maria said. "Soon as the wind dies down it'll start again."

Etta nodded. She swung her bag as she walked. "It'll be April before we're dry."

"At least you've got your Josef home with you," Maria said. She tucked a curl behind her ear. "How nice that he's home," she was saying, "especially with how cold it's been. Maybe they'll send Klaus home, too. He's got more beer than blood in his veins, and it's no good to keep him outside." She was making no sense, and Etta shook her head.

"Josef's not home," Etta said. "He's in the field today and won't be home for hours." *He works longer than all the other men and they don't feed him enough and he's dirty when he comes home and his hands shake from all the digging he does.*

"Klaus is jealous. He's tired of working outside."

Etta wrapped her scarf tighter around her neck. Maria was talking still, oh she went on about Josef and the trouble he made and how he called them idiots and tapped the ground with his walking stick. He lost the buckets and couldn't find them, not even when he retraced his steps. "He didn't want to walk with Klaus," Maria was saying. "He went down by the water instead."

Etta slowed a little then. She stopped there in the street. It sounded right, the way Maria told it. It sounded like the truth. They sent him away, and he made a ruckus. Maybe he went to the river and walked beside the bank, and he cut green reeds and brought them home because that's what he knew how to do. Yes, it sounded right. For weeks he'd been leaving every morning and he didn't return until it was dark, and still he said nothing. The sun went down and the wind blew, and each night he came home to her and told her all his stories, of clearing the roads and moving snow, of loading and unloading trucks and packing up crates and feeding horses and shooting in the field. They were lies, all of them, and he didn't blush or blink in the telling. Her chest went tight, and she put her hand to her throat.

Maria caught the motion. "He might have been wrong." Klaus had been wrong about a lot of things, she was saying. It was the beer that did it. The beer and a peculiar inattentiveness that she'd noticed for years now. "I might not be remembering it right."

They began to walk again, and Maria talked about other things. She wanted to know how Max was doing and if Etta had heard from Georg. "Your boys are artists, the both of them," she told Etta. "Your Max is always in a hurry," but Etta didn't answer. Maria turned at her street and worked her way around the icy patches and banks of muddy snow, mindful of her shoes. Etta waved to her and walked alone the rest of the way.

WILLI HAD BEEN a toothless old man those many years ago, probably younger than Etta was now, but he seemed ancient to her then. He lived with his mother, who swept the school steps and cleaned the church. Etta could hear him still, laughing as he stood there by the bridge and talking nonsense to the passersby. He would chase the river ducks sometimes, too, and flap his arms, and some days he was unhappy and pulled at his hair. He wasn't right in the head, her mother had told her once. He was made in the sauce. It was his parents' drunkenness that caused his problems. He always had his book under his arm, its cover tattered and stained from the dirt on his hands. He couldn't read, everybody knew this, but he carried it anyway, maybe because he liked the weight of it or the feel of its embossed leather binding.

It was spring when she saw him last. The sun was setting behind the hills and the river looked golden in the failing light. The girls in the group had licorice ropes and their lips were red as cherries. The oldest Reisig boy smiled at the others and stepped toward Willi. He gestured toward the book in the old man's hand. "Come on, Willi, let me see your book," he said. "It's such a nice book, much nicer than our old schoolbooks." He leaned in close and smiled at Willi, and Etta felt uneasy when she saw the look on the boy's face. Willi flashed a toothless smile, pleased perhaps that someone had noticed his fine book. The boy pounced then, fast as a tiger the way he snatched it from Willi's hand. Willi cried in anger and in sorrow, but there was nothing he could do. He was too slow for the boys. They tossed it back and forth, to Willi's side and over his head. The girls in the group were laughing at the sorry sight and clapping their hands. The boys threw the book in ever more elaborate ways, between their legs and from behind their backs, then dangling it in front of Willi, only to tear it from his hand. Etta held her satchel close against her chest and watched the old man chase the boys, first one way then the other.

"Stop," Willi said, and he fell to his knees, his breathing ragged. "It's mine," he said, looking around at all of them. "It's from my mother, that book," and he raised his arms and cried out, a horrible wounded sound that came from deep inside his chest. Etta wanted to shout out, to tell them to stop the game because they were hurting the old man and for no reason, but the words didn't come. Ilse stood beside her, holding her licorice twists tight in both fists, and their eyes met. Ilse shook her head and turned to go. Etta watched her walk away, and though she wanted to join her friend, something kept her there. The

other girls had stopped laughing now and were growing impatient with
the game, but the boys kept at it. "Come on, old man," one of them said,
"come and get it. It's right here."

The book flew high into the air. The pages had started to come
undone and fluttered like leaves into the water. Willi cried out and
pushed himself up from the mud. He waded into the river. The sun
shone on his head and haloed his hair, those sorry tufts he had. Etta
shielded her eyes. The sun, the water, the vanishing sky between the
trees, she saw only Willi. She should have tried to help him, but she stood
there with her classmates and did nothing. He reached for the pages,
slapping his palms against the water, and it happened quickly then.
Maybe he slipped in the mud, or maybe it just became too deep for him.
They watched as he went under. Even the boys had gone quiet now. Willi
came up twice, waving his arms as if in greeting, and then he was gone.

They stood still for a moment, all of them. The only sound was the
gentle lapping of the water against the bank, and then the church bells
began to ring, signaling that it was five o'clock already and time to go
home. The sound of the bells brought them back to themselves and they
ran, arms outstretched, each of them going in a different direction,
some crossing the bridge and others heading toward the town center,
but Etta didn't move. She stayed there long after they had gone. She
watched the muddy water. She'd seen a horse wash ashore once, half
rotten and swollen to bursting from its time in the river. She willed
herself to cry for Willi, who was so close to where she stood but
unreachable now. She blinked, but the tears wouldn't come.

Etta had turned to go when she saw the book, pressed facedown into
the mud where the boys had left it. She bent down to look. The binding
was broken, but most of the pages were still intact. It was a history
book, about the Romans and the Greeks, written in the old German

script they had to learn at school, each chapter beginning with enormous scrolling letters as intricate as a wood carving. She couldn't leave it there in the dirt, it wasn't right, not when he'd loved it and fought so hard to get it back, and so she set it inside her satchel.

Her mother scolded her when she got home. "Look how red your fingers are," she told Etta, "look how sticky from the candy." After the dishes were washed and her mother was busy down in the cellar, Etta wiped the pages clean and the tears came then and great rasping sobs that shook her chest and caught inside her throat.

They never spoke of old Willi again, not weeks later when some fishermen caught him in their ropes down by the docks or when his mother fell from the church steps in her grief. They had done something wrong, wrong beyond measure, and it could not be righted in the telling.

THE SNOW WAS fresh on the ground for Christmas, and all the sky was gray. "It's a good omen," the ladies told each other, "it's a good sign for the new year." Max came down and sat in his robe and his slippers and watched Etta work. She sewed the head down tight and stuffed the fish with bread crumbs and made gravy from the juices. She needed only lemons now, but there was no finding them, not in December. All the silver teapots, all the candlesticks and crystal vases she had left wouldn't bring her even a lemon slice. She boiled six potatoes and let them cool, and she peeled them and sliced them extra fine. She turned around to look at Max, and he looked back at her with sleepy eyes and his hair stood up from his head like a rooster crown.

They ate together at six exactly. She said grace, and Josef waited for her this time and squeezed her hand.

"It's a good meal we've got here," he said. He took a second serving of potatoes and then a third, and all the dishes moved toward his end of the table, as if the three of them were on a boat and it tilted only toward him. He burped between helpings and looked around the room.

She gave Max more gravy. "Eat a little more," she said. "Before it all gets cold."

Josef pointed with his fork. "Look at him," he said. "Look how he eats. Like an old woman." He shook his head in disapproval, but Max didn't notice. He looked down at his plate instead and picked at his food. He mashed his potatoes and piled them into mounds and cratered their tops with his spoon, and she could see his collar bones where his shirt was open.

They moved to the living room when they were done. She had put extra logs on the stove, but still the room was damp. It was dark outside and so cold and clear the moon was ringed by a silver halo. *Watch yourself,* her mutti would say on nights like this, *watch yourself because the moon's out twice today.*

Etta set a platter on the table. She had filled it with walnuts and meringues and dried plums. Only Georg was missing now. Only Georg, who always sat closest to the platter so he could take the brownest cookies for himself, who sat beside the tree and shook all the presents, even the ones that weren't for him.

She gave them socks she had knit from one of Georg's old sweaters. She wrapped them in tissue and set a chocolate on each package. She'd given old Frau Ebing a silver candlestick for a box of chocolate bells. Her husband knew someone in the city who could find chocolate even now, who could find liquor and marzipan and butter biscuits.

She took Josef's hand. "You're tired from all your work outside," she said. "I see it in your face." She waited for him to speak. She looked at him and waited, but he took a package from under his chair and set it on her lap.

"Maybe I'll have some peace now. Maybe you won't pester me so much." He smiled a little when he said it.

She pulled open the paper and folded it before setting it aside. He'd carved her a tray of linden wood, big enough for her teapot and her cups, and oiled so fresh it shone like honey. It must have taken him months to carve the flowers, the rose sprigs and acorns and pansy blossoms, and the vine that curled toward the center, heavy with grapes. She held it high to see it better. She shook her head. More than thirty years together, and he could still surprise her. She took his hand and Max's too, and the house wasn't complete without Georg there, but they were together, the three of them, and for that she had to be grateful.

Josef came to church with them. They walked together along the streets, and the wind blew and froze their tears. They kept their coats on because the church was unheated. Old Büchner read from Isaiah and from Luke. "To us a son is born," he said, "a son is given." He spoke of the mystery of that birth, of the son of God who comes among men, and it was easy to forget how ornery the old priest was because his voice was sweet from the pulpit. She held her hands together and tried not to think about Max and the last time he'd knelt in church. Tonight he was wedged tight between them. She'd combed his hair before they left and buttoned up his vest, and he sat straight now and didn't fidget. Nothing could happen so long as they were all together. Nothing could happen because they were in the open and the candles were all lit and she patted her boy on the shoulder the way she did when he was little. She caught people watching Max. They turned around to see him, but he looked at the dark window, at the fat priest and all the candles and how their smoke coiled toward the rafters, and for just a little while the trouble was gone from his face.

*   *   *

MAX WENT TO bed after church and he didn't get up on Christmas or the day after. He leaned against his pillows, and even when he talked he kept his eyes closed. The ticking bothered him, he kept saying. It was in the walls, and even after she stopped the hallway clock he heard it still. He didn't get up for meals or to wash his face, and when she asked him what was wrong he clenched and unclenched his fists. "I'm tired," he said. "All my strings are cut."

He said things that left her shaking in her chair. It stinks like sour milk, he told her, and you don't keep my room clean and things will burn and you'll burn, too, and all the world will be covered in our ashes, and on and on he went. He spoke of fire and machines that cut through bones and rivers under the house. The water flowed through the walls and at night it pulled them all down to the center. It was its own world down there, where the snakes were and the river stones. The men and women looked the same beside the ditches. Could she see them. Could she see how they were piled like firewood and others knelt beside them. Skin stretched tight over bones and faces ageless in their hunger and their misery. Thin as spiders. The sergeant said to shoot because they were partisans, these people, and they fell forward into the graves. They fell and the dirt covered them, and there were red eyes looking through the windowpane. Every night they came, but not when the moon was full.

He scratched his face and his forearms even while she sat with him. She trimmed his nails and took the folding knife from his table before he could reach for it, and nothing calmed him. When he began to beat his head against the wall, she called Josef and together they set him down and tied his hands and his feet to the bedposts. He thrashed like a boar caught in a trap, that's what Josef said. He thrashed like a wild thing and it was wildness she saw in his eyes. "Be still," she told him. "I'm here with you," and he fell back against his pillow and he laughed.

People asked her where Max had gone, and she told them he was down with a cold. Later she told them that he was visiting family in Würzburg. "He's with his cousin the pharmacist," she said, "helping him with his books. He'll be back soon. Any day now he'll be back." She told them these things, and she came home to Max, who lay in bed. His sickness was a fire. This was how she thought of it. It parched him and filled his chest with ash. His eyes glowed from the heat of it. She could beat the flames down in one place, but they'd come back in another. They were stronger than she was, stronger than all her medicines. "Cough it up," she told him, "cough it all up, and you'll be better," but it wasn't true and he didn't listen anyway.

## 12

Her name was Irmingard, but Georg called her Frau Focht. She lived alone. There was no war in her house. No planes flew overhead, and no sirens sounded. She had no radio or newspapers or magazines, and when he asked her for a map so he could see where he was, she laughed at him and shook her head. "You're near Ettlingen," she said, "you're where the foxes and the rabbits say good night." She knew only her fields and her chores and the solitary cow inside her barn. She cooked over a stove so old all its enamel was gone and the metal had lost its luster. He had to take off his shoes and his jacket that first day and every day afterward because she'd have none of his dirt inside. She kept her house neat and didn't need any more work from him. Her floors were covered in old blankets. She covered the window with a blanket, too, a blue one with cornflowers, and tied it back with a ribbon.

Georg sat at her table in his socks and watched her work. She put too much salt in her stew, but still it tasted good. It tasted like home. She talked while she worked. She talked to no one in particular, least of all Georg. She was born in the house and had no plans to leave because nothing good comes of leaving. She said this more than once and with a serious look in her eye. She had four children and they were gone and she didn't speak their names.

"Four," he said. "That's enough for the Mother's Cross." Every German mother with four children was awarded a medal from the state. Two more and she'd have earned silver. She could wear the cross then like the women in Heidenfeld. She could wear it on a ribbon around her neck and make all the others jealous. It was a compliment when he said it, but she seemed offended.

"Don't talk to me about crosses." She waved her spoon at him. "Better to lie fallow." She looked to her window and the field outside.

She set him to work every morning except Sunday. She pulled out a ladder from beside the house and pushed him to the roof because it needed patching. She'd do it herself, she told him, but heights made her dizzy and she'd almost fallen last time, and no one would have found her then. No one would have known. He swept the barn for her and gathered eggs and chopped wood for her stove. He lay on a pile of blankets at night and she had no pillow for him, but he didn't complain because it was good to sleep in a house again and he had no dreams there, not even of Müller. He plotted things before he slept and early in the morning while she stirred the oatmeal pot. He thought of what he needed for the trip and how far he had to go, but he stayed instead and worked for her and ate the food she cooked.

There were all sorts of rules in her house. The longer he stayed the more rules there were, and they were strange ones he had never heard about before. She chopped wood only during a decreasing moon because it would burn better. Killing spiders brought bad luck, especially big ones. She carried them out in her palm because she had no fear of spiders or bugs of any sort, but birds were different. Birds meant something, almost always. They were full of meanings. If a raven sat alone in a tree, there'd be rain. Time to latch the windows and set the buckets by the spouts. It was a starling that gave her cataracts, she told him, a starling that took stray hairs from her comb and carried them to its nest. It was a blessing there'd been only one, or both her eyes would be bad. And when her husband lay dying she opened the windows for him and turned over all the glasses and the bowls, so there'd be no place for him to hide inside the house. He lingered anyway and gasped beneath the sheets, and so she had to climb to the roof and flip a shingle around for him. He was gone by the time she came back in. His eyes were closed. That's what did it, she told Georg, the shingle was the thing, and the crows outside his window.

She poured him a bath the first week, but only after he'd asked. He was so dirty by then he thought for sure there'd be nothing left when he stepped out from the water. She was greedy with the hot water, and so he shivered in the metal tub, but he stayed because it felt good to wipe the dirt and the salt from his skin.

She took his black pants while he soaked. "You can't go out like that," she told him.

She pulled a pillowcase from her cabinet and untied the ribbon at its top. She found him a shirt inside and an old pair of wool pants. They'd belonged to her husband, he knew from the way she unfolded them, and though the shirt was tight around his belly, he stood up straight as he could and buttoned it.

She brought out her darning basket and a pile of old woolen socks, some of which had been patched so often they were stiff like boots and poised as if to march off by themselves. There was something familiar about the way she pursed her lips and held the needle, and he thought of Mutti just then and how she had sat at the table with him. He reached for his rucksack and the pouch where the ladies were. It was habit that made him take them out, habit and the quiet in the room.

She looked up at the sound of money on her table. It was a sound she knew, he could tell. She loved that sweet metallic music. She was a believer in coins and not in paper money. She had told him this early on. She believed in gold coins and silver and better still, in eggs and butter and milk, in pig fat and potatoes, because the belly is better than the bank and more trustworthy. She set down her wooden darning egg. "What do you have?" She reached for one of the ladies. "Let me take a look." She lifted the coin and looked at both its sides. "That's a fine-looking piece," she said, and though she handed it back, she seemed reluctant to let go.

He palmed one of the ladies and held his hands flat over the tabletop, as if waiting for the table to rise and meet his fingertips. He hadn't palmed a coin in months, and still he managed it on the first try.

"Do it again," she said. "Do it slow so I can see." Her eyes followed his hands and when his palming hand tightened just a little and his thumb twitched, she exhaled hard. "I saw you. I saw your hand move."

He shrugged and worked the coin between his fingers, over and under each in turn. It wasn't bad considering his chapped hands and how little he'd practiced since leaving the school. He thought of Müller while he worked. He thought of the evenings they were alone in the room and how Müller sat low in his chair and watched. Once he'd waited until Georg had gone to the window, and he'd reached for Firnholzer's book. He looked through the pages for a good five minutes before Georg saw and pulled it away because nobody was allowed to look inside, not even Müller. "I know all your secrets," he said then, "I know them now," and he looked at Georg for the longest while. Georg palmed two of his ladies and set them down on Frau Focht's little table. How long before the tricks were lost? His memory would fail him eventually, and without the book he had no way to fix his mistakes. It lay under his mattress still, or maybe someone had found it by now and taken it or thrown it in the garbage heap, and he'd forget all the things he ever knew.

She lifted her needle close to her good eye and threaded it. "I can't catch a coin like that," she said. "Not with these old hands."

He worked the coins and she darned her socks, and it was peaceful in her house. He didn't think of Müller again or Mutti or the old man, who was probably sitting in his chair beside the radio. He thought only of the ladies and the stewpot and how good it would be to close his eyes and sleep.

THEY WENT TOGETHER to the garden and cut the chicken from the branch. She liked to take them from the roost when it was still dark outside and the birds were slow. They made no sound when she carried them to the tree. She slit their throats, and they were quiet even as they swung from the branch like ceiling lamps, their wings spread wide, as if caught midflight in a strange downward swoop.

She brought the bird inside and dipped it in steaming water. She waved him down when he tried to help. "You'll be in my way," she said. "I know how to pluck my birds." She pulled the feathers out with both her hands, and his Mutti would have shaken her head at the mess. Everything was strange about this old lady, even how she plucked her chickens.

He sat by the table and watched her work. "There's this ship," he said. "It's got doctors on it and two monkeys."

She lit a piece of paper. "What's that you're telling me?" she said. "You're making fun." She held the flame over the bird, singeing the smallest feathers and the funny hairs that grew between the folds of skin.

He sat back in his chair. It was warm by the oven, and the stories came to him in all their details. He knew them the way people know songs. He knew their characters and their rhythms and how Mutti read them aloud in the chair beside his bed. When he thought of them, he heard her voice. He saw her face and the lines across her forehead and how she held the book close because her eyes weren't as good as they used to be. She saw things through rippled glass, she told him, and all the edges were blurred. He told old Frau Focht about Münchhausen and his crew. He started with one of his favorites. Münchhausen was in peril. He was always in peril, except when he was eating. It was a sea snake this time, enormous and coiling and green like polished emeralds. It rose like a cobra and bucked like a horse, and its eyes were yellow and full of malice.

"I've got no time for nonsense," she told him, but she listened anyway. She tilted her head to hear him better.

He vanished one of the ladies and set her down on the table and palmed her again. Münchhausen was round as a dumpling but fast anyway, and he knew how to move. He ducked and dodged like a fencer and rolled on his back. The snake came close, drawn by his feints. It attacked and Münchhausen moved, and it came so near, the old captain could smell the sulfur on its breath and all its foul vapors. Round and round it went, arching high and swooping low, and it saw only Münchhausen and his fat belly. It thrashed this way and that, tying itself into one knot and another and another still, and it came for him anyway. All its coils were wrapped tight when Münchhausen was done with his dance. Only its head could move and the tip of its tail. It hissed at him when he left the shore and was hissing still when the ship blasted off.

She cut the bird's feet off with a single whack. She worked the knife with the zeal of a pirate. Who paid for the ship, she wanted to know, and what kind of woman goes up with a crew of men, and why did they need monkeys onboard? It wasn't smart of them, bringing monkeys along. You can't trust creatures with long arms like that. They might bite you when you sleep or smother your mouth like cats do. She set the chicken in the pot and scrubbed the wooden block, and when he stopped she told him to keep going. She was nonchalant the way she said it, but she wanted to hear more. He could tell. She was hungry for stories and for talk, and he saw for the first time how lonely she must be, alone in that house with only her animals and the birds by her window.

She set her scrub brush down when he was finished. She dried her hands. "I'll have strange dreams tonight," she told him. "I'll dream of monkeys, and it will be your fault."

THE NEXT TIME she did laundry, she washed his uniform and ironed it for him and set it back inside his bag. He went outside, to gather branches, he told her, though she had plenty of kindling already. He stood on her stoop and looked at the hills, and then he slung the bag over his shoulder. The sky was gray as smoke. Just a little colder and the snow would start again. He took the path that led through her field and to a crescent of acorn trees. A pond lay just beyond the trees. He found pebbles as he went and set them in his pockets.

He walked the perimeter of the water. He slipped twice on the grasses that grew by the edge. When he came round to his starting point, he opened up his rucksack. He held the uniform in both his hands. The pants and shirt smelled of soap and vinegar and they were cleaner than they'd ever been at school. He'd torn the cuffs walking, and she'd sewn them and patched a hole by his knee. He set four pebbles in each pocket of his pants. He took his shirt and unfolded it. Into the right front pocket went three more pebbles, as big as he could fit, and then he took his Westwall medal with its eagle and its gold ribbon and he pinned it on the lapel. He took the pouch with all his pins and set them across the shirt, in no particular order. The youth pin with its eagle head and the marksmanship pin—he poked himself on that one and sucked the blood from his thumb—and that first festival pin from the rally when he was nine, he found a place for all of them and his shirt looked like a general's when he was done.

All the work for those patches and pins. All the time spent running the track and the boxing lessons and taking his gun apart and putting it back together. He'd been the slowest in every race. His team waited for him at the starting mark, hopeless as crewmen watching their ship tilt and sink into the sea, and though their impatience should have spurred him on, it made him tired instead. Müller had tried more than once. "That's not how you do it," he said. "Your arms are all wrong. You start too slow." He took Georg running, and he showed him how to work the boxing bag. "Thumbs down before you connect," he'd always say. "Bend your knees a little. You're a man and not an old lady." Georg listened to all Müller's advice. He watched Müller and how he moved, and he tried to find some kindred grace inside himself, and all the patches he earned changed nothing. He was the weakest link in every chain.

He stood up straight and looked to his left and to his right. Mist had begun to roll in, coming down from the hills and fingering its way between the trees. He dropped the pants and the shirt into the water and knelt by the bank to see. The pants went down fast, but the shirt took longer and fluttered lazily down, winging round like a bird until it was gone. All the pins shone in the water as they sank. They blinked themselves out like stars. He felt a swinging in the air, and he stood up, uneasy. The nearest trees threw shadows over the water. There weren't any boys in the branches, no boys and no straps and no muddy boots, but he hurried anyway. It was dark when he returned to the old woman, who scolded him for bringing mud into the house.

## 13

The days took on a rhythm inside Max's room. Etta brought him his breakfast and sat with him. When he ate, he ate only a little, and most days he ignored the tray, fixing his eyes on the ceiling instead. He ate only bread and oatmeal and unsalted potatoes. He wanted no herbs and no sauces and no color on his plate, nothing to give flavor to his food. It was food for an invalid and not a young man, and when she brought him honey or sweet jam, he shook his head. She brought him more trays at lunch and at dinner. She stroked his hand and talked of trivial things, of the weather and the fishermen down by the bank.

She had nursed her boys through ear infections and broken bones, through spider bites and bouts with influenza and lung infections that lasted for months. She had nursed her mother, too, and her father, sitting beside them and stroking their hands. It was the last thing her parents had taught her, how to sit bedside. She wiped their foreheads with cool washcloths and poured them water from a pitcher and washed and dried their feet. She fluffed their pillows and straightened their blankets, and twice a day she opened the windows so that they could see the sunshine and breathe in fresh air. Sickness brought disorder; it brought fevers and sweats and sour smells. It stopped the clock. Order was the only remedy. Order was a repudiation of the effects of the sickness. In an orderly sick-room, the sun rose again and set. The linens were ironed and smelled of vinegar, and meals arrived at noon and at six exactly, and even if the patient ate nothing, it was enough to see the plates and the silverware set just so. There was a time for reading and for sleeping and for bringing in the trays, a time for opening the curtains and closing them again, and the order worked its way into the patient just like medicine.

She set his tray aside and reached for his bird book. She opened it to the beginning. "Black-throated divers nest in Northern Europe," she told him. She read about tail streamers and migration patterns, about herring gulls and swifts and white-winged terns, and Josef came inside and listened. He sat by the table, his hands on both his knees. His shirt was untucked, and his collar was loose, and each time she looked over at him he sat lower in his chair. They didn't need him today, he'd told her at breakfast, and so he was home and not on the roads or down by the warehouse where they kept the engines. He took the plate from Max's tray and ate the bread and the apple slices.

"He won't eat it anyway," he said when she threw him a look. "And I'm hungry. I'm working the station tomorrow. I'll be clearing fields."

She said nothing. She looked at the book and not at Josef. She turned the page and began the next chapter, but her heart began to pound hard because Josef was still picking at the plate she had made for Max. He was eating the boiled eggs. He popped them whole into his mouth and his cheeks bulged. She kept reading and she didn't stop until Max's breathing was deep and steady.

Josef gripped the chair and pushed himself up. He stood by the table and looked down to the garden and the river and all the bare trees. "There's no fixing him," he said.

She covered Max's feet with the blanket. His feet and his hands were always cold. "You're just bored," she told Josef. "Go work in your shop a little. Finish your carving." Better there than here. He'd have less time to think that way, less time to watch Max and hear his dark stories.

"He's getting worse." Josef set his hands on the sill. His skin hung loose along his jaw. She saw this for the first time. His skin hung loose, and there were rings around his eyes. "One day he's fine and the next he's gone again. Maybe they can help him. Maybe they'll know better what to do."

She stood beside him. Snow covered the beds. It was blown into ripples by the wind. The sky was white and the treetops and the hills, and everything was still outside except for the chimney smoke rising from the houses. "That's not right," she told him. "You know it as well as I do."

He turned away from the window. And though she wanted to stop him and pull him to her, she didn't reach for him. Tell me what you're thinking, you old fool. That's what she should have said. Tell me and we can talk just like we did before. We're the only ones who can help our boy. Be kinder to him and to yourself, too. There's no shame in resting a little. There's no shame in being sent home. Not with all the work you've done already and the students you've taught. She should have held his hand and said these things and more, but she said nothing, and she let him go.


ALL MAX'S BOOKS and Georg's, too, she loved having them in the house. She didn't mind reading to her boys when they were sick. Reading was one of life's great pleasures, and she'd been one of the best students in her class. She helped the others with their schoolwork. She could have gone to the upper school, the gymnasium, if her parents had been able to afford it. The gymnasium was in Lohr, and it sat like a palace on Nägelseestrasse. Students learned Latin there and Greek. They studied together in the library and on the train trip home, and in springtime they went to Würzburg with their class and visited the museums. Etta had been certain she would go. She had the certainty that only the young have. She sat for hours with her books and her dipping pen, and when testing time came she worked all the harder and took her books to bed with her. "Just a little longer," she'd say, "I'm almost done." She studied even in summer. She sat under the trees, and the breeze flapped the pages, and nobody was surprised when her score was highest in the class.

Three pfennig is what the train cost back then. Three pfennig a day and she could have gone to the gymnasium, but it was too much, her father was sorry when he told her. He held out his hands. She went to the handelsschule instead and learned to sew. She learned how to embroider and keep a neat house, and all the things she'd studied before fell away. The arithmetic and the composition and all those history lessons, how easy it was to forget them. Josef saw her one day when she walked home from class. She'd dropped her satchel and all her notebooks, and he stopped to help her. He carried her books for her, and though she was certain all the neighbors were watching from behind their curtains, she let him walk her all the way home. He wrote to her when he was back at the university and sent her soaps and fine silk scarves from the city, and for each present to Etta there was another for Mutti, a silver comb and a matching pillbox and sweet jellies rolled in sugar and crystal candleholders shaped like stars. "There's a reason for things," Mutti told her then. "A reason you were at the handelsschule and not the gymnasium and a reason you took the long way home." Mutti had seen a pattern to things. Everything that comes before takes you where you need to be.

Josef's mother had been unhappy with the match. "You can do better," she'd told him, with Etta standing right there in the Huber kitchen. She wasn't *standesgemäß*, she lacked social standing because her father was just a baker and not a teacher like old Herr Huber. He should marry a doctor's daughter. The pharmacist in Zimmern had a daughter who was almost twenty and pretty, too, but Josef was resolute.

"Gain a daughter or lose a son," Josef told his mother, "the choice is yours." He reached for Etta's hand and squeezed it, and how she loved his stubborn face. His stubbornness was his greatest strength and his greatest failing.

IT SNOWED ON Three Kings' Day and the day after. Even the big linden tree at the waterspout had started to hang low. She took the decorations from the tree, and Josef pulled it out to the garden. He was happy to be outside, she could tell, and he leaned in close as he swung the axe. She gave him a thick piece of chalk when he was done and held the ladder for him. He wrote c+m+b above the lintel, for Caspar and Melchior and Balthasar, who rode to Bethlehem. He was unhappy with the way it looked and wiped the lintel clean before beginning again. He asked them for protection while he wrote. *Protect this house*, he said. *Protect us from fire and from water.*

She left Josef with Max and walked to the stand and the butcher— blutwurst and nothing else in the window—and she stopped by the pharmacy to look at the creams, but the shelves were mostly empty. She walked past the gasthaus and down by the hotel where Frau Steinmüller was sweeping snow from the walk. The beauty shop was empty and the stationery store was closed, and she looked in all the windows anyway. She walked for the sake of walking. She'd tell Josef that he was on leave. He was on leave with all the other men whose names began with *H*—Herr Hallbach was on leave and Hinkel and old Heisenberg. They were all home with their wives, and he should stay, too, and wait for them to call him back. If that didn't work, she'd tell him that she knew and there was no shame in being home.

She stopped by the church. It was Monday and late and she usually only went on Sundays, but she went inside anyway and knelt with the old ladies, who were in their usual spots. They wore the shine off their rosary beads, those ladies, they knelt twice every day. She set her hands together. "Fill our family with Your light and peace," she said, "have mercy on all who suffer." She knew the words from her childhood, prayers for the sick and for the closing of the day, for children and for family, prayers to Mary and the saints, prayers she'd forgotten she ever knew. She worked her way through them, and when she could think of no more, she looked up to the windows and the marble saints. She prayed for Georg, who lacked the resilience of his brother and the physical strength. Watch over him because he's alone somewhere by the wall. Even in the middle of a crowd he's alone and he needs watching. Watch over Max and Josef and all the boys who are gone from home. Her breath rose in the cold air. Take me and not Max. Take Josef instead, who's old and spiteful sometimes and he forgets most of what I say. These dark thoughts came and undid all her prayers. She wrapped her scarf around her neck and prayed anyway.

She came home, and Josef was dozing by his radio. She set her bags on the table and climbed the stairs to Max's room. His bed was empty, and his suitcase was gone and his winter shoes. He'd left by the back door. Someone had gone with him, she could see from the marks they'd left. The tracks had gone crusty already, half-moons that broke through the snow skin to the powder beneath, from the door to the garden gate and then away from the house and its warm kitchen, away from Josef and from her.

She ran to Josef, ran to him and told him. He didn't turn when she shouted his name. He hummed to the music, and only when she shook his shoulders did he open his eyes. He blinked hard. "It's been hours since they left," he said. He set his hands on his knees and rocked back in his chair.

14

Old Frau Focht pulled a file from her pocket and worked the hatchet head, starting at the cutting edge and moving inward, taking out the burrs. She worked the metal like his father worked his wood, with an easy hand. It was warmer in the barn but the light there was no good, and so she worked outside instead.

"The heads are coming loose," she said. "I've been soaking them in buckets, but the wood won't swell." She gave up squatting and knelt in the dirt. Sharpening was hard work and called for leather gloves, but she had only mittens and she didn't wear them while she worked. The skin on her knuckles was cracked, and her eyes watered, but she didn't complain, and when she was done with the file, she looked up. "Go get me the whetstone."

The wind was starting up, and Georg walked fast, setting his hands deep inside his pockets. She was impatient when he came back. She took the stone and didn't thank him. She moved it in circles against the blade, sharpening first one side and then the other. He offered to help, but she didn't trust him with her hatchet heads. He'd make them uneven. He didn't have gentle hands, and if the heads cracked there'd be no fixing them.

"Don't just stand there," she said. "Tell me more about that fat captain."

He'd told her so many of the stories already, but he started again with one of his favorites. There were these scorpions. They glowed at night just like fireflies do. They had poison in their stingers and they were quick the way they hopped, and Münchhausen whacked their tails with the axe he carried. He chopped them all to bits, and even then the stingers were still moving and stuck fast to his boots. She shook her head. "That can't be right," she said. "Bugs don't glow," but she smiled anyway as she sharpened the heads. He was her radio. She shook her head when he talked about generals or the places where the fighting was. She didn't know those names, but she knew the spaceship *Sannah* and all the men and women on its crew and where they went and the creatures they found.

"Tell me another," she said when he stopped. "Tell me one I haven't heard," and he stomped his feet to keep warm and set the collar up on his jacket.

How easy it would be to stay with her and to work her fields when spring came. She'd cook for him, and he'd wear the clothes her husband had worn, and there'd be no fighting and no soldiers and no border police in their green uniforms. They'd be alone as shipwrecked sailors. They'd plant potatoes and carrots and fat red beets, and he wouldn't go to school anymore or listen to the radio. There'd be no books in the house except for the Bible she kept inside a drawer with her spare blankets. She'd shown it to him once, that old leather book, and inside there was a photograph taken years before. She was proud of that picture, he could tell, proud of how young she was and how she looked straight at the lens, and both her eyes were clear and pale as sea glass in the light.

Going home had its dangers. The old man might send him back. He might shut the door on Georg or report him to the schoolhouse where they kept the list of names, and not even Mutti could sway him then. Not Mutti or Max or anyone else could change his mind. And still he felt the tug. He felt it when the old woman looked at him and when she oversalted her stew and especially when he told the stories that Mutti had read aloud. Max was at school and the old man was in the classroom, walking up the aisles, and it was only Mutti with him in the house. She rocked in her chair, and the sun shone behind her and haloed her dark hair.

Irmingard nicked her thumb against the blade, but she didn't curse or tend to the cut. The wind blew harder. The bare branches swayed, and he covered both his ears.

"Go inside," she said. "No use having us both out here."

He ignored her. He watched the winter birds circle the pond and told her about the nearest comet and how warm it was. Even the wind there blows warm, and strange fruits hang low from the trees. A shrike settled on a branch over his head. It trilled and chattered and tilted its head, and Irmingard kept working but Georg stopped at the sound. It was a butcher bird. He'd seen them in the Heidenfeld churchyard spiking crickets and sometimes mice high on the thorns. He found a rock and threw it against the tree, but the rock fell short and the bird didn't move.

He rubbed his hands together. He turned back to Irmingard. "It never rains there," he said. "It never rains and it's never cold, and the sun shines even at night." The stories needed Mutti's voice and not his. They needed the chair and the window and the chiming of the hallway clock, but he stayed outside with the old woman and told them anyway because he liked the company. He liked the way she shook her head and squinted. "Your stories make no sense," she always said. "That's not how things work," and she smiled when she said it.

He wanted to leave, and he wanted to stay. This is how it was, how it always was. He wanted Mutti but not the old man. He wanted his room and his chair and his magic table, and he wanted Kaspar pecking in his cage. He wanted to see Max again, too, who was touched by some strange grace. Max had caught a bird in his hand once, caught it in midflight and then opened up his palms. He'd leapt off the woodshed, too, and somersaulted in the air. A whole group of them squinted into the sun to watch him jump. He finished the turn early and seemed to hover above them for the longest while, and when he landed on the balls of his feet, he just smiled and wiped his hands against the side of his pants. Georg clapped along with them. He was proud of his brother, who waved down the applause. He was proud and sorry both because things came so easily to Max. Why couldn't it be him for once instead of Max? How sweet to be at the center of things and not outside, to hear the applause like Max did, to brush it aside and walk away.

Irmingard stood up straight when she was done with the second hatchet. She pulled her mittens on and gave him the file and the whetstone. "You're a credit to your mother," she said. She walked quickly to the house, without waiting for him or turning back to look his way.

THERE WERE FOUR empty jugs by her door. He saw them and knew it was time to go to town. Her house had no plumbing, and the water from her well was sour. It was better for washing than for drinking. Might as well drink rainwater. She liked her water fresh from the spout. "It's worth the walk," she said, "it's worth the shoe leather." Its minerals were good as medicine and helped with rheuma and the gout. It came from a deep well, she told him, drawn from the same sort of spring that flowed to Bad Nauheim and Bad Orb and all the other famous resorts where people with money went to cure themselves.

He didn't want to go. He resisted and tried to think of reasons to stay inside her hut. People might see him and wonder who he was and why he wasn't fighting, but she shook her head and gave him two pitchers to carry. "It's only old ladies in town," she told him, "old ladies like me and they won't pay you any mind." They walked along a footpath too narrow for cars or buggies. She walked fast, swinging the empty pitchers at her sides, and he fell into rhythm three steps behind her. She sang to pass the time, her voice clear as a soldier's and low. Though the melody was familiar, the words she sang were new to him and sorrowful as a dirge. "*Evening has come,*" she sang, "*time to ride the train. The dry branches break, but the green ones remain.*" She knew no happy songs as far as he could tell.

He waited until she was finished. "What's wrong with the trees here?" He pointed to the nearest oaks. "They don't look right."

"They've got weevils." She was cheerful the way she said it. "They bleed from their branches, and the weevils come and eat."

"Trees don't bleed," he said. "Maybe it was sap you saw."

"Serves them right." She shook her head approvingly. "They wanted to cut them, and now the wood's rotten and there's nothing to cut."

He caught up to where she was, and they walked side by side the rest of the way to town. They crossed the stone bridge—it had only four arches and not six—and went to the square where the waterspout was. The houses were half-timbered and built close together, just like the ones in Heidenfeld. There was a shuttered butcher shop and a pharmacy and a gasthaus with empty tables. The women on the street looked the same and the balconies and even the grasses by the bank. What was to keep him from walking into the schoolhouse here and starting his lessons, from having an apple juice at the café or going down to the river and catching frogs? What was to keep him from staying, he thought, when things were the same everywhere, when the towns blended one into the next, with their church steeples and stone roads, their ironwork and their cemeteries and empty flower pots, all the town shields swinging over all the doors and the ladies who walked with their heads held low. The buildings and the people inside them, he knew them already. He felt for a moment that he'd uncovered some great secret, a pattern hidden in things, and then the feeling was gone, and he knelt down by the spout and filled the pitchers.

If the water were special in the town, it didn't show. The ladies he saw were in sore need of curing. Their legs were bent from age and the damp air, and they looked like wishbones and not women. They greeted each other on the street. "Smells like rain," they said, "or maybe snow," and they raised their fingers to see how the wind was blowing. They waited in lines for milk, for bread and flour and sugar, and they looked to the sky where fat clouds were gathering. "Better hurry," they said, "better run if we want to beat the storm." They pounded the last of their comforters and brought them back inside. The town was in mourning, it seemed to Georg, it was covered with a shroud. There were only women left and babies and he didn't see any men, not a single one, not even grandfathers or crippled veterans.

Frau Focht talked while he worked the spout. She stood with another woman who wore only black, and they looked toward the bridge. "Every time it's more," the lady from town was saying. "They ate all my chickens. And my laying birds, too."

"They're passing through," Frau Focht said. "They come and they go again." And while she spoke the horns began to sound.

The trucks came from the west. They crossed the bridge and rumbled up the street, more than Georg had seen since he left the supply road, two dozen at least, with others still coming. Opel Blitz trucks and towing tractors and half-tread cable tractors and fire tanks with their hoses wrapped neatly behind them, one after another they came, and the old ladies raised their handkerchiefs. They stood on the curb and down by the bridge and waved like schoolgirls. The trucks were muddy and the soldiers were muddy, too, and they looked tired and didn't wave back. A driver shouted when a woman crossed the street too soon. She dropped her shopping bag at the sound. "Idiot," he yelled, "damned woman," and the wheels ran over the bag, crushing it flat against the stones. Her bread was gone and her sugar, and the flour was just a puff of white smoke under the treads.

Georg knelt behind old Frau Focht and raised his arm by his head, but one of the soldiers noticed anyway and turned around to see him better. He stood up in his seat and shaded his eyes though there was no sun, and Georg could see how he opened his mouth into a perfect O. Against his better judgment he met the soldier's eye. They looked straight at each other for the longest time, and then the truck rounded the corner by the church and was gone. They were going eastward. They were falling back, back from the border and the fighting, and soon they'd be in all the fields and sleeping in the houses and the barns.

Irmingard didn't look. "They're just workers," she said. "They're going north. They're going away from here and won't be back." She said these things without conviction, and Georg nodded without conviction, too. "Yes," he said, "you're right," but the soldiers were faster than he was. They moved like a river over the land, and there was no outrunning them.

The woman who'd been careless before knelt on the street. She cleaned up the mess, sweeping the crumbs and the torn paper and the broken tins that dripped their juices, and threw it all away. The last of the ladies went inside then and drew their curtains against the clouds and waited for the storm.

SHE LED HIM outside when they were back at the house. They set their jugs down and walked past the oak trees and the pond. All the ice had gone soft and water flowed over it. He looked for his shirt, certain that it had come to the surface again, rising through the water like a drowned sailor, but only twigs poked through. She took him toward the hill where the trees grew thicker, and when she stopped he saw four crosses. They had settled into the dirt, and one was crooked and leaned away from the others.

It took him a while to understand. She had buried her boys like soldiers. She buried them in a field and not in a cemetery where they belonged. Who knew how she'd done it. Bodies were supposed to be kept at the house for only two days. Two days in their beds while their families sat with them and then they went to the corpse house in the cemetery and were buried. She must have bribed the gravediggers and the coffin maker. She must have given them cigarettes and wine, just like Mutti when she wanted to find her mother a better room at the old people's home or when she needed a favor from the priest. Chocolate pralines and wine and oranges, plum schnapps and marzipan, this was the currency in all the towns and cities. Old Frau Focht had paid them, and they brought her children home. And still how hard it must have been to see those crosses every day and watch their wood go to silver.

She knelt by the nearest marker and brushed the snow and dead leaves from beneath it. "I set them here so they'd be close," she said. This one was her youngest. He was walking before he was one. Every night she had to chase him around the house to put him to bed. He was never sick, not even for a day. Never sick and always hungry, this is how he was, until that last morning when he choked on his food. Choked on the milk and the potatoes she mashed, and then he went blue and she left all her babies and ran for the doctor, along the path and into town. It took a while to find him because it was lunchtime and he wasn't in his office. The doctor closed her baby's eyes when he finally came. He set his hands over those blue eyes and rolled them shut.

"That's all they ever do," she said. She rubbed her palm along her skirt. "They're useless, doctors. They have no cures."

Bad luck settled over her house after that. It brought the crying disease. She lost her other three in as many years. They were gone from a fever, gone from a lung infection, from stomach cramps. And then her husband had his first gout attack, and his legs swelled up fat as sausages and he couldn't work the fields. Each time she fetched the doctor and each time he did nothing, and now they were buried and she had no need anymore for doctors or for nurses. "Boys always leave," she said. Georg didn't understand what she meant, but he nodded anyway. "Easier growing oranges than boys." She wiped the wood on each of the markers and ran her fingers where the names were carved.

She was in a funny mood at dinner, setting her spoon down as if to say something and picking it up again. She waved him aside when he started to tell a story. "I'm tired tonight," she told him. "You're not the first one who's come to my door. You're not the only one. I'm an old lady, but I do what I can." She left him alone at the table and went outside to sweep her stoop. She went to bed when she was done and snored loud as a man through the thin curtain.

He waited in the kitchen, poking the log in the oven and listening to it burn. He wasn't sleepy yet. He waited for sounds outside, for the turning of wheels and shouts from the soldiers, but it was quiet. They were gone to wherever they were going. They were sleeping somewhere else tonight and not in her field and not in her barn, but another few days and they'd be coming to her door. Almost thirty years since they'd come last. He looked around the room, and he could imagine how it was. She wasn't young then but she wasn't old yet either, and she let them inside. She opened her door and her eyes were clear and the house was warm. Maybe she cooked for them. Maybe she washed their clothes and brought out the soaking tub. Her boys were buried already and her husband was gone, and the soldiers were falling back. They were coming home, the fathers and the grandfathers of the boys who were knocking now. They ate her food and smoked their cigarettes and brought mud into the house, and she outlived them all.

He went to the window. No sign of rain yet. The moon was bright behind the clouds and threw long shadows. It was a night for walking. Mutti took him to Rothenfels on nights like this or farther on to Lohr, to visit her aunt or the cousins who lived past the quarry. He was only five or six and he'd fidget in his chair when the talking went late. He fell asleep right at the table, and Mutti roused him when it was time to go. She lifted him and buttoned his jacket, and he breathed in the smell of her and pulled at her pearls. They walked the last part home, down the stone steps and along the river, and sometimes the gypsies were there dancing by their wagons. Mutti covered his eyes then and ushered him along, but he saw them anyway and they were beautiful, how they arched their backs and swung their skirts around. He held tight to her wrist. He walked but was only half awake and had no memory of taking the steps, and then he was home again and in his bed. He pretended to sleep so she would pull his blanket up for him, and her hands were soft when they touched his face.

He pulled his rucksack out and began to pack his things. He took one of the old woman's blankets and rolled it up tight and pushed it to the bottom. He went to the cupboard. It was wrong to take her food, but he'd eat it anyway if he stayed with her and so what matter if he took it from her now. This is how he thought of it, and he opened the cupboard door. He stepped back at what he saw. On her shelves there were dried apple slices and a half dozen cured pork sausages, a fresh loaf of bread and a handful of sugar lumps. She had set them on napkins for him and filled his lard tin. She'd packed his food for him. She must have known that he'd be leaving, if not tonight then the next night or the one after. There'd be no more stories when he left and nobody to help patch her roof, and she'd packed for him anyway.

He took the bundles and set them inside his bag, and when he went for his shoes there was an old shotgun leaning beside them. She'd set it there so he wouldn't miss it. It probably belonged to her husband once, that old Behr gun, and years before he'd tied a leather sling around its barrel and its stock and carried it in the fields. Georg could see only two shells for it, just the shells in the chambers and none more. The barrel had no engraving, no antlers or scrollwork or stags, and the wood had dried in places and begun to crack, and still he was grateful and set it over his shoulder.

The old woman's breathing was deep now and slow, and every now and again she talked into her pillow. He set four of his ladies in his pocket and the last one he left at the center of the table. He snuffed the lamp and dipped his fingers in the blessed water she kept beside the door. He closed the door gently so she wouldn't wake.

## 15

E tta went to see Dr. Kleissner first. She climbed the stone steps and walked the hall to his door, but his office was dark and there was no note posted by his name and nobody at the desk. She pressed her face against the glass of the office door. Neat stacks of paper lined the desk and the two side tables. Papers for her Max were somewhere in those piles, she was certain. They'd tell her where Max had gone, and she wanted to break through the glass. She'd read those papers and burn them because it was paper that kept you prisoner and paper that could set you free, everyone knew this was true. She rattled the handle of the door. She pounded on the wood in case somebody was in a back room. "Herr Doktor," she called, "Herr Doktor Kleissner, please let me in." She pounded harder on the door, she pounded with both her fists, and a lady came out from the accounting offices across the hall. "Ma'am, please," she told Etta, "you're causing a disruption." She was young, maybe twenty, but her face looked pinched. "You're disturbing our clerk and he's not here anyway, your doctor. He hasn't been here all morning."

"I'll wait," Etta told her. "I'll wait right here until he comes," and she paced along the narrow hall, stopping every now and again at the window to watch the street. The sky was gray and the clouds looked like snow. What should she tell Kleissner when he came back? What could she say to help Max come back home? The authorities could have taken Max while he was fighting. They could have sent him to a work camp or shot him for insubordination, and who knows why they didn't. They sent him home instead, but there was no more shelter in Heidenfeld than there was on the front. She waited a half hour and another half hour, and the church bells chimed eleven, and still the doctor didn't come and his office stayed dark. It was almost noon when she climbed back down the steps, and she didn't stop to chat with the ladies on the street, not even old Frau Fader who waved to Etta from her stoop.

Josef was already gone when she came home at lunchtime. Who knew where he was. Not working, that was certain. Not clearing the roads or working with the other old men who were gathering wood that day and bringing it to the schoolhouse. The house was empty, and she went to Max's room and made his bed so it would be ready when he came back. She smoothed the down comforter and fluffed his pillow, and she went into Georg's room, too, and straightened the books on his shelf, the Latin and the Greek grammars he loved best, and the snow had started to fall, small needling flakes that hit the windows. Just beyond the trees the fishermen were by the banks, and how could the river flow when her boys were gone? It wasn't her world, this strange place. It wasn't any world she'd ever known and the men were out there angling and the ladies with their purses and the sun would set and it would rise again and her boys would still be gone.

SHE WENT TO see Ushi Hillen next, because they'd taken her Jürgen just last fall. He was only a little younger than Max, and his face was soft and girlish and had been since he was little. He didn't play with the other boys, young Jürgen, he didn't play soccer or race along the river bank. He stayed inside, and Ushi did too. She went to no klatsches and she didn't chat with the ladies while they waited at the stand. It wasn't snobbery, though the other ladies thought so. It was shyness, Etta was convinced, a reticence that she'd had even as a girl, and it kept her from joining in their talk. Sometimes weeks went by when nobody saw her and people wondered then what she did with her time inside her grand stone house.

Etta rapped the iron knocker and waited on the steps. Ushi took a long time to open the door. She didn't look surprised to see Etta standing there, though Etta had visited her house only once, years before. She stepped aside and took Etta's coat and her wool cap and hung them on the wooden coat rack in the hall. Her eyes were rimmed with red. She'd lost weight since Etta had seen her last. Her wool tights hung loose around her ankles.

"They took my Max," Etta told her when they were both inside Ushi's kitchen. She should have made polite conversation first, but she couldn't think of what to say. She sat at the round table with her coffee cup and the wood popped and hissed inside the stove. "They came yesterday and I don't know where they went."

Ushi nodded. "That's what they do. They take the weak ones." It was Kleissner who came and two other men she didn't know. They pounded on her door and they came inside and they didn't listen to her pleas. It wasn't right how they took him. She'd go to the ends of the earth if only she knew where he was. There was no sweeter boy anywhere than her Jürgen, but he was soft and that's why they took him. He was soft and he left the girls alone. She rubbed her eyes with the back of her hand. She looked like a woman of seventy and not the pharmacist's wife who used to walk along the streets with her back so straight and her only boy beside her.

"Don't give up, Ushi. You'll get him home. You have to keep looking until you find him."

"He's not coming back," Ushi pushed her cup aside. "People leave and they don't come back. My Jens is gone and my Jürgen, too." Her voice quavered. "They've wrecked the world, these men, and still they're not done. They'd take the sky if they could. They'd take the air we breathe, and there's nothing we can do to stop them."

Etta shook her head. "I'm bringing Max home. I'll find him and bring him back."

Ushi smiled at that. "God bless your Max and keep him safe. He's a good boy. I saw it for myself, how kind he was to Jürgen. If I hear anything, I'll tell you," she said. "And you'll do the same for me. We're just the same, though we never knew it. We're sisters in our loss," and she patted Etta's hand. Something about the gesture brought the tears to Etta's eyes. She cried there in the kitchen, she cried though she tried hard not to, and Ushi fetched a handkerchief for her and held her by the shoulders.

She walked with Etta to the door when it was time. "I don't know why I keep it locked," she told Etta. "I have nothing left to take." She squeezed Etta by the shoulder one last time. "Don't go to Kleissner. He'll give you nothing but more trouble," and she opened the door and waited until Etta was down the stairs before she closed it again and turned the latch.

JOSEF WAS IN his workshop when she came home. He was carving a flower into a square of butternut wood, working each petal with his gouge and then sanding it down just a little. He lifted the carving and angled it toward the light. She stood by the door and watched. He set down one gouge and picked up another, a V-shaped one. He was adding the veins to the petals now, pressing the metal into the wood.

"We have to find him. We have to bring him home."

Josef nodded while she talked. He looked toward the window. "Bring me an apple," he said. "Go bring me a glass of water."

"We need to write some letters." She folded her arms. Nothing moved him. Nothing touched him where he was, and the anger rose inside her then. Let him forget things. Let him be like his father and suffer in his chair. Why couldn't he listen when she talked? They could sit together at the table if he'd only listen. They could sit and plan things out. She tightened her scarf over the ears. Oh, it was work to bring him round. It was work, and she was tired and lacked the will. She knew when to push and when to step back, when to be stern and gentle and when to cry. She knew all these things, and still there was no hurrying him. He made everyone angry. He fought with the priest and his cousins and all the union people. For years he'd needled people and frowned at their diction. *Be nice*, she'd tell him, *try just a little, even if it rankles. Bend with the grain, with the grain and not against it*, and it wasn't any use.

"Maybe Pfarrer Büchner can help," she said. "He might know people in the city." She waited for him to raise a fuss, to shout the way he sometimes did, but he blew the dust from the wood. She needed to reach him, but she didn't know how, and so she left him to his carving.

SHE TOOK MAX's medals off the wall when she came back inside. She had caught Josef staring at those medals and the clippings from the papers of the local boys who fought, and his face went puckerish sometimes and he looked toward the window as if trying to find a way out. Coming home wasn't easy for him. He'd returned from the war and from his post at the school and now from the field, and she needed to be patient. The first weeks were hardest, Etta knew, and it was best to leave him to his workshop and his exercise. She'd learned this the first time he came back.

His mother had insisted on having a dinner for him all those years ago. "To welcome him," she said, "to bring him home." Etta told her to wait. Better to wait a week or maybe even two, but no, Mutti Huber had started the stew already and set the table. Even the cousins from Würzburg were invited. The good china came out and the candlesticks were polished and all the cakes bought, and Etta almost dropped the lid when she saw the rabbit head floating at the center of the pot.

His hands began to shake at dinner. They shook harder by the time the cakes were cut. They were worn raw, his hands, and dark from the sun. People lingered over coffee. They spoke of his brothers who were gone still, of Erich and Oskar and Richard. How good when they come back, how good it will be, and he fidgeted at their names. He looked down at the teacup in his hand, then lifted it high over the floor, as if raising it in salute. The others weren't paying him any attention, but Etta caught the queer look in his eye and put down her fork to watch. He let the cup drop to the floor, where it shattered and threw shards over the tiles that Mutti Huber mopped every day. "Idiots," he said, "you're all idiots," and he left them gaping and walked back home. Etta walked with him, struggling to keep up with his long strides. He came back to himself within a week, but Mutti Huber had stayed angry for months afterward.

Etta took Max's medals now and set them in her purse, shaking her head the whole while because Josef looked for reasons to be unhappy. He was jealous of his son. Jealous of his medals and how long he fought, jealous when he should have been proud.

SHE WROTE TO the clinics next and all the hospitals and even the barracks just in case they'd taken him there. She spent days writing at her table, beginning letters and tearing them up and beginning again.

She worked her way through the uncles and aunts in Bamberg and the cousins in Würzburg, Josef's old colleagues, anyone who might know anyone else who might help. Her fingers went stiff from the pen, and she stopped to rub her palm. Each letter said the same thing. Max had come home, but they took him from his bed. Did they know anyone who might help, she wanted to know. Anyone who might listen.

She went to see Ilse, who cried when she heard. She went to Maria and Regina and old Hansi and when no one could help her, she went to see the cousins in Würzburg who lived in a fine corner house on Semmelstrasse. They were party members, but they were family and they'd seen Max just a few months before. They'd spent the morning with him and taken him back to the station. She took the early train and brought them a bottle of wine and a thick piece of smoked ham that Ilse had given her. They lived on the second floor and rented out rooms to a bookkeeper and a retired attorney, and they were proud of their house and their tenants, who were educated men.

She sat with them and drank their coffee. "Max is sick," she said. "They came at dinnertime and took him from the house."

Cousin Hilde's jaw went tight. Her husband Gerhard left the room to fetch his paper and didn't come back.

"He needs doctors if he's sick," Hilde said. She smoothed her skirt across her lap. "He needs medicine."

"They took him and didn't tell me where."

Hilde reached for the coffeepot. She shook her head. "Look how bad things are," she said. "The trains don't run the way they used to. Half the time the milk is spoiled." The grocery stores had closed, she was saying, and children were chewing yeast to keep their bellies full. And what about the house at the corner of Harfenstrasse. What a shame. Two dozen died there, and babies, too. They died at their dinner table and in the stairwell, and even the ones who were quick and went to the basement breathed in the vapors and died together on the floor. "People are starting to leave. Another month and we'll go, too." She poured more coffee.

"Maybe Gerhard knows someone," Etta said. "He sees doctors all day long. Maybe he knows somebody who can tell me where Max is."

Hilde looked at her teacup. She turned it around and around on its saucer. "If Max is sick, he needs doctors," she said. "He needs his rest. They're helping him wherever he is. They're curing him." She set her hands together.

When the coffee was gone, Hilde didn't brew another pot. Etta held her empty cup for the longest time because she didn't want to leave. She understood she was imposing, and still she tried again. "Let me know if he hears something," she said. "Call me at the station. Send me a wire." He's your cousin. You've known him since he was a baby. He toddled around this room.

"We'll come see you in the springtime," Hilde said. "When things are better we'll be by." Etta shook her hand, and so it went. All her letters and all her visits came to nothing.

JOSEF HAD BEEN to the movie house, and he came home happy. "I needed the rest," he told her. "All those days clearing the road and my legs are tired." He sat with her in the kitchen and talked about the newsreels, which were much better than the radio because you could really see how things were, you could see them with your own eyes. He told her about stone buildings burning from their windows and planes dropping their loads. Silesia and Pomerania, Elbing and Posen and Marienberg and the Bolsheviks coming up to the Oder. The Führer wasn't on the newsreels very often now, and not his generals either. They were busy, that was the reason. They were busy getting ready. It was only a matter of time before the German wave rose and pushed the Bolsheviks back. No one sat still this time around. There was no sitting in trenches and waiting. It was all movement and hauling things uphill and downhill and over bridges. It was horses and bicycles and enormous trucks, men marching and commanders pointing. He jabbed his finger in the air. *Curse the Bolsheviks*, he said, *curse them and their fur hats. Curse the British and the Amis, too, those gum-chewers. What a sorry bunch. I saw the pictures. I saw them at the movie house, how the Ami soldiers wrecked the fine buildings where they were quartered. They ripped the books from the walls and broke the arms off all the statues.*

She listened to his stories, and when he was done, she leaned in close so he could hear. "We have to do something," she said. "Kleissner can't help us, and not the cousins either."

Josef flinched a little when she said Kleissner's name. The muscles tightened in his jaw. "I don't know any Kleissner," he said. "He's no student of mine."

He went to the living room and turned the knobs on the radio. He sat in his chair and she stood by the door, and he didn't look her way. The radio played a march and two sad folk songs and then another march, and he closed his eyes. His chest rose and fell. Maybe he'd forgotten Kleissner's visit or maybe he remembered the visit but not the doctor's name. There was no telling how his mind worked.

The announcers were listing some of the dead and the places they'd fallen, and the march played low. Josef's fingers curled like a baby's in his lap. Just yesterday he had started the clocks again. He had risen from the table and wound the hallway clock. "Leave it the way it was," she told him, "leave it alone. Max will want it peaceful when he comes back. All that ticking bothers him." She stilled the pendulum, and the house went quiet, and when Josef reached for the clock again, she set her hands on her hips. He'd taken his pewter beer cup then and left the house.

They hadn't even finished with *M* yet; they weren't halfway through, and the list went on and on. Maier, Marlin, Matthäus, Maurer, Mehlinger, Meister, Meltzer, Metzger, the names went, and Josef's head began to dip. The announcer said Metzger twice, and then Mittelmann and Müller and Münch and on to the *N*'s. Josef snored. "You're not helping," is what he had said that night in Max's room. "It's no good," and he spoke like a stranger and not a father. All at once she could see how it might have happened. She saw him walking up the hill to Kleissner's office. He worked his way around the snowbanks. He swung his walking stick and nodded at all the ladies who greeted him. "Guten Tag, Herr Lehrer," the ladies said, and he touched the brim of his hat.

How it must have tickled as it grew. How hard to sit and watch his boy and to listen as she read from those books when things called for action and not for patience. She should have known from the way he looked at the medals she'd framed. His brothers had brought honor to the house, and now his son did, too, and what good was her talk about the teaching he'd done and the commendations and all his years of service. What good when all he wanted was framed on the wall, and he couldn't have it. Yes, it was her Josef and no one else. He went up the hill to Kleissner or to somebody else and that's why they came and took her boy. It was Josef, and it couldn't have been, because he loved his boys, loved both of them, even if he couldn't show it. She knew and she doubted, and her hands began to shake. She wanted to choke him back to himself. She needed him the way he used to be. She couldn't fix this thing alone. His mouth was open, and he'd started to snore. It wasn't right to suspect him. It wasn't right, and still her chest was tight as she crouched down beside him and set a blanket across his knees.

## 16

J ust before the sun rose, the snow began to fall. Georg squatted in the reeds and looked upstream. The ice had gone soft by the bank, and there were no rocks in the water and no branches. He walked back and forth between the trees until he found two thick sticks. They were each as high as his shoulder, and one of them was forked at the bottom. He took off his boots and his socks, and he tied the laces together and set them like skates around his neck. He wasn't sure how deep the water was at the center, and so he took off his pants, too, but not his underwear because he didn't want to stand naked in the cold air. Max had stripped plenty of times, even in winter. "It's only water," he'd say. "Last I checked we're not made of sugar," and if Georg hesitated, Max laughed and called him sugar boy, and once he'd pushed him in and Georg's best boots were ruined after that. The soles warped, and they smelled like herring even after Mutti had scrubbed them clean.

He took a deep breath and stepped in. The shock left him wordless as a baby. He coughed and his eyes brimmed and he almost dropped his sticks. The water rose from his knees to his hips and then to his belly. It pushed the wind out of him, and for a moment he wanted to yield to it. He wanted to dive under, but he shook his head clear and pushed the sticks hard into the bed. When he reached the other bank, his capacity for cursing came back to him. He shouted and hopped from one foot to another. He put his pants back on and his dry shoes. He was hot now that he was out of the water, and he sweated even as the snow fell against his hair. He missed the old woman and her stone hut and most of all he missed her stove, which crackled and hissed and dried the air.

He stopped to cough. He pressed both his palms against a tree trunk and bent low. The snow was falling harder, and though sweat ran down his forehead and into his eyes, he shivered and held his collar shut. All day he'd felt a burning in his chest, but coughing did no good and brought up only ropes of yellow spit. It was the damp that clogged his lungs. It squeezed out all his air, and he walked only a few kilometers before he had to lie back down.

The path crossed a paved road and curved between the trees. He walked the road because it was less likely to take him to another bridgeless river. He carried the shotgun over his shoulder. He walked during the day now. His discipline was gone. He had no patience for walking in the dark. He thought of stories in case someone stopped him or asked him where he was going. Trucks came down the road every hour. Trucks and the occasional car and he didn't look when they drove by. He kept his head low. He was a farm boy walking to his uncle's house. He was on leave and helping his mother, who had no one else at home. His name was Markus, and he didn't have his papers. His name was Müller, and he had four older brothers and they were all fighting, but not together. They'd been sent to different places, and it wasn't good to separate brothers like that, to keep apart the ones who knew each other best.

He sat beside a birch tree and ate from the stash the old lady left him. He went behind the trunk so that nobody on the road could see him. He rationed out the food tighter than the ladies who worked the stands. Three thin pieces of sausage and a half apple and a single slice of bread, which was soggy and went down hard. Everything tasted wrong. It tasted like metal, and his throat hurt when he swallowed. He drank from his canteen and wiped his mouth and when he heard sounds on the road he pushed his back against the trunk, but only partway, so he could see. Every day now he had vanishing dreams. He wanted to disappear like his ladies, to be palmed and hidden away.

A truck stopped near the trees. It was a fuel tanker, one of the snub-nosed Opels he'd dug out from the mud when he was at the wall. The driver climbed down. He wore field gray, but his uniform had no bars and no badges. He kicked the right front tire and cursed at it. "Useless," he said, loud enough for Georg to hear, "what useless shit they give us." He climbed the side to reach the spare. He was high on the rear wheel housing when Georg began to wheeze. It started in his chest, that terrible tickling, and worked its way up, and he set his fist against his mouth to keep the cough inside. The driver squinted into the falling snow. He waved toward the trees. "It's no use hiding," he said. "I see just where you are."

The driver stood with his arms on his hips. His cap was low on his head and Georg saw only his lips, which were thin and pressed tight together. Georg stood motionless behind the tree. He thought about running the other way. He could take his rucksack and run to the trees. He could take his gun and his rucksack and chances were good the driver wouldn't follow him. He wouldn't leave his truck to chase him down. Georg reached for his gun, reached for it out of habit, and then he set it back. It was the pull he felt, had always felt, that strange inevitability, and he didn't run. He went to the driver, who was waiting for him.

"My spare was leaking," the driver said. He talked to Georg as if they knew each other already. "The lieutenant didn't listen. Shortages, he told me, shortages all around." He took the hubcap off and then the lug nuts. "I found a good spare and took it for my own." He jacked the truck up, huffing with each pump. Georg could see that he was old now, almost as old as his father, and his hands were spotty. "Right from the lieutenant's own truck I took it." He smiled at that. He looked at Georg, and his eyes were tinged yellow.

Georg held the wrench for him. He looked to see if the old man had a gun, but he didn't see a holster or even a knife. He pointed to the other tires. "They've all gone thin," he said.

The driver ignored him. He grunted and pushed the spare into place. He took the wrench from Georg. He tightened the top lug nut and then the bottom one, and he crisscrossed his way around the wheel. When he finished with the wrench, he tucked it inside his belt. "Why were you in the trees?" He reached for Georg's wrist. He was quick like a snake, the way he pounced. "What were you doing out there?"

Georg pulled at his hand, but the old man was stronger than he looked and didn't let go. He held fast to Georg's wrist and looked up and down the road, and Georg could smell his sour breath. There were no other trucks in sight and no cars and nobody was walking. It was quiet as a cemetery, and only the snow was falling.

"How old are you?" The soldier was breathing hard, and all the muscles of his face had gone loose.

"Thirteen. I'll be fourteen in May." The lie came easily to him. He was thirteen and not fifteen. He was only in his third year at the gymnasium. He hadn't been called up, he never went to the academy or worked at the wall. He nodded at the soldier. He looked into his eyes, and he wasn't ashamed.

"Thirteen," the old man said. "Not even any whiskers yet." His mouth opened a little and his eyelids fluttered. Their breath steamed together in the cold air. Georg stepped back to get away from the smell of him, that strange sour smell of vinegar and sweat. He moved, and the soldier moved with him. The wind picked up. It blew beneath the skirts of the evergreens and made them dance.

 He saw how dirty the man's nails were, as dirty as his own, and he tried to pry those fingers loose. All the pain was gone from his chest. He could breathe again, and he saw things with a strange clarity. He should have taken his gun. He shouldn't have left it leaning against the tree. The fingers tightened their grip. He wanted to pull the old man with him, to buck against his touch. He'd seen a deer once with a trap around its leg. The steel bit through its fur and into the bone, and it ran anyway. Max needed three shots to bring it down, and he was quiet afterward. "Sometimes it's hard," he'd told Georg then. "It's hard to do what they tell you." The soldier pulled him closer. Georg looked at those eyes. This is what it's like, he thought. Sometimes boys are walking beside the road when the planes fly by. Sometimes they're caught sleeping by a stream and the police bring them back, and this is what it's like. Look for mercy, look for kindness and for charity, but there's only steel, only steel and bored eyes. He shouldn't have coughed just then. He shouldn't have stopped to rest. The soldier laughed. He threw back his head.

 Georg moved quickly then. It wasn't anger he felt and it wasn't fear. It was something more elemental, this need to break loose. He brought his heel down hard across the soldier's foot. He felt the grip loosen around his wrist. It released for just a moment, and he pulled free and he was running.

 The soldier followed him at first. He ran halfway to the trees before stopping. "I know what you are." He bent at the waist. He set his hands on his knees and gasped. "They'll find you," he shouted with his last air. "They'll string you up high."

 Georg went between the nearest trees. He ran away from the road and the truck and he stayed in the hills until it was dark. When the moon was out he came back down and went in circles looking for his gear. The trees all looked the same at night, and it was hours before he found the spot. His gun and his bag were gone, his HJ traveling knife, too, and his blanket, and only the crust was left from his bread. He knelt by the tree and looked to the road, and he wished that he'd shot the old soldier with the sour breath, shot him in the back while he changed the tire, shot him when he reached for the toolbox he kept inside his truck. He'd lost all his things. Only his ladies were left, only the four he carried in his pocket.

He walked that night and didn't sleep. He went away from the road and walked in the fields instead because he didn't want to see any more trucks. He had no gear, nothing to carry, but it was harder now than it was before. The burning came back to his chest. He didn't feel his feet anymore, not even the blisters along his heels, and as he walked, the lie set roots. He wasn't fifteen anymore. He was thirteen because he'd been thirteen once and he wanted to be thirteen again and because people would believe him when he said so. Bless his fat face, his fat soft hairless face and his rounded chin, and bless those hands of his, too, plump as any girl's.

It was the softness that bothered his father, he knew this. It was a flaw that only Mutti could forgive. He'd joined the Deutsches Jungvolk when he was nine. He'd been proud of the uniform that looked just like Max's. He'd trained and marched with the other boys and learned to shoot a rifle and how to put out fires. He'd done everything he was supposed to. The DJ at nine and the HJ at fourteen, but the training didn't toughen him up. *He's too soft*, is what his father always said. *Nothing good will come of it. Work is what he needs. Time away from home. Sometimes it takes heat to harden things up. Heat from the fire and a quenching afterward.* For a teacher he was quick to find inspiration in the handicrafts and in labor, in the language of carpentry and smithing and animal husbandry.

They'd been in the kitchen together, just his mother and father, but Georg had heard them through the door. "All that running will hurt his lungs," Mutti said. She ran the water and turned it off again.

"There's nothing wrong with his lungs." The old man rapped the table with his knuckles. "It's his head where the problem is."

"The doctor will write a letter."

"Let him go with the rest of them," his father said. He was getting impatient now.

Georg pressed closer. They argued almost every week. They argued about school and money and the lease for the hunting grounds, which cost more than everything else combined, and Mutti had to turn every penny around twice because a teacher needed a substantial tract, a place where he could bag a roe buck every winter and all the people could see him cart it home. Georg leaned against the door and almost pushed it open.

"Not even fifteen yet," his mother said, but the fight was gone from her voice. She'd pack his bags when the notice came. She'd take him to the station.

The old man tried to find the toughness in Georg. He tried to grow it the way farmers grow their crops. The branches he kept by his desk, the hours scouting together for deer and the rifles they shot, these things left no mark. Georg was as soft at fifteen as he was when he was eight, and he'd be just as soft at twenty. His father was a teacher and not an alchemist. All his efforts were bound to fail.

And still Georg tried. Every year he went to see the gypsies. It was best to watch from a distance, so he couldn't see their smudged faces or the tangles in their hair. They were just a blur then, all color and movement and brown skin flashing. They wrapped scarves around their waists and let the ends hang loose, and when they danced the fringes swung. They wore bright leather shoes, red and yellow and cobalt blue, but no stockings, and the old ladies in town shook their heads in dismay at the sight of those bare legs. He'd come especially to see them. He waited until Mutti was distracted, until she left for town or was working her beds, and then he went down by the water. He sat with a book and pretended to read, but he watched them instead. He waited for a twinge.

They came through town twice a year, once in spring and again in fall just as the weather started to turn, and they camped down by the river with their wagons and their carts. Their fires lit up the sky at night and shone on the water, and the townspeople could smell the meat cooking all the way up by the cemetery. *Watch for your wallets*, they'd tell one another when the wagons came, *watch your chickens and your milk pails. Lock your children inside.* They'd take the blond babies, the women were sure of it. *They'll take our babies away. They visit the cemeteries at night to steal from the dead. Gold teeth and leather shoes and burial suits, they'll take it all and cart it away and they'll leave the dead naked and dishonored in their wooden boxes.*

They stayed no longer than a week or maybe two, and he missed them when they left. He missed their music and their dancing and the way they clapped and shouted. He missed their naked brown legs. And still they didn't help. The gypsies didn't move him, and old paintings of naked ladies didn't either, and not even the magazines that Max had left hidden in his room. Max had strapped them under his bed so Mutti wouldn't see when she reached down with her duster. Georg had found them the summer Max left. He took them and looked at every page. The pictures were sharp and clear, and the ladies wore garters and black underpants and they looked straight at the camera with no shame in their eyes. Some sat with their legs spread wide and cupped their breasts in their hands, and he waited for the stirring but it didn't come.

\*   \*   \*

TWO NIGHTS WALKING and two days sleeping in fields and empty barns, and he drank only water from the streams he found. His boots had holes already and his socks, too, and his bare toes poked through the leather. All those years that Frau Focht had kept her husband's clothes. She washed and ironed them, and they were ruined now. They were worn through, and she wasn't here to fix them. Maybe Mutti could stitch them again and fix the holes when he came home. He'd bring them back to old Frau Focht then and thank her for her help. He'd bring gifts, too, marzipan and picture cards and maybe some books because it wasn't enough just having one Bible in the house. Mutti would come, and it wouldn't be far if they went together. Just a day on the train. Mutti liked taking the train. She always sat beside the window and looked outside, and sometimes she reached for his hand. "It's not so much money," she'd say, "and look how far we can go," and she seemed almost sad when she said it.

On the third night he couldn't swallow anymore. He went back to the road even though trucks might still come. It was straight, and he could see the trucks coming long before the drivers could see him. He told himself the road was safe along this stretch, and so he walked along the shoulder and tried to ignore the tickling in his throat. He stopped when it grew stronger. He knelt on the ice and choked like a drunkard. Nothing loosened in his chest. He gasped for air and spit himself dry. Another week or two and he'd be home in bed, and Mutti would sit beside him. His room would be warm. He pushed himself up. He rolled back on his heels, and he saw a solitary light farther up the road.

He was shaking with fever when he came to the town. The lights were out in all the houses and the streetlamps were dark save one, and though he stifled his coughing, there was no one on the streets to hear. The snow had gone soft as he walked, and a steady rain began to fall.

The sting was gone from the wind. Every time he stepped he felt the water rise between his toes. He should have hurried, but he was tired and he wanted to take his time, to walk the streets when everyone else lay in their beds. He looked at the windows as he passed. He looked for shadows, for a fluttering behind the curtains. He heard sounds with a peculiar sharpness. He heard the pinging of water from the gutter spouts and door signs swinging in the wind, and somewhere behind the houses a dog began to howl.

He came to a church and sat on the steps. It seemed no bigger than his house back in Heidenfeld. It was built at an angle, straddling the two roads that went through the town. I've found a town of dwarves, he thought, a town with houses and churches and roads all built on a three-quarter scale. He was certain he'd hit his head against the streetlamps if he stood up straight. He'd rest for a little while. Time to stretch his tired legs. He lay back and closed his eyes.

17

Forty days had passed since Christmas. Forty days since Christmas
and another forty until spring. It was time to bring the baby to the
temple, to light the candles to mark his name. The ladies wore their
good hats and carried their candles for the blessing. Most had white
tapers that they bought in town, but a few were lucky and carried
beeswax candles from their people up in the hills, and they smelled
sweet as berries when they burned. Etta brought her candles for the
whole year, thinking it better to bring too many than too few because
it was a long time to wait until the next blessing.

Etta unbuttoned her collar as she walked. Water ran down the
stones, and she slipped in her leather shoes. The ice in the river had
already gone soft at the edges. It cracked like bones breaking, and the
water came up black from beneath. In the afternoon snow slid down
from the pitched rooftops and fell on passersby. The ladies cursed the
sun then and the melting ice. They wished for fresh snow, enormous
drifts of it, and winds that blew down across the hills. *If it warms,* they
said, *the Amis will come. The sun will shine down on them and warm
their shoulders, and they'll cross the fields from here all the way to Kassel.
Let it stay cold. Let the snowdrops freeze on their stalks and break, keep
the buds from the trees.* They wore their coats and their scarves. They

wrapped themselves in felt and wool, and all around them the air went soft and the sun shone on the river.

Pfarrer Büchner stood at the pulpit and blessed the candles. "Light our hearts," he said. "Light them as we light our candles." The sun shone through the windows, and all the saints in the glass were lit and threw their colors across the altar. He read from Luke. He told the story of Joseph and Mary bringing the baby to the temple. Simeon took the baby up in his arms and blessed him. "O Blessed Mother," the priest said, "the sword is in your heart."

The ladies stood together on the steps when the service was done. They wanted to know if there was any news. Every time Etta saw them they asked the same question. "Did it come?" Ilse asked. "Did a letter come?" The others gathered close to hear.

"Nothing. Not even a note."

It'll come and with good news, they said. This is the week. He might not be in the city. They probably have him working. In the fields, that's where he is, that's where they always take people, in the country where the air is clean. They looked up to the sky. She looked with them and wished for clouds, but the sky was clear, and the Allied planes flew undisturbed. They flew over the river, over the hills and toward the city, and everywhere new posters were on the walls. *Frankfurt is the new front city*, they said. *Together we must defend it*, and how could this be? she wondered. How could this be true, when Frankfurt was only eighty kilometers away?

ETTA CHECKED THE mailbox twice a day, and still she was surprised when she saw the letter. She set her finger under the flap and worked the envelope open. She read the letter twice on her stoop and once more in the kitchen. Max was at the University Psychiatric Clinic in Würzburg, it said; he'd been there for weeks. All this time and he'd been in the city. He'd been there when she'd gone to see the cousins. The doctors had him just a few blocks away. The letter spoke of treatments and therapies and the uncertain prospects for recovery. The words slipped away from her. She read the same sentence three or four times and was still unsure of what it said. The signature at the bottom was smudged, and it took her a good while to make out the name. Franz Selig, it said, chief administrator for the intake section. It wasn't even a doctor who wrote to her about her boy, not even a doctor or a nurse. Just before the closing sentence, which wished Max a quick recovery and freedom from suffering, someone had scratched out a few words. They had used a pen with a thick nib, working their way across the words upward and then across until a black box covered what had been written there.

She went to the window and held the paper up to the light, but she could see nothing. She was certain that there was something important inside that blot, and so she took to rubbing it with her fingertip. She licked her finger and when that didn't work, she took a damp rag and wiped against the paper. What had they written there? she wanted to know, what had they said before changing their minds? She pushed harder and harder, and she stopped only when she had worn a hole through the paper. She smoothed the letter then and set it out to dry.

SOMETIMES THE FEELING rose inside her and took away her air. It came while she was washing the dishes or peeling potatoes or sweeping the snow from her stoop. It rose inside her chest, and she wanted to shake Josef then. She wanted to tear his books from their shelves and break his radio and burn all his precious papers, but she pushed these thoughts away. Anyone could have gone and told. All the people who saw Max on the streets, who saw him at mass or pacing in the graveyard and talking to the stones. The town kept no secrets, and still she looked around the empty house and the tightness came to her chest like great iron bands strapped around her ribs and it left her gasping. She fought the feeling when it started. She lived in a new world now, a world she didn't know, and the time for tears had gone and the time for softness, too. Be resolute, she told herself. Be hard like the rock and quick like the water so she could bring her boy back home.

JOSEF SPEARED THE last herring from the bowl. "I'm hungry still," he said. "Fish doesn't stick. It doesn't fill me up." He mopped the juices with a piece of bread. She could tell he was thinking of dinner already, of the plate she would fix for him.

"Come with me to the city," she said. "We'll go together. We'll talk to the doctors." He was a teacher and they'd listen better to him, but only if it was a good day and his eyes were clear. He'd wear his wool suit and they'd take the train, and they'd walk together just as they did when Max was in school there and renting a room on Lindenstrasse. They'd gone every other week that first year. She brought Max food and did his wash and scrubbed the floors, scolding him because his room was messy and he didn't fold his clothes. "What a slob I raised," she told him. "You're living in a rat's nest." He spent his money on books and beer and not on a cleaning girl, and he laughed when she complained. He held up both his hands.

"I've got work," Josef said. "Maybe next week we'll go." He licked his knife clean and set it back, dissatisfied. He looked to the cupboard where she kept the hard candy and the licorice sticks, but she ignored him. Let him get his own. Let him lift a finger for once. She cleared the table, looking straight at him as she took his plate. He squirmed a little then, and his face went puckery. She looked at him as she washed the dishes and as she dried them and set them back in their places.

"You can take a few days," she said. "They'll understand if you need some time to see about your son."

He looked at her for the longest while, squinting as if trying to understand.

"They don't need you until April," she said. "That's when you go back." She heard it from Maria, she told him, Maria who couldn't keep any secrets, not even when she was a girl. "There'll be no resting when they call you back. You'll be working every day."

He scratched his chin and nodded, but reluctantly. He pushed back his chair. "I'm tired," he said. "My knees hurt."

She scrubbed her counters and cleaned the sink and wiped the table down. She wanted to say things that would hurt him, that would make him look her way. She wanted to tell him what she knew. You lost the buckets and the shovels. You spent the whole day retracing your steps, looking behind buildings and digging up fresh snow with your hands. They sent you home when you couldn't find them. They took your armband and your gun. All the men knew. They came home and told their wives, and now she knew, too. She wanted to say these things, but it wasn't any use. She'd have to bring her boy home without anybody's help.

He was back in his chair, his pant legs pulled high over his ankles. She set a briquette for him and drew the curtains. He nodded at the radio. A few boys spoke, their voices earnest and upbeat, and some hadn't broken yet. They sounded like choirboys and not soldiers. "It's an honor," one of them was saying, "a real honor to be here." And Josef nodded, yes, an honor is what it was. He shut his eyes when the music began. She left him to his song. She pulled her step stool to the cupboard and climbed up. She reached behind her tins and her empty canisters of sugar and flour. There were only four squares left, and she had no other bars. She broke him off a single square. She set the chocolate and two hard candies on a saucer and sliced an apple so the plate looked full.

He ate the candies first, sucking on them until they went soft. When announcers came back on, he tapped his feet. "That's right," he said, "just right. That's what I want to hear." He looked like his father then, and his jaw went slack. She tried to stay angry while she watched him. She tried to keep herself sharp like a blade, but it was no use. He was falling away from her. He reached for her like a man pulled by the current, reached for her and pushed her away.

Sometimes when he slept she could still see the young man he'd been when he left for the front thirty years before. She'd gone with him to the Würzburg station and he waved his hat from the window like every other soldier on the train. They waved hats and handkerchiefs and the women on the platform waved back, and only women were left in the city after that, women and children and old men. Every letter that had come from Josef while he was gone, every smudged letter was a gift, and she read them all until she knew the words by memory. The land was a moonscape, he'd told her, with no trees, no flowers, nothing green or growing and no birds in the sky, only rats and mosquitoes that sucked the blood from the dead and the living alike. She wrote back with news from Heidenfeld and from his teachers and from church. She didn't tell him about the boys from town who had died or how food was getting scarce. She focused on the silly things. The Hankels' shepherd wandered into the gasthaus and stole a sausage from the mayor's table. Just as the mayor raised his glass in a toast, the old dog made its move. The Baiers and the Mecklers were still fighting about the boundary between their land and everything was just the same and he needed only to come home. He stumbled on the platform the day he came back and she caught him by the sleeve, and he wasn't himself, she could see this, but he was with her and he was alive and that was enough.

She roused him when it was time for bed. He sat upright in his chair, his chin tucked tight against his chest, and his snoring was louder than the radio. "I'm not sleeping," he told her. "I was just resting my eyes."

"Better to rest upstairs," she said. "You'll give yourself a crick."

He grumbled a little and pulled his arm from hers, but he went with her anyway. They climbed the stairs together. He walked fast just to show her that he hadn't been sleeping, and when they reached the bedroom he took off his shirt and his pants and handed them to her. By the time she had hung them on their hooks and changed into her nightgown, he was snoring in his bed.

He was still sleeping the next morning when she left for the station.

# 18

Georg dozed and woke and dozed again, and each time he opened his eyes a young woman was sitting by his bed. Her face was dimpled and flushed from the heat in the room. She raised his head from the pillows so he could drink the tea she'd brewed. It was lung moss, she told him, and she picked it from the beech trees behind the cemetery.

"I scraped the fattest lobes for you," she said. She brewed it fresh, and even with the honey she added it was bitter enough to make him spit.

He tried to talk, but his throat was swollen and no sound came out, not even a croak. He looked around the room, at the cross beside the door and the curtains that she'd opened. It was raining. The wind blew the drops slantwise and he saw no streetlamps outside and no trees. She laid his head back down, and her face leaned over his and she looked like Mutti the way her eyes slanted upward. He tried to follow what she was saying, tried to listen because she was pointing her finger and her eyes were solemn, but he caught only a few words. "Sleep," she was saying. "Sleep a little longer," and her fingers were rough against his cheek.

He shivered under the down comforter. He burned and shivered and drenched the sheets with sweat. He heard Mutti's voice while he slept. She was sitting beside him and reading from his books, and there were bells in every story. They rang so loud he couldn't hear her voice. He knew the girl's name was Ingrid when his fever broke, though he didn't remember talking to her. She lived in the rectory and cooked for the priest, and he remembered the priest's name, too— Zimmermann—and how his face was thin and had no softness to it.

She led him to the kitchen when he was better. She took him by his arm because he didn't want to leave his bed. "Bed is where people die," she told him. It wasn't true, he knew this and she must have known it, too. People don't die in bed. They die in distant places, on the field and in trenches and up in the hills. They die at the dinner table and in shelters, but he got up anyway and went with her.

She had the water ready for him, and every time he tried to talk, she shooed him back beneath the towel. "Don't waste the steam," she said. "Don't waste the chamomile I dropped in fresh." She talked as much as Frau Focht, but her voice was young as a girl's. He'd slept so long she'd started to worry. He slept through the ringing of the bells and a storm that rattled all the windows. Any longer and she'd have called the doctor. She'd have brought out the salts to wake him up. Another few days and the priest would be back. Every month he went to the monastery. "It's good that you're up," she said. "He'll want to talk to you when he comes back."

Georg coughed over the bowl. His lungs were clogged tight. They were dry as they'd been when he was ten and he'd slept all summer in his bed. He sat in the chair, and twice he had to hoist up his pants. For the first time in his life his belt was loose.

"It's the last storm of winter," Ingrid said. She was working by the sink. He could hear her work the knife against the cutting board. "It'll start to turn now." She spoke a funny German, the way she rolled her r's. Just a few more days, she was saying, just a few more cold ones. She could tell from the way the clouds hung, and just yesterday she saw the first snowdrops poking through. Spring would be short this year and the summer hot, and so it goes.

He stayed under the towel and closed his eyes and her voice rose and fell the way young girls sang when they were skipping rope. It made him dizzy just to listen to her. The priest didn't eat enough and her husband had been gone too long. It made no sense how they sent him east, when the fighting was so much closer. All winter she'd worried about him because the snows there were different. They were heavier than the ones she knew. They could work their way through boot leather and freeze a man's foot to the bone. *There's no telling why he's there and not here*, she said, *and there's nothing I can do anyway.*

He worked through his stories while she talked. He set aside the ones he'd started on the road. They were too elaborate and didn't sound right, and he began again with what he knew. He was at the wall. They sent him north for just a day but the truck was hit. They walked together all night and into the morning, and he lost them when he stopped to rest. He woke, and they were gone, and it was luck that brought him to the town and to the steps where Ingrid found him. It sounded true as far as it went, but he had no answers to questions about his parents. Let's write a letter, the priest might say, let's send your parents a wire. Where are your papers? Tell me about your unit and your commander and what happened to your uniform and why don't we call your group. It won't be a day and you'll be back with them. Georg tried to think of answers, but he needed quiet and not the sound of Ingrid's voice and the closing and opening of the cupboard doors. He needed time alone.

She asked him questions once the water had gone cold. "Where are you from?" She set her hand on her hip and cocked her head. "Tell me about your mother." But when he tried to answer, she waved him down. She took the bowl from him and emptied it. "It's better not to know," she said, and she left him in the kitchen.

*   *   *

THEY WENT UPSTAIRS together when she came back. Georg went with her because he wanted to see Zimmermann's room. He was at the monastery still and would be gone for another two days, and she looked happy when she said so. Those trips were a blessing, she told him, because she could listen to the radio announcers then, and they might have news from where her Richard was. It was dark inside the room because the winter curtains were drawn, but Georg could see the radio on the table even in the half-light. It was a Lumophon just like the old man's, ten years old at least and shaped like a cathedral.

"I almost dropped it last time," Ingrid said. "It slipped when I took the stairs." She knelt below the table and reached for the plug.

Georg helped her carry it down. She went backward and he went forward, and he looked around the room as they left, at all those books on the shelves and the armchair where the priest kept his notebooks. "He's messy with his papers," she said. "I sweep around the piles because he doesn't let me sort them."

They put the radio in the kitchen. Georg sat over another pot of steaming water. She wouldn't let him sit down unless he breathed in steam. You don't want a lung infection, she told him. You need to loosen up your chest. She got anxious every time the announcements began. She remembered all the places from the letters Richard had sent. She wrote them down and kept the list inside the pantry. She tilted her head when the announcers spoke, worrying their words around like rosary beads. She closed the cupboard doors too hard when the alerts were done and she was almost spiteful, the way she worked her kitchen knife. "He's gone already from all those places," she said. "And I don't believe them anyway with that strange German they talk. They sound like criminals." She whacked the knife against the cutting board.

Georg nodded. "Maybe you shouldn't listen anymore," he said. "We can put it back upstairs." He missed the quiet of Frau Focht's stone house. He missed not knowing things, but still he was drawn to the sound. He sat like his father and listened. Lodz and Tarnów and Kraków were lost and Budapest was falling and Warsaw, too, and the boys were coming home for the final push. Belgium was gone and the Amis were pushing on, past the wall, toward the Mosel and the Rhein, but wait until they come closer, the announcers were saying, wait until they cross. They'll see then what trouble they're in. Our boys are falling back on purpose. They'll squeeze the Amis like a snake.

A march came on the radio next and then trumpets followed by an announcer with a solemn voice. *To commemorate the twelfth anniversary of his coming into power*, he said, *our Führer will now speak to the nation.* It took Georg a moment to realize who it was when Hitler began talking. Even through the radio his voice was tired. It lacked the fire from his earlier speeches. *The Bolsheviks want to destroy Germany and all of Europe*, he said. *The Bolsheviks from the outside and the Jews from within, but we won't let them take us down.* No, it was up to the people now, every person in every city and village. *We expect every healthy man to fight with his body and his life, and we expect the sick and the weak to work with their last strength against the Kremlin Jews. People in the city must forge the weapons to fight and the farmers must feed them no matter the cost, no matter the hardship, because they will destroy us and all we represent. Together we will overcome this calamity*, and Ingrid's face was pinched. She whacked the knife harder now, so hard Georg was certain the blade would break loose from the handle.

He went back under the towel. He breathed in more steam and coughed over the water. He didn't want to hear the rest of the speech. He could see already how things would go. The Amis had crossed the Moder and the Sauer, and the Rhein was next. They'd cross at Köln or Bonn or Koblenz, and if the bridges were gone they'd make their own.

They'd build new ones and come across. They rolled across the fields like waters from a flood, and it was just the same in the East, where Danzig was gone and the Bolsheviks had crossed the Oder, and soon the waves would meet. They'd surge to the center. They'd cover all the towns and the cities. Bombs over Nürnberg and Goch and Kleve, over Kalkar and Reichswald and Karlsruhe and now Dresden, Dresden where a hundred thousand people burned, maybe more, and the announcers kept talking just like before and the music played. Fight more, the Führer was saying. Fight harder, as if winning were a choice when everyone knew it wasn't. Priests spoke from the pulpit and ladies came with their coupons and their net shopping bags. They went about their business and they kept quiet because what good was it to say what everyone already knew.

He stayed under the towel even after the water was cold. He didn't listen to the announcers when they came back on. He didn't want to hear any speeches, any voices from the front or the names of the newly dead. He stayed there coughing until she tapped his shoulder, and together they carried the radio back upstairs.

FATHER ZIMMERMANN CAME back late Saturday, but he made no effort to see Georg. On Sunday Ingrid told him not to come to services. "Stay inside," she said. "Stay where nobody will see you." He needed warm air. It was cold outside and damp, and he should stay beside the oven, but Georg went anyway. He was restless, and he came through the doors just as the bells began to ring. He sat in the back with the old ladies and a man with a cane. He set his hands together.

Zimmermann's voice was an instrument of uncommon power. His hands shook when he talked. His face went red and his eyes bulged, and Georg was certain the old priest was not just communing with the angels but had swallowed them whole. He spoke of duty in his sermon. He spoke of Abraham and his sacrifice. Georg knew the story and all the verses, and still he leaned in to hear.

"God told him to take his son, his only son Isaac, and to lay him down." Zimmermann raised his hands and looked at the parishioners, who looked back at him and some of them nodded in rhythm to his words. Three days it took to reach the mountain, three days and three nights, and they built the altar together and gathered the wood, and Abraham offered up his son. He didn't waver. He held the knife and raised it.

Women should have wept at the story. They should have wiped their eyes, but they were hard, even the ones who wore their mourning coats, and they weren't moved by sacrifice. They knew loss already. They knew about altars and dead sons. The priest drew himself up. He looked even taller in his robes and he spread his arms wide. "Lay not thine hand upon him. For now I know thou fearest God, seeing thou hast not withheld thy son, thine only son from me." And so Isaac is spared but not Jesus. One son dies while another lives, and don't try to understand. There is no understanding perfection with our imperfect minds.

Ingrid was in a sour mood after the service. She didn't like talk of butchery and knives and strange tests of faith. What kind of example is it, what kind of story, where fathers have to kill their sons? She shook her finger at Georg, who shouldn't have gone outside. Winter wasn't done yet, and why bother with compresses if he was going to breathe in that cold air? And besides people saw him in the church. They turned to look when he came in. She swung her iron in the air, and the coals crackled and hissed.

"He thought he had no choice," Georg said. "God told him what to do."

Ingrid shook her head. "It might have been the devil talking and not God. You've got to do the right thing. You've got to use your mind," she said. "That's what the real God wants. People should do the right thing but they never do." She'd learned this when she was little, she told him. She learned it from her father's mistress who lived just across the street and the whole town knew. She bore him two sons and they wanted for nothing, and she never worked a single day, and when the old man died, and wasn't even cold yet in the ground, she came for his things. The woven rugs and the fine table linens were piled high, and she filled a cart with them. The silver, too, and the good clock, she took it all because Ingrid's father had made arrangements for his sons, and all the neighbors watched from their windows. They were doctors now, both those boys, and they lived in Karlsruhe in fine stone houses with house-keepers and nannies and motor cars. One of them even had a cook. It was almost too much, that final detail. It just went to prove that there was no moral reckoning in this world.

Georg stood up and walked to the window and came back again. She shouldn't be saying things about her father and how he had a mistress. He was uneasy with her talk of private things. He tried to think of the stories he'd polished while he was walking those days after he'd left old Irmingard's hut. He tried to remember their details.

"I know about you," she said. "There's no shame in it." Her voice was low and easy and absentminded, the voice of a woman sharing a recipe or looking at the clouds and predicting snow. She held the priest's trousers by their cuffs to make sure the pleats were straight. "I wish my Richard would run, too, and bless every woman who helps him on his way."

"I'm going back," Georg said. He pushed his hands into his pockets. "As soon as I'm better I'll find my group." He tried to make his voice convincing, but she knew just what he had done. He could tell when she looked at him.

19

Men worked the roads in Würzburg, pushing barrows and hauling bricks and roof tiles and branches. They stopped to wipe their faces or to take a drink from their bottles and they spoke in low voices. The city was quiet. No one shouted or whistled, and no children played. Women swept the alleyways. They carried brooms and buckets and even the nuns were working, their habits gray from ash. Etta nodded at them as she passed. She swung her bag and her umbrella, and the sweat rolled down her neck. The old town wasn't so far away, and the Dom St. Kilian. The bones of the saint himself were inside, and all his helpers, too. The Residenz was nearby, and the palace gardens where the vines hung black against their arbors. Her eyes itched from the smoke, and tears rolled down her cheeks and into her scarf. The clinic was on Füchsleinstrasse. It was just a little farther now.

She stopped for a moment to tighten her bootlaces. An old woman leaned down and took hold of her elbow. "Do you know about the toy factory?" she asked Etta. "Do you know where it went? It was right here, and now I can't find it." She looked upward with red-rimmed eyes and moved on and asked the next person and the next, and they all ignored her and waved her aside.

They didn't want to let her see Max when Etta arrived at the clinic. Two nurses and a woman in a brown wool suit stopped her at the front desk and told her that visiting hours were done for the day and that a written request was required regardless. "Would you like to come back in two days, or perhaps the following week?" the woman asked. She pointed at Etta's bag. "If you have something for your son, I'll give it to him in the meanwhile."

Etta shook her head. "I've come all the way from Marktheidenfeld," she told them. "I took the early train, and it's not even noon yet."

She set her bags on the floor. The wool of her sweater itched against her skin. She was sweating in her winter coat, and her face went hot just looking at those women and the way they had their hands on their hips. "It's been weeks since I've seen him." Her voice was rising now, and people stopped in the hall to look. "It's been weeks, and your letter didn't say anything about a written notice."

The woman nodded. Her hair was short as a man's and combed back from her face. "Come back," she said. "Come the day after tomorrow and you'll see him."

Etta drew herself up. "I didn't come all this way to turn around again and leave." She unwound her scarf from around her neck and set it with her bags.

The woman stepped back and spoke with one of the nurses, who looked over at Etta. They talked for the longest while, and the nurse shrugged. She gestured to Etta and led her down one long hall and then another. Etta lost track of where they went. The clinic didn't feel as clean as a hospital should. She expected to see spiders in the corners and dust piles, and more than once she felt something brush against her skin. Unease is all it was. She wiped her cheeks with her palm. They turned to the right and to the left, and she was certain when they rounded the corner that she'd see the front desk again and they'd be back where they had started, but it was just another stretch of hallway. She looked inside the rooms as she passed. Patients lay on their beds or sat upright against their pillows. A few were strapped around their waists. They made strange sounds when she passed. They clicked and hooted and shouted toward the hall, and their eyes rolled back in their heads.

The nurse stopped at an open door. There were six beds inside the room. Men slept in the two beds farthest from the door. One of them was bald and he snored and swatted at his face. The other lay with his back to her. She knew from the tilt of his head that it was Max. She went beside him and set her hands against his cheeks. He was thinner than he had ever been, so thin that she could see all the bones in his throat. She held his face until he opened his eyes and looked at her, and she pulled him up and propped the pillow behind his back. She cut the sandwich into pieces and peeled two apples.

"The food is sour," he said. He ate the sandwich slowly as an old man, and one of his front teeth was chipped. "There are worms in the oatmeal. I see them in the bowl."

"Look how thin you are," Etta told him. She pulled the covers up around his waist. "You need to eat what they bring. You can't be picky with your food."

He bit into the apple slices. He didn't finish any of them, not a single one. He pushed the napkin aside.

"I'll bring you meat next time I come," she said. She knelt beside him so only he could hear. "Take his in the meantime if he doesn't want it." She pointed to the bald man sleeping in the other bed.

Max shifted against his pillow. "The wind blows at night."

"Promise me you'll eat," she said. "Promise you'll leave them only empty plates." She set a slice of bread under his covers and closed his hand around it, but he closed his eyes and didn't answer. She sat with him until he slept again. She held his wrist and felt it flutter.

She wasn't ready to leave when the nurse came back, but she stood up from the chair. She stroked Max's cheek and picked up her bags. She walked slowly and looked at all the doors and watched for their numbers so she could remember how to come. A few visitors sat in chairs by the wall. They looked down at the floor, at their hands, at their purses. Somewhere a man laughed and shouted, but she couldn't understand his words. Max didn't belong here, not in a place where they strapped people to their beds and nurses came running with needles. A girl sat upright just as Etta passed her door. She sat straight in her bed and screamed. Etta stopped at the sound, but the other patients in the room paid no attention. The girl screamed again and beat her fists against the bedsheets. She was thin, and her skin looked blue from the veins beneath, but her voice carried. She could have been ten or twelve or twenty-three. There was no telling because her cheeks had gone hollow from sickness or from hunger. Where were her parents, Etta wondered, and why weren't they bringing her any food? Etta wanted to give her something, to peel the last of the apples in her purse and set the slices by her bed, but the nurses came. They came quickly and shut the door, and then the ward was quiet.

HE HAD NO one but her now. She was the only one who could save him. Her boy, her perfect boy, who was born in the Heidenfeld schoolhouse on the classroom floor. They had planned to go to the hospital in Würzburg because Etta was older than thirty and the doctors feared there might be complications. They had ether there and new sleeping drugs for a painless birth, and she kept her bag ready so they could take the train as soon as the contractions started. She'd walked to the schoolhouse that morning to tell Josef it was time. She moved as quickly as she could, stopping every now and again to catch her breath, and she knew already they wouldn't make it to the city. All the stories from her mother and the women she knew best. All their talk of the hours or even full days spent working, working to open themselves up and push the baby out, and her baby was in a hurry. He had already started to crown. She held her belly as she climbed the schoolhouse steps. She made it to Josef's classroom and knocked hard on the wooden door.

Josef came running when he saw her. He dismissed his students, and Jutta the old secretary ran to fetch Dr. Ackermann, who wasn't even forty then but his hair had started to gray. Josef spoke to her while they waited. He folded his coat into a pillow for her and patted her forehead with his hanky. She watched his lips moving, but she didn't listen to the words because her baby was coming, any moment he was coming. She pulled down her underwear and clawed at her skirt buttons and Dr. Ackermann was in the room now. He knelt on the wooden floor and Etta heard old Jutta praying somewhere behind them, "Hail Maria," she was saying, "the Lord is with you," and Max was born before the prayer was done. He came into the world with a shout. He raised his fist like a little boxer, and Josef wept beside her. He held his boy for the longest while before setting him against Etta's chest. "He's going to be a fine student," he told her, "he's at home here in the classroom," and he kissed her on the forehead. "Just look how he wiggles. We've got ourselves an athlete." It was her world there inside that class-room, her entire world, and she lay back against Josef's coat.

ETTA DREAMED OF the clinic when she was home again. She dreamt of the apple-green floors. They unrolled before her like a ribbon, pulling her past open doors where people shouted and laughed and swatted their faces, and old Willi was inside one of the rooms. He waved at her with both his arms. The tiles dipped and rose and dipped again. They were covered with pine needles, and they led her past the chamomile fields and into the hills. She had her berry basket and her walking stick, and she stopped every little while and knelt. The blackberry bushes hung thick with fruit. She picked the fattest berries, and the juices ran dark and stained her fingers. Max waited for her. He stood under the branches, and his shoulders were broad again and his legs were straight. "Come help me," she told him, "come help your old mother," but he just smiled. She set her basket down, and when she turned back to him there was only a sparrow on the branch. It watched her with eyes shiny as marbles, and then it was borne upward.

## 20

The telegram came from Berlin. It sat a full two days before the postman found it. "It fell against the wall," he said. "I didn't see it until I bent to tie my shoe." Ingrid took the paper and didn't read it, and when the postman turned to leave, she tried to keep him at the door. There was fresh bread. It was cooling on the rack, and he should come inside and have a warm meal, but he shook his head. He'd brought the paper only because the party official was in Bretten and wouldn't be back for few days. Georg stood in the hall and listened, unsure of whether to leave or to stay.

"I'm sorry," the postman told her. He touched his hat and bowed. His hands were scabby and his fingers bent. There might be a picture of the grave, he was saying, they might have sent it already, but she had to be patient because it took weeks sometimes or even months and other times it didn't come at all. He looked at her feet and at the doorframe and the iron handle, anywhere but her eyes, and he squinted because the wind was starting and the raindrops blew against his face.

She watched him go down the steps. He held the railing to keep from slipping. When he reached the bottom she shut the door. She went to the kitchen and cut three fat slices of bread, and when Georg tried to say something, to find a word of comfort, she put her finger to her lips. She wrapped the slices and put them in his hand. "Hurry," she said. "He walks fast for an old man."

She stayed inside her room that night. She didn't open the door, not even for the priest. Georg heard drawers opening and closing again, and just after midnight she began to move things, heavy things that scraped along the floor. When she came out the next day her face had settled into creases. She peeled potatoes and set the herring in a bowl, and she looked like a drier version of herself, the way he imagined her mother or her grandmother. Grief had etched lines into her face from one day to the next. It was real as a disease, the way it changed her.

She didn't wait to sort through all her husband's things. She set them in boxes and in crates. His socks and his pants she gave to Georg, who resisted at first and relented only when her face went quivery and she began to shout. The shoes and the work boots and his winter coat went to the old people's home, and his best pipe she threw on the compost heap so no one else could smoke from it. She carried the telegram while she worked, in her apron pocket or tucked inside her bra. She carried it as if it were a lock of hair or a tombstone rubbing, and she went peevish when he noticed. Time will make things better, he started to say, and she shook her fist. Going to God, freeing the spirit, leaving the stage, finding peace, joining the angels. So many ways to say it and all of them meaningless. "He belongs here," she said. "He belongs with me and not with the God who took him."

She had trouble picking a poem for the notice cards. None of the verses sounded right, she told him. None of them was true. In the end she chose a simple couplet. *He gave his utmost*, it said, *and I gave my happiness*. She had no patience for poems about courage and the afterlife and eternal rest. They were just words, she said, and they gave no comfort.

He helped her with the notices when they came. He folded them lengthwise, and she addressed the envelopes. The cards were thick and rimmed in black, and each had a photograph of Richard in his dress uniform and his winter cap. He was younger than Georg expected. His front teeth were crooked, and he smiled anyway, broadly as a boy.

She was left-handed just like Mutti, and sometimes she smeared the ink. She looked up from the cards every time he coughed. She frowned over her glasses and scolded him. He coughed too much and the priest didn't eat what she cooked for him and the postman should have seen the notice sooner. Her voice went hard. That was no way to handle the telegrams, she said, letting them fall into a crack. And what about all the letters she hadn't sent. She should have written every day and not just twice a week, especially once the omens turned. She'd known for at least a month before the notice came. Dogs barked when she passed, even dogs that were old and friendly and knew her voice. Crows gathered by the door and didn't move when she threw stones, and just two nights before the postman knocked she'd dreamed of her grandmother, her mother's mother who had passed on years before. "You've married a good boy," she told Ingrid, "a real fine boy, but he's too thin." The dream was real as her wedding band or the crucifix on the wall, and still she didn't write.

"I brought him bad luck," she said. "I wasn't minding the signs."

"We never know how things will be," Georg said. "God doesn't give us clues."

"You'll understand when you're older. When you're married." She reached for her handkerchief. "If you ever get married." There was something spiteful in her voice, he was almost certain, but when he looked at her, she was rubbing her eyes.

He cut his finger on the edge of one of the cards. He wrapped a napkin around the cut and kept on folding.

"What about your mother," she said. "When was the last time you sent her a letter? She'll want to know you're well." She looked at Georg and pointed her pen at him, and he didn't want to think about writing to Mutti because his father would be there, too. He'd be sitting at the table.

Georg finished the first stack of cards and began with the second. He didn't meet her eye, but she watched him anyway and he could tell she wasn't going to let it go. There'd be no peace until he lifted his pen.

SHE WENT THROUGH the books last. They were in his trunk, and it wasn't easy bringing it up from the cellar. Georg pushed from below and she tugged at the handle and together they hauled it up the stairs. She looked for marks he might have left in them, for scribbling in the margins and slips of paper he might have forgotten, but he kept his books clean and she found only a braided green ribbon that he'd used once to mark his place. She sent the books to the schoolhouse, all except for one that she saved for Georg. It had maps of the provinces and the cities from the French border all the way to Freiburg and Sulzbad, and alongside each map were pictures of cars that someone had glued in one by one. *Cruising with Abdulla—Through the World!*, it was called. Abdulla was a cigarette and not a person and so the ladies in the back seat were smoking, those glamorous ladies in their hats and gloves. They were smoking as their driver took them to the Brandenburg Gate in Berlin and the Roland Fountain in Hildesheim, to the Hofbräuhaus in München and the harbor in Hamburg. They went past the Acropolis, past quarries on Malta and those famous steps in Rome and the race-track in Monte Carlo, and from one page to the next they were in America, in Arizona and Colorado and the forests of Arkansas. The maps bore no relation to the picture plates, and so the map with Dresden was framed by pictures of Kansas and Massachusetts, as if to say, look how big the world is and how different one place from the next.

"He smoked a lot of cigarettes for these pictures," Ingrid said. "His teeth were brown by the time the book was full." What a waste, she must have thought, look at all the places he'll never see.

Georg flipped through the pages until he found the map with Heidenfeld. He pointed to the spot, and she looked at it and shook her head. "It's not so far," she said. "It's closer than I thought." She pulled the book away from him. "It's yours if you want it. Write a letter to your mother, and it's yours."

She had the paper ready, and she left it on the table. She took the paper away before lunch and set it back afterward, but she didn't pester him or remind him about the book. He knew she was right. He should write to Mutti and tell her he was safe. He could tell her that and nothing else, and it would be enough. He had known this even at the wall, but he always found reasons not to. He didn't write because he had nothing interesting to tell her, because he was unhappy and she'd sense his misery even if he only said hello. He didn't write because Müller was with him and later because Müller was gone and because they might open his letters and read what he had written. They had offices that looked at the mail and they stamped it when they were done just so people would know. There was always a reason.

He took the paper and went to his room. He began and stopped and threw away the sheet and began again. One version told the truth and said how he had run, and in another he wrote about the fighting as if he'd been there himself. He pretended he was Müller, who was alive and with his group and they'd fallen back from Vossenack. They were out of the forest now, where it was dark even in daytime because the fir trees were old and leaned one into the next and knitted themselves together. It was a different world under the branches. Sometimes the compasses spun around for no reason, as if the polarity of things had been reversed, but he was healthy and he was with other boys he knew, and it was easy writing as Müller. He'd thought so much about him and how things might have gone. The repetition brought familiarity, and over time this familiarity began to feel like truth, and so the words came and he wrote them down. He folded the letter when he was done and gave it to Ingrid.

She left the book on his pillow. When he was alone in his room, he took a piece of string and measured the distance to where Müller's family lived. He traced the finger lengths across the pages and wrote each number in a column. He added them all up and checked his work, and he dreamed of maps that night, of maps and wooden crosses and those ladies in their convertible driving along the shore.

THE AMIS HAD Köln now and the last of the Westwall, too. All that work digging, all the boys who'd been sent to fight, and none of it mattered. The Germans had flooded the Rur valley, but how long could they keep the Amis out? Any day now they'd cross the Rhein, too, and their planes would fly over the cities and drop more bombs and those cities would burn and all their people. Ingrid didn't listen anymore when the music stopped and the announcers came with their reports. She scrubbed the floors and cooked the old priest's meals and she didn't sing anymore either or stop to chat with Georg. He helped her in the kitchen as best he could. He peeled potatoes and scrubbed the dirty pans and he worried for Max because the Russians might have him. They might have taken him prisoner. The world was spinning, faster,

faster. The world was burning, but it was calm inside the rectory, and the rain turned to wet snow and the flakes melted on the street.


MEN CAME KNOCKING after the notice came out. Old men and veterans on crutches and soldiers home from fighting, they all came, and she opened the door for them and let them inside. The sounds carried all the way to his room, gasps and the bedsprings creaking and sometimes things knocked against the wall, and only the priest didn't hear, old Zimmermann who slept on the other side of the rectory and up the stairs. She looked just the same in the morning. Her hair was pinned back and she wore the same sweater and the same housedress with its faded collar, and she never said anything about the men who came to see her, all those men who knew just when to visit and when to take their turn. She took her anger and made them moan, and it was hard to look at her.

## 21

The liquor jars came out before the coffee pitcher had gone cold. It was getting late in the season, but Ilse still had elderberry and juniper and a half jar of plum. The ladies reclined in their chairs and sat with their hands across their bellies. It was warm in the room. The light went rosy as they drank, and their talk fell into the familiar rhythm. A letter from Georg had finally come while Etta was in the city. Josef had thrown away the envelope so she didn't know when he'd sent it, but he was well, her boy, he was alive and he'd made it out from the Hürtgen Forest. *Thank God*, they all said, *thank God in heaven. Both your boys are alive and soon you'll have them home.* They raised their glasses.

Maria had more news. Fischer was back at work. He was clearing roads up by Lohr and the officers were making him shoot now, too, and they'd set a ring around the barrel of his rifle so he could hold it with his stump. *Poor Beate*, they said, *and just when she thought her boy was home for good.* Young Dr. Ackermann was still in the East somewhere. He wrote when he could, and all he ever talked about was snow. It was a world of sun and snow, and the cold worked its way through the soles of his boots because they were made of cardboard and not leather.

"No proper boots for the boys out there," Maria said. "Not even for a doctor." She stopped to sip from her cup.

Etta cleared her throat. "I'm going back. I'll find a room and stay for a while."

Maria set her glass down. "People are leaving the city. Wait a while longer. Wait before you go."

"I can't do anything here," Etta said. "They don't answer my letters."

"My sister left," Maria said. "Three weeks ago she took the train and she's in Hafenlohr where it's safe."

Ilse held up her hand. "It's the right thing. They'll listen if you're there."

Maria still looked doubtful, but the others all agreed. They sat like conspirators around the table. *You need to pester them*, they said. *You need to show your face. Write letters and bring them to the hospital in person. Better still, befriend the nurses. Bring them bottles of wine, and bring the director the finest liquor you can find and wrap it with a ribbon. Be pleasant and smile, but don't yield when they say no; don't bend, not even a little.* They nodded as they spoke. *You'll have him home before summer. He'll be back with you and eating at your table.*

"I'll cook for Josef while you're gone." Regina set her hands flat on the table. "He'll be lost in the kitchen without you."

"Keep your food," Etta said. "I'll cook ahead. He'll be fine with what I make."

It was too much. They shouldn't be giving away their food, especially not to Josef because he was picky and he wouldn't be gracious. He'd give them trouble no matter what they brought him, especially Ilse.

"I'll take Wednesdays," Regina said. "And Fridays, too, if nobody objects."

They fought for the chance to feed him on this day and that one. Even Maria agreed to bring a plate. He'd be fat from their cooking by the time Etta came home. The dirty plates would be piled to the ceiling.

There was no fighting them and the plans they made. When they left, Regina squeezed her hand. "You'll cook for us when he's back home. You'll make lunch for every one of us."

"That's right," Etta said. "You'll eat your fill," and she couldn't look at them because she didn't want them to see her cry.

Ilse waited until the others had all left. "Don't bring him home," she said then. She refilled both their glasses. It was the last glass of the day. The clouds outside were going to gray. Women were on the streets finishing their errands. They were racing the sun. Time to go home. Time to set the table.

"The director doesn't answer when I write," Etta said. "Who knows if he even reads my letters."

"Bring him here instead." Ilse's eyes were bright. All that liquor and she wasn't even a little drunk. "He can stay at Ute's farm. He'll be safe up in the hills."

"Josef doesn't miss him. He sits and sleeps by the radio and doesn't say his name."

Ilse narrowed her eyes. "We'll go at night, and nobody needs to know."

Etta clasped her hands together. The cousins and the colleagues and the students in the city, they fell aside, and she saw only Ilse. She saw her when she was young and her hair still had its color and all her fingers were straight. She'd left the bank that day because it wasn't right the way they teased poor Willi, it wasn't right to take his book. Even then she'd been kinder than the others. She had a grace about her. They were old now, the both of them, but they looked out at the world through the same eyes.

Etta drank the last of the liquor and licked the syrup from her lips. Max would stay in the hills. He'd eat good food, and he'd work outside in the springtime air, far from the hospital and from Josef and his sour looks. She'd visit him twice a week and sit with him on the folding chairs Ilse's daughter kept outside her door. The work would bring the shine back to his eyes. She sat with her friend and it was thin as a thread, this hope she had, thin as a filament, and she reached for it.

JOSEF WATCHED HER pack her bags, and it wasn't right how she was humming. He sat in the living room, and she didn't check on him like before. She left him to his radio and his pipe. She was happy to leave. Happy to go to the city without him. He set his pipe down. How long had it been since he'd gone to see the doctor? How many weeks had passed? The days were all the same. All those mornings she went to the milk stand, and she stayed for hours because that's where the ladies all were, and who knew what they talked about. They saw each other in church and by the cemetery, and still they greeted each other like long-lost cousins. And now she was leaving and he'd be alone in the house.

The doctor's fat face had made him nervous at first, how soft it was and his hands were soft, too, and hairless, and Josef talked more than he wanted because it was so quiet in that office. No typewriters or radios, not even the ticking of a clock.

"Someone moved my buckets," Josef had told him. "I won't lose them again." He held his walking stick across his knees and looked at that round face. "Next time I'll make a note of where they are."

The doctor was polite, how he listened. He sat like a student and took notes in his book. He nodded when Josef paused. He smiled and waited.

"I want to work," Josef said. "I want to help since my boy can't." He gripped his stick tight. "He talks nonsense." Josef leaned closer to the doctor, who had stopped his writing. "He talks about fires sometimes and water behind the windows. He sits in the cemetery for no reason."

The doctor had questions. "Tell me about the visions," he wanted to know. "Tell me what he says and when he sleeps." They were scientists and scholars, the both of them. They were learned men. Together they'd find the truth, and Josef sat a little straighter in his chair. He cleared his throat and talked like the teacher he was, and Kleissner picked up his pen again. He dipped it in the well and wrote down what Josef said, wrote it down and listened and he asked questions that made no sense. "Tell me about your parents and their parents, about your brothers and sisters. Tell me about your other boy."

Josef moved his chair closer to the desk. He tried to see what the doctor had written, but the paper was too far away and the doctor covered it with his hand. Down the hill the church bells chimed, calling the ladies to afternoon mass. The doctor asked his questions, and Josef answered them. He'd see about getting Josef back to work. They needed men, especially now. He'd do his best.

Kleissner was polite when he reached for Josef's hand. He shook it the way colleagues do. He shook it with respect. Josef should have been relieved once the meeting was done, but he was restless instead. He went the long way back. Down the hill and along the bank so she wouldn't see him from the stand. He swung his stick and scared away the birds, and all the doctor's questions and all his promises, too, they slipped away. They faded like photographs, and Josef set them aside.

ETTA KNELT BY the liquor cabinet and pulled out all his best bottles. She took out the Ettaler liquor from the cloister and the Jägermeister and far in the back the Asbach Uralt brandy that Josef loved most of all. She gathered up the bottles and dusted them clean and tied a ribbon around each of them. She was no better than a thief, the way she took them. Ilse gave her the last of her jars, too. "They don't have this in the city," she said. "Poor people living in those houses without any plum trees or berries to pick. Those gardens they have aren't nearly big enough."

Etta rolled the bottles in sweaters and wadded stockings in between. Her bags were heavy with all the liquor.

She cooked red cabbage for Josef before she left because the ladies might forget or he might not like what they brought him. She cored the cloves to keep the bitter out and set the apples in the pot, and she looked to the cabinet while she worked. How long until he noticed? How long until he saw the empty spaces where his bottles had been? "Give me some yellow," he'd say even now, "give me the green," which tasted like herbs and burnt grass. The monks knew just which ones to pick and how to brew them. "It's medicine," he'd say, "it's good for the heart," and he was almost tender when he held the cup. She hoped he'd be too lazy to reach for the cabinet while she was gone. Let him sit by the radio and write in his journal, write just what the announcers said and forget about everything else.

He ignored all her packing and her preparations. He didn't talk about her trip, but when the bags were by the door and her coat was buttoned, he fidgeted in his chair. "There'll be someone different in the house every day," he said. "I won't have any peace."

"It won't be long," she said. "Two weeks and I'll be back." She kissed the top of his head, and he didn't resist for once. He pressed his head against her belly and touched her hand.

"It was wrong how they took him," Josef said. "They came like thieves into our house." She pulled away from him and looked at his face, but he said nothing more. His eyes were dark like his father's, and he closed them.

SHE FOUND A room in a third-floor apartment off Ludwigstrasse in the northern part of old town, not too far from the university and the clinic. She slept on a child's bed. It creaked under her weight, and green paint curled from the metal frame and fell to the floor. The windows were boarded shut, and the electricity stopped and started and stopped again. The old woman who lived in the flat took no money from her.

"Help me pack instead," she told Etta. "My son is gone already. He's gone to the country with his wife and daughter. Help me bring the boxes to the station. Better you than somebody else. Better you than having it lie empty." The woman shook her head though because it made no sense that anyone would come to the city. People were leaving from every neighborhood. They took trains and buses and the poor ones walked with their babies, and they all went toward the hills where the planes didn't fly. The old woman had rolled her rugs and set her best pots in boxes, and only the furniture remained, pushed to the corners and covered with blankets. She sat in her kitchen in the afternoons and watched the shadows grow across the floor.

"What a shame I've lived this long," she said. "Better to die than see the city burn." She set her hand across her mouth and rocked in her chair, and once the sun had set the sirens started again, and people ran along the streets.

ETTA MADE AN appointment to see Herr Selig, and she took the new bottle of Asbach Uhralt with her. She wore her mother's pearls and pinned her hair and wet her fingers to keep the curls tucked back. She'd taken her wedding band from the cord around her neck and forced it back onto her finger. Selig made her wait a half hour before he came for her. He was younger than she expected, no more than forty, but the veins had broken across his nose and his hair was thin as a baby's and waved like wheat every time he nodded. She sat across from him with the bottle in her lap.

"There's been a mistake," she said. "Max belongs at home." She tried to take the shrillness from her voice. She tried to smile.

Selig steepled his fingers and sat back in his chair. Papers lay across his desk and on the ledge by the window, neat stacks set one beside the next, and atop each was a glass paperweight. Max's papers were somewhere in there. She'd give her house and all her precious things to have that file, to set it in her purse and leave with it. The doors would open for him then.

"There was a mistake," she said again.

Selig rubbed his chin. He nodded while she spoke and furrowed his brow. Just outside his window men were pulling hoses. They pointed and ran between buildings, and others followed with shovels and buckets. A woman lost her shoe by the curb. She slipped once, twice, and fell to her knees, and all around her people worked. The dirt had started to heave early. It made a mess of all the streets and the fields. It's worse than ice, they said, the way it slicks the road. The woman was up again, and her skirt was brown from the mud. Water sprayed against the windowpanes, but Selig didn't turn at the sound. It was a world of water out there, of running people, and he couldn't see it where he was. Peaceful as an altar boy, the way he sat and looked at her.

"He was gone for two years," Etta said. "His boots fell to pieces from all the walking he did." She held the arm of her chair. "He's home not even five months now. Not even five months and he's gone again." She forgot all the things she meant to say. She'd noted them before she left her room, and still she forgot them and new words came in their place. He'd won medals. He fought where it was cold even in April, where the snows didn't melt. Two years without boots or warm coats and sometimes he fought hungry and there was only ice to eat, he'd told her this himself, and men lay where they fell and he climbed over them. "He's war sick," she said. "He needs his bed and his books."

Selig waited until she was done. He cleared his throat and said all the things he'd written in his letter. "It's a serious condition," he said. They didn't know yet how long the treatment would take. They might have to send him someplace else. She should go home in the meantime. They'd send her letters to tell her how he was doing. Every week she'd get a letter. "Go home, Frau Huber," he said again, and his voice was almost gentle.

"Better to save his spot for someone without family," she said. She held the bottle of liquor. It was heavy in her lap. She held the bottle by its neck and thought of ways to turn the talk around. "All those sick people and not enough beds." It was a matter of duty to free the beds for those who needed them most, that's what it was, and her voice picked up. "I'll do just what you say. I'll give him all his treatments."

He didn't let her finish. He rose from his chair and held the door for her. She wasn't ready yet. She set the bottle on his desk and went anyway, and the ladies were typing still, filling in those forms, one after the next, rolling them around the bar and pulling them out and setting them in piles, and the room echoed with the sound of the keys. She had his medals in her purse. She had his Iron Cross. She reached inside but didn't take it out. She hesitated and they were past the ladies now and Selig was extending his hand, but he looked over her shoulder and toward the door where people were waiting on benches.

She was in the hallway when one of the secretaries found her. She was almost at the steps. "You forgot this," the secretary said, and gave Etta back her bottle.

EVERY TIME ETTA came to visit there were fewer patients in the beds. Sometimes in the morning gray buses drove behind the hospital and pulled away again, and she walked a little faster then, unsure if her Max would still be there. She gave the rest of the liquor to the nurses, but they fussed anyway and weren't any nicer. They frowned when she came to visit and when she brought him food. "It's too heavy for him," they said, "he can't digest it all." They fed him only oatmeal made with water and not with milk. It wasn't even warm when they brought the bowl, and it needed sugar. It needed honey.

She hollowed out his book for him. She took his bird book and cut through the pages a few at a time until there was a hole, and when she closed the covers it looked just the same. She set apple slices inside and boiled eggs, sausage and pieces of hard cheese, all the things Ilse had given her for the trip. She sat by his bed with the books on her lap, and when the nurses left, she brought out the food. She hurried him. "This is no time to be picky," she said. "Be quick before they come and see." She stood between him and the door, and when he pushed the food away, she gave him a look. She wagged her finger, and sometimes she sat on the bed and fed him. He pressed his head against her lap then and opened his mouth for her, and when he was done eating, she rocked him in her arms.

People were walking outside when she left the hospital. She took off her mittens and her coat because the breeze was blowing warm from the hills. She didn't look up at the sound of the first planes. Not even dinnertime and the sky was clear and still they came. Every day more planes flew. They came with the thaw. They came just when the birds began to sing again and when the crocus leaves pushed through. The Marktbreit and Seligenstadt trains were hit and the Gemünden station destroyed, and people climbed aboard again as soon as the tracks were cleared. "If it happens," they said, "it was meant to be," but they were nervous anyway and the trains were quiet as schoolrooms because people were looking out their windows to the sky.

She didn't go straight back to her room. She went to the movie house instead and waited because she wasn't ready yet to sit with the old woman, who had nothing good to say. *The Lady of My Dreams* was playing in color, and *A Night in Venice* and *Music in Salzburg*, and in another week, *The Orient Express* would show every day and twice on Sunday. She paid her money when it was time and sat at the back, and the weekly newsreel came on first. All the Volkssturm soldiers gearing up, the women sorting boots and sweaters and coats. Everyone smiling, the old men with their rifles, all those gray and balding heads, and the German refugees coming from Prussia, thousands of them pushed out by the Soviets, and they smiled for the cameras, too, and none of it made any sense. It was too much, these pictures, and she stopped watching halfway through. She looked at the people in the theater and not at the screen. It was all women and a few small children sitting in their chairs. They looked like angels in the dark, their eyes silver in the light from the screen. Just two rows over she saw a little boy who curled his hands like Max and another with Georg's round face, and she had to stop herself from reaching for them.

She walked circles around old town when the movie was done. None of the clocks was working in the city. The clock on the Domstrasse tower stood still at 8:28 exactly and didn't start again, and other clocks stopped in trolley stations and down by the post office and at the St. Adalbero church and the Grafeneckart. And after the electric plant on Theresienstrasse was hit, the electrical clocks stopped, too, and half the people in old town couldn't hear the radio anymore or play records. They sat home and waited, they didn't know what for, and all around them a strange sound worked its way through the walls and into their darkened kitchens. It pulsed from beneath the streets and inside the building walls, steady as a heartbeat, that intake of breath and the release.

The old woman was in her spot when Etta came back. She was watching for the door. "I hear it again," she told Etta. "Every night I hear it."

Etta nodded. "I hear it, too." She pulled a chair to the table. The noise unnerved her and made it hard to sleep. Who knew what it was. It's birds, some people said. They're on the roof. They're in the walls, caught in the plaster. Or maybe it was the tower out by the barracks. Experiments or signals from the planes.

"It's the waiting that does it," Etta said. The waiting made people strange. Just yesterday she saw an old man wander the streets in his pajamas. Women carried around water pumps and set sandbags beside their doors. They walked with gas masks in their shopping bags. Three reichsmarks, those masks had cost them, and though they'd grumbled at the time, they were glad to have them now. There's no knowing when the gases will come, the ladies said, best to be ready. They'll come rolling in waves beneath doors and around window frames, and the air will turn golden and then brown. They set their masks across their laps and waited. And even on quiet days, when planes flew overhead but no bombs fell, people shook their heads. Shoot them down, they said, why don't they shoot them down before they come back, but the planes kept coming and the city lay open as a flower.

"Go home to your husband," the woman said. "Go to him while you can." She pushed herself up from her chair.

"There's time still." Etta set Max's hollow book on the counter. "I'll get him out, and we'll leave together. We'll be taking the train." She'd been in the city ten days already, and she had two Heidenfeld tickets. Two tickets when she only needed one. "We'll leave together," she said again. She spoke louder than she meant to because it wasn't right, what the old woman was saying, but when she turned around from the counter the woman was in her bedroom already and didn't hear.

## 22

Georg watched Ingrid work the stove. Father Zimmermann was at the nursing home across town, and any moment now he'd be back. He went to the home on Wednesday mornings because some of the old people there couldn't walk to services. He sat at the long tables with them and visited the ones who were sick in bed, and the sickest ones he anointed with the oil he carried in his case. Lunch was ready for him when he came back. Ingrid was like Mutti. She served at twelve exactly.

Zimmermann lifted all the lids when he came into the kitchen so he could smell the meat. Before he went back to his room, he waved his hand at Georg. "You bring me the tray today," he said. "We'll eat together."

Ingrid nodded at Georg when the plates were ready. She spooned out a little more gravy and gave him the tray. "Don't talk too much," she told him. "He can be prickly sometimes. It's better just to listen."

Zimmermann was waiting in his chair. The lights were all on, but the room was dark anyway and the curtains were drawn. He pointed to a round oak table by the window. "Set that table," he said. "And take the dishes off the tray. I don't like to eat on trays."

Georg fumbled with the silverware, but Zimmermann didn't seem to notice. He reached over to turn the knob on his radio. The reception was spotty in his room. The radio crackled and faded and sometimes there was nothing but a humming sound like bees, but Zimmermann listened anyway and the way he sat reminded Georg of his father, who listened to the announcers but never to Mutti. She'd have better luck if she found a way to speak to him through the radio, Georg had thought this more than once. The old man would pay more attention if he couldn't see her face.

Georg sat across from the priest, with his back to the window. He tried to eat slowly, but it made him nervous to sit so close to the priest, and it was easier to eat than to find something to say. He looked around the room while he ate. He took a closer look at the books that were stacked along the nearest wall, more books than even his father had, and the shelves sagged at the center from their weight. Aquinas and Amort and Albertus Magnus, the sermons of Faber and the mystical works of Hildegard von Bingen, Zimmermann had them all. He'd wedged them between Latin grammars and anatomy texts and gardening books, and the overflow sat on chairs and on the windowsill. Georg could have spent months beside those shelves. He'd learn his declensions again and the constructions he'd forgotten since leaving school, the ablative absolute and all the contrafactual clauses and when to use *ut non* and when to use *ne* instead. The nuances would come back, and the other things would fall away and he wouldn't have to know about rifles anymore or the Panzerfaust.

"I built them myself." Zimmermann pointed his fork toward the bookcase. "I built the table, too." He cut a potato into quarters and dipped a piece into the sauce. He was methodical as a surgeon, clearing one dish before proceeding to the next. His fingers were long like a surgeon's, too, and his eyes sloped downward and made his face look sad even when he smiled. He finished the potatoes and started on the cabbage, and he blinked the whole while, as if eating were an effort for him and not a pleasure. "You're looking better," he said. "It's those herbs she picks. She'll walk all day for a basketful of leaves."

"Yes, sir," Georg said. "She knows about plants." He smoothed the front of his pant legs. "She's better than a doctor with all those compresses."

The priest lifted his glass. His Adam's apple moved up and down while he drank. It was big as a goiter, and Georg couldn't help but watch. The music had stopped and the announcers were talking about Dortmund. The city was in ruins, they said, only ashes were left. There was no counting the dead because most of the bodies were gone. They were burned and the wind carried them away. Pforzheim was hit, too, and another seventeen thousand were dead or missing, and Zimmermann shook his head then. He turned the knob so he wouldn't have to hear. "Just last year they hung a man. Three days they left him on the branch." He pulled the toothpicks from the rouladen and licked them clean. "They'd have left him longer, but he was drawing flies."

"I've seen men hanging," Georg said. "I've seen it myself." It was only a few months ago that they ran. They ran and Müller didn't and they were all gone now anyway, and it didn't matter what they did, it seemed to him, because there was an inevitability to how things came out. One boy walked along the road and lived, and another died only a few feet away. All their work on the wall, and it wasn't enough to keep their enemies from crossing. Their boasts and their quibbles about uniforms and who was the best shot and who was fastest around the track and none of it mattered because the pattern was working its way out.

Zimmermann pushed his plate aside. "They're gathering up the old men and the boys," he said. He was dainty as he folded his napkin, and it was hard to believe he was the same man who stood so tall on the pulpit, whose voice rolled like a wave over the parishioners and rose high as the rafters. "You'll need to see them now that you're better.

THE VANISHING SKY 215

They've got a table at the school where they keep the names." He looked toward the window. "That's where you need to go."

INGRID WALKED THE hallway at night. She said it was the sounds that made her nervous, the marching and the shouting and all the men shooting their guns. They were exercising in the fields every day and some were leaving in groups, going as far as Trier and Koblenz. They'd be coming back soon, everybody knew. They'd be coming back in bandages if they were lucky, falling back to their towns. The wheels were turning faster now, people could feel it. All those years when nothing happened, nothing but notices and funerals and planes overhead, and from one day to the next they smelled burning in the air. They could hear the first shells already, and the sky shone red some nights as if the world had reversed itself and the sun were rising from the west.

She forgot to give him a fork with dinner. She spilled the water and burned the bread. "We have only a little time," she said. "Another week and the town will be full with them."

"They'll want my papers," Georg said. He didn't want to leave again. He didn't want to start his walking, but he didn't want to stay either and give them his name. He'd pick a cap from the table and a rifle if he was lucky. He'd march with the old men and the altar boys, and what difference did it make. Home or the uniform, these were his choices. They had always been the choices. Home meant being with Mutti, seeing her eyes again and sleeping in his bed, but the old man would be there, too, and they'd know just what he'd done because they always knew. They saw it in his face.

"He's gone all day today." She sat down beside him. "He's visiting the monastery again and won't be back until late."

"They'll ask me where I've been," Georg said.

"You could pass for fourteen." She reached for his hair. "Thirteen if we comb your hair down low."

She had no relatives left, no husband or brothers or uncles, and so she worried for him instead. Somebody might ask for his papers and if he didn't have anything to show, they might take him from the station. He could wear a sling on his arm. She could dress him in a young boy's clothes, and nobody would notice him if she did it right. He was just another boy going to the hills, going to see his grandparents who lived far from the fighting.

There might be dozens of soldiers on the train or none at all. They might be looking for men and boys because the posters were up and a few had even been called down from the old people's home. It was a scandal the way they took men whose eyes were bad, who hobbled on canes and could barely hoist themselves up, and when they did their joints all cracked.

"I'm tired," Georg said. He set his head on the table. Home or the uniform, these were his choices, and he wanted only Müller. He wanted a chance to visit with the dead. Every day he felt the pull of their voices. They were sitting in the hall and joking like before. Schneider was reaching for his book and they looked together at the pretty ladies and it was always the same how the talk went. They were at the table and in the gymnasium and down by the trench, and they were complaining about the buckets and the sergeant and the food. It needed seasoning. It needed butter, and the dumplings were cooked too long. Müller sat with them. He sat at the center, and he laughed at all their talk and closed his eyes. They were ghosts around the table, and sometimes they saved him a spot. They called him fatty and butter boy though he was thin now from all the walking he'd done. "It's not enough," they said, and pointed to his tray, "you're a growing boy and need more bread."

All the people he knew, Müller and Mutti and Schneider and even Maus, all the living and the dead and the people from his books, they were jumbled together. They were telling the stories they always told and they looked just the same, and it was hard to remember sometimes where he was.

She tapped his shoulder and smiled when he turned around to look. The windows had gone dark. She was done with the kitchen work. The dishes were washed and the counters wiped, and it was time for bed.

"We're leaving early," she said. "It'll be dark still when we go."

SHE USED A plain wooden walking stick, planting it into the ground with every step, and when they stopped to rest, she leaned on it as if it were a banister. He struggled with his rucksack because it was bigger than he was used to and pulled him backward. He held the straps in both his hands to lighten the load. She'd given it to him just before they left and filled it with her husband's pants and his clean undershirts and socks that she knotted together and pushed down the side. Every place he went, he wore dead men's clothes. She packed apples and dried plum slices and pork sausages, thick slices of smoked ham, a bar of hard cheese, three tins of sardines, and half a stollen left from Christmas that smelled of rum and butter. She gave him flat bars of grape sugar, too, for energy, and a bar of milk chocolate, which was much better than the Scho-Ka-Kola bars he ate in school. "That dark stuff's no good," she told him, "it's medicine and not chocolate. It'll make your heart thump hard inside your chest."

She knew the trees and the rocks the way other people know houses and streets and shops. She pointed things out to him with her free hand: where the lung moss grew and the tree where Richard had proposed seven years before, the mushroom path and the skating pond and the spot where old Herr Melzer had fallen from his cart and died under the trees.

"He didn't tell his wife where he was going," she said, shaking her head. He might have lived if she'd known where to look. He was careless instead and his wife lived only a few years longer. Loneliness is what did it. His going took away all her air. That happened sometimes, she said. People were like trees. Their roots grew together, and there was no untangling them.

He stopped to drink from his bottle and she stood beside him, tapping her fingers against her stick. She combed his hair across his forehead with her fingers, first one way and then the other.

"It's good you look so young," she said.

He wiped his mouth with the back of his hand. "Soft as a girl is what my father always says."

"You don't look like a girl." She pulled his cap down low on his face. "You look like a schoolboy. Not even sixteen and they take you from your home. The grown men will be all right and the little boys, too. But I worry for the ones like you." She cupped her hand against his cheek. She kissed him on the lips. She kissed him like a mother, and he didn't pull away.

It wasn't even noon yet when they came to the first houses. "Look like nothing's the matter," she told him. "If you look that way, people will think it's true." She looped her arm in his and pulled him by the crook of his elbow. They passed the post office and the bank and a pharmacy where three old women stood in line. A young woman was washing windows in the warm air, wiping them down with a white dish towel when she was done. She'd rolled the sleeves of her housedress up, and droplets flashed in the sun as she wrung out the rags. They walked past two inns that sat across one from the other. Each inn was its own world, Georg knew, and the boundary between them was real as the boundary between the town's two churches. Men drank in one and not the other and worshipped in one and not the other, and the circles around people grew smaller and smaller still.

The train station had its own lobby and a small café. All Ingrid's talk about soldiers and there wasn't even one on the platform. There were only women and a single old man who talked to himself and pointed to the trees. It was a revelation how thin the people were without their winter coats, how knobby they looked and haggard. Only the priests ate well, the priests and the farmers and the officers at the academy. The best cuts went to a few, the finest meat and butter cakes and noodles. He shifted the bag on his shoulders. For the first time he was ashamed of the food he had.

Ingrid stepped up to the agent and bought a ticket. Georg reached inside his pocket out of habit, though he had only his ladies and no good money. She waved him down. "I've got nothing to save for," she told him.

They sat together at a small round table and drank apple juice. "You've been good to me," he told her. "Better than I deserve." He almost reached inside his pocket again to give her a coin, but he needed four for his tricks. Three wouldn't be enough.

She looked at her fingernails. "I've got a washerwoman's hands," she said. "He wouldn't recognize me if he saw me. He'd walk right by." She looked young just then. It was the way the light came across her face and how pink she was from walking.

"He'll know your eyes," Georg said. "He'll spot you right away." People don't change, he wanted to say, not at their core. He'd know those grey eyes if he saw them again. All the time he had left, everything good that might come, he'd trade it all away to conjure them back. He drained his glass.

She stayed with him until boarding time, and even after he was in his seat and the other ladies had left the platform, he could see her still, waving at him with her walking stick.

# 23

Etta stood in the Bahnhofstrasse shelter. She was pressed tight against the earthen wall. A lady coughed by her ear, and somewhere in the crowd a baby cried. An old man cursed Hitler. "He poked the lions and now they're loose," he said. "He's unleashed them on us all," and his wife nudged him with her elbow. It was true what he said, but his wife was right. He needed to keep quiet. The shelter lights flickered, and smoke came through the cracks around the door. People stood quietly and listened to the tut-tut-tut and the whirring of the planes. A single alarm started and stopped and sputtered, high-low, high-low. Etta leaned her cheek against the wall. Max wouldn't go with the nurses if they tried to take him to a shelter. He'd raise a fuss as they pulled him from his bed. And the others wouldn't come either, the ones who shouted for no reason and pulled at their hair, and who knew how long the nurses would try to coax them out.

She closed her jacket. What good was it to be in the city if she couldn't be with him after dark? Eleven days she'd been in the city already, and the planes came almost every night. They came between eight and ten, just as people were finishing dinner or getting ready for bed. "Time to go," the nurses told her every afternoon, "time to let him sleep." "It's not even five yet," she'd say, "give me a little while longer," but they just shook their heads. They gave him his pills and shut the door, and there was no kindness in the way they touched him. They were starving him, starving them all. Everybody knew, and nobody spoke of it.

The siren outside changed to a roiling low sound. People went up the stairs, and no one pushed or shouted. Smoke hung over old town and down by the power station. The hills were bright with fires. Their flames shone on the river and lit the smoke clouds from beneath. The railroad tracks were hit and a few buildings in the center city, but the skies were quiet again and people went back to their houses.

The old woman was in her kitchen when Etta climbed the stairs. "You're dirty from all those vapors," she said. "Wash up. Wash the smoke from your face."

Etta sat with her until after midnight. "They're coming," the old lady was saying. "Any day they'll come, and then we'll burn like they did in Dresden." She rubbed her eyes with her palm and she didn't answer when Etta wished her a good night. When Etta woke, the old woman's shoes weren't in their spot, and her umbrella was gone and her only jacket. She'd taken her purse and her hat and her market bag, and she'd watered the herbs she kept by the window and folded all her towels. The crucifix was gone from above her iron bed. Its outline showed in the paint. She'd left the house and the last of her things and hadn't said good-bye.


ETTA WENT TO Max that morning and asked him where he went. "Where did they take you?" she wanted to know. "Where did you go when the sirens sounded?"

"The snow is piling on the sill," he said.

"There's no snow," she told him. "It's warm outside today and all the roads are muddy."

"It blows in at night. The wind brings in drifts."

She pulled him up. He swung his legs to the floor like an old man. His feet were blue with veins and spotty, and he ignored the slippers by his bed. He walked with her to the window and watched the people outside. The bald man was gone, and Max had the room to himself. She steadied him against the wall so he could see. Girls were setting up the lunch truck on the street. They were bringing out the soup pots and slicing loaves of bread. The sky was blue and streaked with clouds, and men wiped their brows and rested and set to work again. Max watched it all, and the light reflected in his eyes. "When will it stop?" He set his fingers against the glass. "All night long I hear the sounds. I hear running in the hall."

"Lie back down," Etta said. She took his hand. "It'll be quiet tonight. You'll sleep the whole night through."

She left the room and walked the hallway until she found a nurse. "Where do you take them?" Etta didn't know her face. She wasn't one of the nurses who'd taken a bottle of schnapps. "When the sirens go, where do you take the patients?"

The nurse stopped. She looked over her shoulder. "I wasn't here last night." She stepped forward, and Etta touched her elbow.

"How do you get them to the shelters? It must be hard to move them all."

The nurse pulled her arm from Etta and walked past. She held her charts against her chest. "I wasn't here," she said again. She turned the corner, and Etta looked for someone else to ask, but no one knew and no one stopped to talk to her, and when she left at five o'clock the hospital doors closed behind her and were locked for the evening.

MAX WAS SLEEPING the next day when she came into his room. He lay on his back with his hands across his belly, which was swollen under the blanket. He'd gotten thinner even with the food she'd brought him. She could see every vein in his temples as he slept. The clinic wasn't going to release him. She'd tried to see Herr Selig again, but the secretary just shook her head. She'd been in the city for thirteen days. Two weeks was what she'd promised Josef, two weeks and she'd come home, but the days had passed too quickly and all her visits had accomplished nothing. "I'll be back soon," she told Max. She leaned in close so only he could hear. "I'll come back and then we'll leave together." He didn't stir at the sound of her voice or when she kissed him on his forehead. He lay there and she set an apple under his blanket so he'd have something when he woke.

There was no shelter without her sons. This is what she knew. She could run when the sirens sounded. She could go to the cellars and wait for the signal, and there was no shelter because Max and Georg were somewhere else. She could go home to Heidenfeld and sit with Josef by the table and fix his meals. She could stand at her window there and watch the river, and there was no shelter for her and no peace.

SHE HELD HER ticket and waited for the train. Men stood by the benches in shirtsleeves and the women beside them wore thin cardigans. It wasn't even three in the afternoon, but the sky was pale already and streaked with gold. "It's warmer than April," someone said, "it's strange how warm it's been," but once the sun had set the air would go chilly, and the people in old town would sleep under their thickest feather quilts. They used cardboard and bits of wood to seal their broken windows. They hung their winter drapes, but the night winds blew and worked their way inside.

An old man sat down beside her, and she moved her purse to give him room. It was getting crowded on the platform. People were leaving the city. They took the train northward to Lohr or farther still to Gemünden, where aunts and uncles and cousins met them and took them to houses up in the hills. For weeks they'd been moving out their things. They'd sent the silver already and the radios and all their best clothes, and a few sent books, too, and chess sets and woven rugs. The women packed, and the men moved the boxes, and the houses stood half empty when they were done. And even then they found reasons to stay. They waited one day and another and another still. "Time to go," the men said, "time to take the train before the Amis bomb the tracks," but the women stood in the houses and touched all the things that remained, the mantel clocks and the fine wooden dressers, fringed lampshades and serving platters and the soup pots that hung on hooks by the stove. "This is no time for weeping," their husbands said, "and we'll be back anyway. We'll be back by summertime." And though they were glad to leave the smoke and the sirens, it was no easy thing to turn the key.

The old man coughed. "It's the air," he told her. "All the smoke has got me wheezing." His hands were huge as oven mitts, and all along the tops they were puckered with silver scars. He took a pipe from his pocket. He covered the bowl with his palm and blew hard through the stem. He set his Tiedemanns tin on his knee and filled the bowl and tamped it down until the spring was right. He struck a match and let the sulfur burn off and passed it over the bowl, puffing deeply the whole while. The tobacco fluffed a little from the flame, but he didn't bother to smooth it.

She moved a little farther down the bench, but the smell of his smoke followed her. "It's a wonder we don't all choke," she said. She looked around for another spot, but all the benches were full already and she didn't want to stand. Half an hour and the train would come. She'd be in Lohr by five and in Heidenfeld by five thirty, and Josef would be sitting at the table when she walked in. What's for dinner, he'd ask her before she'd even hung her coat. What are you making, and he'd rub his eyes.

The man beside her puffed contentedly on his pipe. His eyes were halfway closed. He had four bulging satchels, each of them patched in so many places she couldn't tell what color they'd been. His wife must have patched them over the course of many years. She'd used dish towels and faded housedresses and at least two pieces from an embroidered tablecloth, taking care to center the roses and the circling vines.

He caught her looking. "I've got my best hammers." He pointed with his pipe. "It wasn't easy making them fit." He leaned back against the bench. He was a blacksmith, he said, and he'd made hanging signs as far as Schweinfurt and Bamberg. The finest scrollwork on Domstrasse and the repairs to the Marienkapelle and every flower basket by the south train station, they were all his work, and his son was a smith, too, before leaving for the front, and they'd pounded together in their shop. It took them time to find their rhythm, but they knew one another now, knew when to hit and when to step back, and it was like having four hands instead of two. "It's hard with him gone," he told her. His boy had left and then each of his apprentices, too, and there wasn't any point now to firing up his forge. He shook his head. "I've forgotten how to work alone." He looked like Josef, the way he held his pipe, and he sounded like him, too, when he talked about his son.

Josef had always wanted them to come out to his shop. For years he tried to coax them. *Come on*, he'd say, *there's fresh wood in the pile, there's a nice piece for carving*, but they didn't listen. Georg stayed inside with his books and his coins, and Max was no better, how he ran along the bank. One was too soft and the other too wild, and Josef just shook his head. No good will come of it. They don't listen, especially Max, who should know better. He's wild like an Indian the way he runs.

Brown as a walnut from May to October. Where is he, Josef wanted to know, where'd he go this time, and she just shrugged. He'll come when he comes, she told him, he'll come when the table is cleared and all the dishes washed. She tried to summon her anger when Max finally sat at the table. She shook her finger in his mud-cracked face and did her best to shout.

But all she knew is that they were wonders, all three of them, and blessings to her. She knew this even in summertime when Josef was home from school and they argued almost every afternoon. She knelt by her beds and picked the hornworms off the tobacco leaves, and she wanted things to stay just as they were. Keep Josef in his woodshop and Max by the banks and Georg in his room where he was happiest. Keep them all in their places and let the sun never set. Let it shine through the bottles she kept on the sill. Leave them alone, she'd tell Josef when he started in, they're fine boys. You were young once, too, and made plenty of your own trouble. She flashed him a look, and he went quiet because she was right. His eyes were clear and there was no sign yet of the clouds that were coming. He took her hand, and she was certain then that things could be no better.

The crowd was moving toward the tracks. Men were hauling their boxes and their bags. A young woman cradled a baby in her elbow and pulled a little boy behind her, and she hit his hand when he started to complain. "Behave," she told him, "be good for once." The blacksmith set his pipe back in his pocket. He stood up straight and tipped his hat. "It's time," he said. "Here it comes."

She reached for her purse. People were inside and finding their places. It was her train, the Lohr train, and she closed her eyes.

Josef was in the kitchen. He was at the window, and the house was quiet because all its clocks had stopped. Georg's room was dark and the door was closed and his table was inside and Kaspar's wire cage. *Damn that bird and all its nonsense,* Josef always said, *look at all the dirt he makes,* and still he fed it when no one looked, and he pushed his fingers through the bars. She could see him and the house and the streets that led to the bridge below. She could see the fishermen down by the banks and the solitary ferryman in his boat and the tracks that followed the river up to Rothenfels and Lohr. They went past the fields where the best strawberries grew and past the grounds where Josef had hunted in better days and he came home with a red deer one year, the biggest she'd ever seen. Past the steeple and the spot where Willi fell and the trees that grew over the tracks. Children were climbing the branches again. They were waiting for the sound. It's almost here, they said, I can feel it coming.

She gripped her bag, but she didn't rise from the bench. Max was here in the city and Georg was somewhere fighting, and she couldn't help either one. Her Georg, her baby with his sweet face. She'd give everything to have him home with her. She'd bring him his meals and his books and she'd watch all his magic tricks, and she'd nurse Max, too, she'd hold him until the dark thoughts faded and he came back to himself. She'd give up all her remaining days and Josef's, too, to have them both back safe, to see them sitting again around the dinner table.

The doors closed, and the train began to move. It went straight toward the river and then turned right. The old man was in his seat, with his satchels and all his hammers, and the mother with her boys and all the women who had packed their things and wept. They were gone from the city. Etta sat until the platform was empty, and then she stood to go.

## 24

Georg walked along the Würzburg streets and how sweet it was to see the churches again and the station and the lions on the bridge. The city was pocked in places and the squares felt deserted, but the Madonna was still there and the old crane by the river. There weren't any more trains to Lohr and Heidenfeld. "The tracks were hit just this morning," the ticket taker told him. "It'll be a week before they're running," and so Georg walked toward the university with his bag. A beautiful spring day, a day like any other, and the sun was shining high in the sky. All those weekends he'd taken the train and visited Max, those lazy afternoons they'd walked together to Market Square and he'd been certain that he'd go to school there, too, someday. He'd learn languages and not even his father would understand them.

He came to the conservatory building and sat on an ironwork bench. The windows were open, but no music came from the classrooms. Just the sounds of boys talking and someone pounding a hammer. He reached inside his pocket and felt his ladies to make sure they were all still there. He needed to think about where to go. He could try the old cousins on Semmelstrasse. He could probably find their apartment, but what then, what would he tell them? They hadn't seen him in years. They might not even open the door for him. They might call the operator in Heidenfeld so Etta could bring him home, or maybe they'd know what he'd done and they'd call the police instead. He could walk the rest of the way to Heidenfeld. He was so close now. Another forty kilometers and he'd be home. He reached inside his bag and pulled out the lunch Ingrid had packed for him.

A boy came up behind him and tapped him on the shoulder. "What are you doing out here? The sergeant wants us ready." He tugged at Georg's arm, and he didn't look older than ten in his knee socks.

Georg stayed on the bench. He took a bite from his sandwich.

"Come on," the boy told him. "He's in a foul mood today."

"I'm not in your group. I'm here alone."

"What do you mean, not in the group? Everyone's in the group." The boy folded his arms. He was wearing an HJ uniform that was two sizes too big. "We're sealing up buildings today. We're just waiting for the wood." He leaned in closer. "Is that ham you've got there?"

Three other boys came down the steps, older boys this time, twelve, maybe thirteen years old, and they stood around Georg and watched him eat his sandwich.

"Get in there, Franzi. Get in there quick. And you, too," they told Georg. "Lunchtime is long over."

The double doors to the building opened and more boys came out. "The crates are finally here," they said. "They've got enough for everybody." More people came out with hammers and sheets of plywood they set in wagons. Old men and boys in uniforms and even a few schoolgirls who huddled close together. It was the most people Georg had seen in one place since Father Zimmermann's sermon. Dozens of boys from nine to thirteen probably and some refugees, too, judging from their accents, and the sergeant came out to the steps. He carried a Dreyse pistol in his holster, and there were other men with pistols, too. They stood beside him at the door. "Everybody inside who doesn't have a hammer," the sergeant shouted. "Everybody inside now," and

Georg looked around at the boys who were running to the door. He hesitated, unsure of where to go, and then he hoisted his bag over his shoulder and climbed the steps with Franzi.

They all went in different directions once they had their hammers. The sergeant had a long sheet with buildings they needed to seal, and the boys signed their names on the list so there wouldn't be any gaps. Georg and Franzi and a few other boys worked on windows in the stores of the old city, pharmacies and fabric stores and bank branches with empty bays. The younger boys hoisted the wood from building to building and the older ones sealed the windows. The sergeant came by only once. He walked with a limp, but his eyes missed nothing, Georg could tell. He came and was gone again, and some of the boys started to sing to pass the time. "*The day of revenge will come,*" they sang, "*and then we will be free, break your chains O Germany,*" and Georg pounded the wood into the window frames and looked out to the street below. The first trees were well into bud and the hills were green already in the distance. He could work a hammer for a few days. He'd pound nails and hide here in the city until the Heidenfeld train was running, and then he'd leave while the others were busy. He'd walk if he had to. He'd sneak out with his bag.

"You're too slow," young Franzi told him as he sealed the window next to Georg's. "You've got to be fast now, you've got to be quick because the Amis are coming and the Tommies, too, and then we'll use our Wonder Weapon."

"There's no such thing, you idiot," an older boy told him the next window down. He was Prussian and had a funny way of talking. "If there was, they'd already have used it and we wouldn't be closing up our windows, would we." He pointed his hammer at Georg. "How old are you? I haven't seen you before."

Georg pounded a nail crooked and the plywood splintered at its edge. "I'm thirteen," he said, reaching for another nail.

The Prussian boy nodded, satisfied. "Same as me then. That's what I figured," and he smiled at Georg after that and rolled his eyes at the other boys and how naive they were and how young.

Just before dark a few old ladies came with a cart and ladled out bowls of watery soup. The boys stood around under a budding linden tree and drank the broth and they talked about tomorrow and how the sergeant might let them practice with the Panzerfaust in the field. "It's the easiest thing," one of them was saying, "the easiest thing you'll ever do. You just load it, screw it tight and pull the trigger. A monkey could do it."

At night the boys and the old men laid out straw mattresses in the gymnasium and they slept without blankets or pillows, all of them together on the dusty wooden floor, and Georg reached for his bag the way he used to. He should sneak out. He should cross the river and walk the rest of the way home, but he ate instead. He finished all the food Ingrid had packed for him. He ate and thought of home, and when he slept he dreamed of Mutti and his room and Kaspar chirping in his cage.

MAX HAD LIVED in a tiny apartment near the university, and every time Georg visited him the books were piled high on the table and on the floor beside his bed. Botany and biology and chemistry with its strange reactions, all those books, they tugged at Georg, who would have been happy just to stay in that cramped room and read beside the window, but Max took him to all the places he'd loved best. The Ringpark with its flower beds and the markets on Domstrasse and once they went to the Residenz palace with its scrolling mirrors and tapestries and they lay on their backs to look at the ceiling frescoes until the guard chased them out. Everywhere they went Max saw people he knew, other boys from the university and professors and girls in sundresses who stopped to chat with him, and they blushed and held their books against their chests. One of the girls meant more to him, Georg could tell from how Max greeted her. A tall girl with strawberry blond hair. Her name was Klara, and he bought her a bottle of Fanta and they walked together, the three of them, they walked for hours in the sun.

The trolleys were running to the squares and the vendors sold their fruits and flowers and young people were everywhere. They sat on benches and at outdoor cafés. They played soccer in the park and read books on the grass, and the world was waiting for Georg, for all of them. This is your city, too, Max had told him. You'll be here soon enough and the professors won't know what to do with you. Keep your nose in the books and you'll know as much as they do. He set his arm around Georg's shoulder, and Georg felt so grown up just then and he stood a little taller as he walked beside his brother.

THE BOYS CROUCHED on the gymnasium floor in the morning, and Georg sat with them. They reminded him of the boys from the academy, the way they jostled and bickered and teased each other. They talked about Pforzheim and Mannheim and Köln, how they'd burned one after the next. All those cities gone, consumed by fires that sucked the air from the sky, but the numbers didn't sound right. It couldn't be thousands dead, one of the boys said. People were probably in the hills or in shelters and they hadn't been counted as safe yet. They hadn't found their families. The Germans needed to shoot down the planes in the meanwhile. It was the British who were dropping the bombs, and not just on factories and railway stations. No, they fell on houses and churches and cemeteries, too, and they needed flak from the ground and German planes to take the Tommies down. They're soft, those Tommies and the Amis especially, little Franzi said. They're not brave like us, and one of the older boys mussed Franzi's hair so he looked like a rooster.

Pforzheim, Mannheim, Köln, Pforzheim, Mannheim, Köln. Berlin before that and Dresden and Chemnitz, Georg thought of their names as he worked that morning. Cities died like people, and what good was it to hammer windows shut when the buildings were going to burn.

## 25

Etta walked along Augustinerstrasse and Brücknerstrasse and up by the Juliuspromenade, looking for a bakery or a butcher shop, but all the stores were boarded shut. She looked in the little streets, the ones she didn't know, where the houses sat close together. If only she knew the city better. If she had paid attention when she came to visit Josef all those years before or when Max was still at school, she'd find her way now and she'd have meat for him and not just apples. She had looped around old town already and walked the length of Domstrasse all the way to the river, and the sweat ran down her neck. She turned to a side street and saw the sign. ZELLER'S BUTCHER SHOP, it said, METT-WURST FOR SALE and KATENRAUCHWURST. It had prices for all the cuts and for fresh slicing sausages, for bierwurst and schinkenwurst with bacon inside and garlic, and there was tongue and sülzwurst and teewurst for spreading on bread, peppery tongue sausage and knackwurst that popped open when you boiled them. Sausages of every sort and some she hadn't eaten in years, and still she remembered just the way they tasted.

The store doors were locked. She leaned against the glass and looked inside. The cases and all the hooks inside were bare. The only meat was in the pictures on the walls, colored drawings of pigs and mournful cows and sausages spread on a tray. A note by the stairwell door listed half a dozen family names. For the Zellers ring three times, it said, and for Fritz Drescher ring twice, and for the family Bauer give one long ring. They're living together like bees in a hive, she thought; they're squeezed in tight. Someone had set a brick inside the door so people wouldn't need to ring the bell. She climbed the stairs and knocked at every door, and no one answered. She climbed to the fourth floor and knocked with both her hands. She waited a half minute and knocked again.

After a long while a man opened the door. His head was smooth as an egg.

"I'm here for some sausage." She held her purse against her belly. "I'm looking for mettwurst."

"I've got no sausages." He shook his head. "I've got no meat at all."

"I'll take blutwurst then, as many as you have."

"I haven't had meat since January." He rubbed his chin. "There's no meat in the city and no blutwurst either."

She pulled the silk from her purse. She opened it and showed him the pearls. "I can pay."

"If I had meat I'd eat it myself."

"There's no finer quality." She held them to the light. "They're white as the day my mother bought them. And look how they shine."

He opened the door wider. The apartment was dark and smelled of cigarettes and boiled eggs.

"They're yours for some eggs." Her chest was tight now. She wanted to be rid of them. "Just think how your wife will love them."

She sat at the table while he brought out the pot. Dirty dishes were piled by the counter and on the tabletop. The faucet dripped, pinging water into the basin. She shifted in her seat. What a scandal, what a shame, for an old man to live like that. A cat lay across the sill, trying to catch the last light. It fixed a green eye on Etta and closed it again, unimpressed.

"I can give you six." He set six brown eggs inside a bag. "My wife is gone to the country already. She's safe up in the hills." He reached inside his cupboard and brought out a wedge of Swiss cheese. He laid the bag and the cheese in front of her.

It was less than she'd hoped for. She could have gotten all this and plenty more from Ilse, but she wouldn't go home even if the trains were still running. She took the pearls and spread them on the table, and they looked warm like skin in the light from the window. They were her mother's and they'd have gone to the girl Max married, and still it was easy to let them go. The bald man touched the strand and its fine gold clasp. He hesitated, and something flickered in his eyes, and then he took the pearls and set them in his pocket. "It's late," he said, and he latched his thumbs around his suspenders. He looked at the floor and not at Etta. He was ashamed to take them, she could tell. There was more food where he was going, but he kept the strand anyway and walked her to the door. He didn't thank her and didn't say good-bye, and so it was that she gave her mother's pearls to a bald man in the city and she never learned his name.

EVERY NIGHT SHE dreamed of food. She'd been frying fleischwurst this time, and Georg was back home, too, and sitting at the table. Her kitchen smelled of butter and onions. There was freshly ground horse-radish and mettwurst and tongue sausage sliced extra fine. Her kitchen was full with butter cakes and bacon and herring, with oranges and cut lemons and loaves of rye bread soft still from the oven. Her pantry shelves sagged from all the weight. This was how her dreams went, how they always went. She was cooking, and the house smelled sweet and both her boys were with her and Josef sat with them and he didn't grumble for once. He smiled the way he used to.

THE AMIS BOMBED the main train station. Two hundred bombs and the building was destroyed and all the tracks behind it, and people were almost relieved. *The Amis won't come after us anymore and not the English either*, they said. *They've gotten what they wanted. Churchill himself studied in our city and he doesn't want to see it burn*, and people began to clear the rubble and they worked all the harder to board up the buildings that still stood. The last of the trees began to bud and flowers bloomed in flower boxes though the apartments were empty and their windows dark. Every day Etta went to visit Max in the clinic and she came back to the old woman's apartment and wrote letters to Georg and to Josef. She told Josef that Max was eating again and the hollows had gone from beneath his chin and he rested most afternoons and sometimes he walked to the window and watched the people working on the streets. She told Georg to be careful, to take care of himself and his room was waiting for him and all his books. Things were just as he had left them. She took the letters to the substitute post office near the old Ludwig station, where lady train conductors in gray skirts stood outside and collected them because there weren't any bays inside and nobody to sort them. They set them in enormous burlap bags and piled them by the curb, and the piles grew higher and the bags didn't seem to move.

"When will the mail go out?" Etta asked the lady who took her letters. "It's no good keeping it on the street."

The conductor held up her hands. She looked at Etta from beneath her cap and said nothing, and the next time Etta checked, the conductors were gone, but the bags were all still there.

## 26

G eorg was working on a second-story window near the Ludwig station in old town when he saw a woman on the street who looked just like his mutti. It was late in the afternoon already. It was warm outside, but a breeze blew through the shattered windows and raised goose bumps on his bare arms. Something about this lady pulled at him. Her brown wool hat, the ankle boots she wore, the way she held her net shopping bag. She'd stopped to look at something. She was standing beside the burlap letter bags that were stacked along the street, and Georg leaned out the window to see her better. It wasn't her, he knew this, it couldn't be his mutti because she was in Heidenfeld and not here in the city, but he was drawn to this lady and her knitted cap.

He set his hammer down and started for the door. "Where are you going?" one of the boys asked him on the stairway. "We're not done here yet," but Georg went down the stairs two at a time and out the broken wooden doors. He walked toward the station, he walked and then he ran, but the lady was gone and only the burlap bags were there, and when he couldn't find her, he kept on walking, away from his group, away from all the boys working their hammers and toward the center of the city. He'd been working with them for more than three weeks already, but it was so easy to leave them.

*   *   *

HE HID IN an empty apartment building on Augustinerstrasse until the streets were dark. He waited in the alcove by the mailboxes and not a single person came into the building while he stood there. No sound came from any of the flats. It was deserted as a Roman ruin, and he waited in the corner, unsure. What to do, what to do, the city was an island and he was afraid to leave it.

How easy things had been when he was little, and he hadn't known it then. The teasing at school, the looks from his father, they didn't matter and they never had. He held the ladies in his pocket. He squeezed one against his palm, and he was sweating though the air was growing cool. Get out there, Max had told him just before he'd left for the front. Get out there, you're not the only one who's afraid. Anyone who's got any sense at all is afraid sometimes, but you have to go forward because that's the only way there is. Forward and through, and he felt his brother with him now. Max was leading him by the hand.

GEORG WAS ALMOST at the bridge when the first flares came down over the center city. The markers fell next, green and red, and lit up all the buildings. He ran with other boys and old women and mothers with their babies, and the voice over the speakers told them what they already knew. Planes were coming to the city. Everyone needed to seek shelter, and people trampled each other in their running and a mother cried because she couldn't find her daughter, "Somebody help me, help me," she shouted, "Helga, come to your mother," and nobody slowed down and nobody stopped for her. Georg ran to the Domstrasse shelter. Down the steep stone steps and into the cellar room where dozens of others were already waiting. HJ boys and a few old men and mothers with their children, and within minutes the first bombs began to fall. Georg could hear them whistling. Even underground the walls shook and glass broke above them on the streets. The lights went out in the cellar. People stood together in complete blackness. The mother next to him began to pray. *"Five little angels around my bed,"* she sang, *"one at the foot and one at the head,"* and she rocked her baby in the dark.

Georg coughed from the dust. People squeezed against him on all sides. Some of them wept or covered their heads with blankets. Others stood motionless or tapped their fingers against the stone walls and they all waited, pressed tight together but each alone. Ten minutes, twenty, Georg wasn't sure how long, but he pushed his way toward the stairs as soon as the bombing stopped. None of the others budged from their spots. "We better stay," one of the boys told him. "Any time it could start again," and he grabbed Georg's arm, but Georg pulled himself free because anything was better than staying in that room and waiting.

## 27

E tta was at her window when the first alarms sounded. The colored markers began to fall in every corner of the city, and it wasn't like anything she'd ever seen before. First dark red and then red and green, the sky was bright with them. The smoke settled low over the streets and the buildings and circled the moon. She hurried down the stairs as the sirens started, and all around her people ran. They pulled her with them, sweeping her along the street.

The air went thick and smelled of blood and powder. She had nothing with her, not even her purse or a scarf to keep out the dust. Her eyes burned and dripped tears down her cheeks. Hands pushed her forward into the smoke, and people appeared beside her and were gone again. She lost her bearings. Where was the hospital and where the river and the bridge and the tower on the hill? The dust and the smoke were substantial as dirt, and she was certain that they were buried already, all of them. They were beneath the city, beneath its streets and its buildings, beneath the bridges and the river, and they were falling together to the center of things.

She moved with the others, not knowing if she was getting closer to Max or farther away. She held her arms out like a sleepwalker, and her shoe hit something soft in the street. God help us, she thought, they're laid out like cobblestones. A young woman ran alongside her. Etta saw her for just a moment and she looked like Ilse when she was young. She wore a fine wool hat with a brooch pinned to its brim, and when the hat fell from her head, she didn't stop to reach for it. People spoke to themselves as they ran. They shouted and waved their fists. Etta's throat went tight at the smoke and all the dust raised up from the sandstone and the plaster. She coughed as she ran and gasped for air, and when she couldn't clear her chest, she stopped for a moment by the curb. She spit on the stones like a farmer, choking up black ash and strings of powder. Church bells rang somewhere through the smoke. There was no one pulling the ropes and turning the wheel. The rumbling had shaken the bells in their towers. Some rang fast and others slow as passing bells, and the sounds confounded people and led them astray.

Someone pushed her, and she was spun around. She looked up, and for a moment the smoke separated. She saw the ruined train station, and she knew just where she was. She turned into the crowd. She ran to the hospital and not any of the shelters. As she got closer, nurses passed her by, stumbling down the street in their starched caps and their uniforms. *They're leaving the hospital without the patients. They're leaving them all in their beds.* Her heel caught in the cracked pavement, and she fell hard on her ankle. People went by her, splitting to her left and to her right. They were a river and she was a rock, and they didn't stop to help her. She pushed herself up with both hands.

The doors were open when she came. Some lights were working and others weren't, and it was quiet inside. No one walked the halls, no doctor or nurse or orderly. Patients lay on their beds and listened to the pounding. Somewhere a woman was singing. Etta knew the song. "*When spring is coming, when the snows all melt,*" the lady sang, "*when the finches have their nests all built, when the air goes soft and the skies are blue,*" the voice went deep now, deep as a man's, "*then I'll come, then I'll come, then I'll come home to you.*" The woman laughed when she was done and started again, and the windows in the building shook and rattled.

Etta walked past all the open doors. She should have been afraid, but she felt only gratitude. She could take him home now, away from the hospital and the heavy camphor smells, away from the doctors and the nurses and all their medical charts. She could take him, and by the time they noticed, he'd be far from the city and from Heidenfeld, too. He'd be in the countryside. He'd be up in the hills eating like a farmer and letting the sun shine across his face, and all around him the cherry trees would snow down their blossoms and sweeten the air. God bless the planes and their pilots because they'd done what all her letters couldn't. God bless them and, forgive her these thoughts, God keep them over the city for just a little while longer, just long enough to get Max through the doors.

The last of the lights went out in the hallway. They flickered and went out and didn't come back on, and all the windows were lit orange. They glowed like embers and threw strange shadows. She knew the path to his room, knew every turn and every dip in the tiles. As she got closer, she ran faster, and by the time she rounded the last corner, she was going so fast she almost missed his door. Max was inside, just as she'd left him. He was alone in the room. The books were still on his bed table, and an apple lay unbitten by his pillow. His hands were folded across his belly, which rose and fell just a little with each breath.

"Get up." She shook his shoulder. "Wake yourself up and come with me."

He looked up at the ceiling and said nothing. His eyes shone in the light from the window. "I don't see the sky," he told her. "They took it while I was sleeping." A deep rumbling came from outside and shook the window frame, and he didn't stir. Somewhere on the street glass was breaking.

She set aside his blankets and pulled him up. He didn't resist. He came up easy, and he stood there in his nightshirt and thin cotton pants. She looked around the room for shoes but found only cloth slippers. Where had they put all his clothes and his good leather shoes? Thieves is what they were, when there was a trunk right by his bed with plenty of room for his things. She set the slippers on his feet and wrapped a blanket around his shoulders, and they walked together down the hall. Each time he slowed, she pulled hard on his hand.

"Be quick," she told him. "This is no time for strolling."

He looked past her when she talked. His slippers came loose from his heels, and he stepped right out of them. He walked barefoot then on that dirty floor, and the blanket hung like a cape from his shoulders. He looked straight ahead and didn't flinch at the noise outside, the droning of the planes, the bombs loud as thunderclaps when they fell. He had always resisted when she tried to hurry him. "Come on," she'd tell him, "this is no time to stand there and look at the river, come home before your father takes out the strap." But he smiled at her, and his eyes shone with trouble, and they walked home together nice and slow, and sometimes he'd hold her hand and swing it high with every step.

She ran ahead, stopping as she went to see about finding him some shoes. She was shameless the way she walked into the sickrooms. Patients lay in their beds and slept. Some laughed at the rumbling outside. They slapped their palms against the bedsheets.

An old man gave her a long look. "It's about time," he told her. "I've been waiting all day for my medicine." He held out his hand, as if expecting a tablet or a cupful of syrup. She found a pair of scuffed leather shoes in his trunk. She looked around for socks, too, but found none.

"Forgive me," she said, reaching for his hand. "I've got no medicine for you." She squeezed his fingers. The old man held on to her hand, and when she tried to step back, he pulled her close.

"They're coming," he said. "They're finally here." She unhooked his fingers from around her wrist and took the shoes.

She went to Max, who was leaning against a doorway. She knelt at first, but her ankle hurt and so she sat down hard on the floor. She looked at her foot and saw for the first time that it had swollen around the top of her shoe. Max held on to her head for balance. The shoes were two or even three sizes too small for him, but he didn't seem to care. She loosened the laces and stretched the tongue to give him more room. "They're tight," she said, "and you'll blister." He smiled and walked with her, and he would not be hurried.

THEY WENT TOGETHER through the doors, and no one stopped them or asked for papers. They reached Bahnhofstrasse and everywhere people were coming out from the shelters and their basements, pressing close together and pointing to the sky. They stood on the curb and turned round in circles to see what the planes had done. Fires burned by the dozens along the streets of the old town and up into the wine hills. The city was bright with them. They burned around the Marienkapelle and the Dom St. Kilian and all along Theresienstrasse and on the rooftops down by the river. Copper melted from the spires and dripped to the streets below, and people didn't run yet and they didn't shout. They felt the pull of what was coming. They stood on their tiptoes to see.

Etta raised her hand to her forehead and shielded her eyes, but it did no good. The light found its way in. A walnut tree was burning in the courtyard. It shed flames from its trunk. It stood real as a person, that tree, real as a man with arms stretched wide, and still it turned to powder.

The flames quivered for a moment and then leapt across to some juniper bushes and to another tree and rose again. They twisted and dripped and fed themselves, and the smoke wound ribbons in the air.

"We can't stay here," she said. She reached for his wrist. "We need to go down by the water." They'd follow the bank, follow it all the way home, and then they'd pack him for the hills. Trains were running just outside the city. Things were fine in Ochsenfurt and Klingenberg and farther out by Heidenfeld. Things were just as they'd always been. The sky was dark there, and the stars shone, and people were sleeping in their beds. She pulled again on his wrist, and when he didn't move, she set her hands against his cheeks and turned his face toward hers. "We're going home," she told him.

Something quivered in the air just then. It was real as the beat of wings. The air turned, and from one moment to the next those many points of light found each other. The flames ran together like water and gained a terrible power, and the towers began to burn, all of the towers in the city. They shot flames into the sky, and only the golden Madonna atop the Maria steeple tower was untouched. She held out her hands and watched from above as people ran and shouted and fell on the streets. They beat against their chests and gasped. They crouched low against the cobblestones and scratched like cats. The air rose all at once. It bucked up and rose to meet the flames, and it bore people upward as if making an offering. Metal burned easily as wood in the heat. Things turned to powder and drifted back down. People lay outside the buildings and on the riverbank and in the squares of old town. They lay on their backs and on their sides, and some of them looked up toward the sky with eyes wide open, and the ash fell over them all and covered them.

*   *   *

THE CLOUDS WERE orange again. The bells were ringing in the tower. They rang five times, and when they were done they rang again. Her mutti was calling. *It's time to come home,* she said. *Don't make us wait.* The sun came slantwise through the walnut trees that grew along the bank, and gnats hovered in the light. Etta pretended not to hear. She dug her hands into the mud and let it slip between her fingers. It was the best time of the day just then, when the light was soft and flecked the water with gold. The apple trees were blooming in town, dropping their blossoms on all the roads and gardens. The ladies were out sweeping every day, sometimes two or even three times. *What a mess,* they said, *what a mess those trees make,* and the air was sweet with the smell. She looked up at the sky. Mutti was getting impatient, Etta could hear it in her voice. *Don't make me come after you. Be good for once and come when I call.* A little longer, and the wooden spoon would come off the wall. She mounded the mud with her palms. A breeze blew down from the hills and ruffled the water. She went goosebumpy then, but still she lingered beside the trees.

Her mutti was on the stoop when Etta rounded the corner. Her hand was on her hip, but she wasn't riled, not even a little, and she held the door for Etta and took her muddy shoes. They sat together and ate, and the sun shone through the window and slipped down beneath the sill and was gone.

## 28

S omething flashed in the light. It was a switch plate he saw, maybe even copper though it was too dirty to tell for certain. Georg reached for it and felt the familiar sting. He sucked the blood from his thumb. All along the pile he could hear the curses of men who cut themselves. There were no bandages below, and so they stayed in their places and dug. Best to let it bleed. Let the ash staunch the flow. Ten days after the bombing and the ash was falling still. It floated down from the branches and stung his eyes, and no matter how much water he drank he felt a strange burning in his chest. They were all coughing. The men working the piles and the ladies with their push carts, they wheezed like asthmatics. They spit up dark clots and gasped for air, and one man choked in his sleep, his fingers wrapped around his throat and nobody could pry them loose.

The city he knew had vanished. He'd come out from the shelter that night and nothing was the same. The detonating bombs had opened the buildings and the incendiary bombs that came next had lit them up like torches. The bombs had fallen between Neubaustrasse and Hofstrasse, on Theaterstrasse and Bahnhofstrasse and in the Hofgarten and over the St. Laurentius church with all its flowers from the forty hours' devotion that had ended the night before. They landed on Winterhäuser Strasse and on the Katzenberg and right by the river, and the buildings shook and buckled. The people outside wandered along the wrecked streets. They stepped over the bodies that lay across the broken stones and some of them sat down like visitors and watched the fires grow. The St. Stephan church was burning and the university buildings, the houses, all the houses in old town with their wooden timber frames, and Georg ran toward the river, which was black even as the city burned.

Georg waded knee-deep into that cold water. An old woman beside him slipped in the mud and he took her by the hand. "Let me go," she told him, pulling her hand away. "Better to drown than to burn," and there were people all around him. They stood together in the water. A little boy jumped from the bridge and others lay dead on the river-bank, and somebody must have found a wine cellar with a few unbroken bottles. The ladies carried them to the river, two and three at a time, cradling them like babies against their breasts. They drank while the city burned. They drank and wept and shook their heads, and Georg took one of the bottles and finished it.

The old Ludwig station was gone when he came out and all the letter bags that sat outside its doors. The English Institute and the University Church and St. Michael's had burned, and the nuns died in their convent and one was thrown up into a tree from the blast and flamed like a torch between the branches. The nursing school and the regional archives were gone and all the files for all the patients. Anyone who had stayed too long in the shelters was dead. They'd choked on the fumes. Thousands dead, thousands under buildings and in the streets and nowhere to put them because the cemetery had burned, too.

Some of the survivors walked the back roads toward Zellingen and Höchberg and all the little towns along the river and up in the hills. Their faces were black from the smoke, and their eyes were black, too, and looked straight ahead. Others climbed the piles instead and looked for each other in the ruins. They wrote messages in chalk. *Has anyone seen the Becker family?*, they wrote, *Has anyone seen Jürgen Schiller? Here rest in God the residents of Marktplatz 5. God rest the Melzers*, and *Mariette Heissler, your parents are at 147 Helmstrasse.* The notes they wrote covered all the walls that were left in the city.

Georg was so close to home. Just two days walking and he'd be there, but it was walking toward the Amis and not away from them, and so he stayed instead and dug in the piles and pulled out what he found. Every now and again the men looked west over the river, and the clouds were brown from smoke. The city was calm and no wind blew, but they felt the strange charge in the air. It was coming from the west. Coming like a wave, and soon it would break over them.

Georg reached inside the pile again and grabbed hold of the copper plate. He didn't look down at the street because that's where the bodies were. He looked up instead at the yellow sky. He should feel anger at the Amis and the English who burned his city. He should feel sorrow for the dead, but he felt nothing at all but the need to sleep. At night he lay on the ground with all the other men and boys who had no place to go and he closed his eyes but sleep didn't come and during the day he worked the piles in a daze. Russian prisoners cleared the bodies out. Even now they were looking. They found them by smell and marked the spots with circles, under fallen doorways and in cellars where people had suffocated. The Russians stacked them high like firewood. They dug the graves and rolled the bodies in, and they threw lye between the layers. The old women waited with their shovels and their barrows. Not even a blanket to wrap them, not even a marker for their names. God help them, the women said, God give them rest. Let the earth fall light upon them. They crossed themselves and waited for more.

Georg filled his bucket, and the men grunted around him, and their faces went shiny from the heat. "They're coming to Kassel." The old man below him was shouting again. Every morning he claimed his spot, and sometimes he laughed for no reason and clapped his hands. "Any day now they're coming." He smiled at Georg, and both his front teeth were gone.

"Yes," Georg said, "yes, they're coming for certain." He dropped the plate into his bucket. Even in the heat the old man talked without stopping to rest. He heard things down at the station or along the cots where the officers slept. He repeated them throughout his shift and embellished them. Kassel and Gemünden and Rieneck, they were taking them all, but not Hammelburg. No, the Amis ran back like women there. They choked on their chewing gum. He looked up at Georg and smiled again. The city burned from below. It wasn't the bombs that did it. It wasn't the planes. It came from the tunnels and not the sky.

Georg pretended to agree, "That's true," he said, "you're right," and he wanted to finish the pile so that he could move away from the old man and all his strange talk. It would be weeks before the trains were running. Weeks or months, and the Amis were coming anyway. The crazy old man was right about that much. Any day now they'd be here, and what would it matter then if the tracks were fixed.

Someone shouted from the street below. An HJ boy with dark brown hair was waving his arms. Men gathered around him. They were leaving their carts and standing in line. "Don't go," the old man said. He drew his fingers across his throat. Georg looked up and down the street. There were dozens of Wehrmacht and Volkssturm soldiers at both ends, and who knew where they had come from. They were ready to defend the city. They were going to keep the Allies out. "Russians this way," they were saying. "Russians and women to the left and Germans to the right." The soldiers swung their rifles high. They were gathering up all the German men and boys. An old woman shook her fist. "Idiots," she called to them. "What have you done to us," and she set her scarf around her head, but they didn't listen. They pushed her along.

Georg climbed down. He looked for openings between the men and boys who stood in line, but they were grouped tight together all along the street. Even the old man with the missing teeth came down, but only after an HJ boy shouted at him and began to climb the pile. They walked together to the station, where a sergeant examined them in turn. They waited in lines, soldiers and men with gray hair and boys whose voices hadn't cracked yet. One of the soldiers scratched under his dressings. "It's these lice," he said, "look how they itch. They've worked their way inside," and Georg stepped away from the soldier and his blood-rimmed eyes.

He tried to look like a sorry specimen. He stood crooked, and he would have crossed his eyes, too, or limped to the inspector, but his courage failed him, and he signed his name on a stained sheet of paper and went on to the next table. An officer gave out tunics and steel helmets from the Faulenberg barracks, and they changed their clothes right on the street. The helmet didn't sit right on his head. He pushed it to one side and to the other. More men kept coming in. They'd pulled them from all the piles and from the nearest towns. By noontime the courtyard was nearly full. There was no leaving this time. The Russians were gone and the women, too, and Georg didn't know where they went. Only German men were left in the city, as far as he could tell, German men and German boys.

Georg took a rifle from the table. All this talk of shortages and look how many there were. Old hunting rifles and farmers' guns with cracked stocks and even a few good ones that hadn't lost their shine. He carried it on his shoulder. It was heavy already, and he wanted to set it down. They gave him guns at the academy and at the wall and even old Frau Focht had a gun for him and he set each one aside and walked away and there was always another.

Men coughed while they waited. They rubbed their eyes. An infantryman stretched his arms and bent at the waist, and the light shone on his hair. He turned around, and he looked nothing like Müller, but Georg watched him anyway. *I'll go see your grave if I live.* He reached for his ladies. He squeezed one in his palm and made promises to his boy. *I'll bring news from your family.* How good it would be to meet his parents and his brothers and all the people who loved him best, to see the lines of his jaw again and to sit with them and eat from their table. *I'll plant flowers for you. I'll change your wooden cross to a stone one and set a wreath of evergreens around it, and your marker will be the best one in the field. Everyone who comes will see it first. They'll wonder who lies under that fine stone.*

A Wehrmacht officer climbed the steps. His uniform was clean compared to the ragged jackets of the men in the crowd. He had two green stripes under his garland, which meant he was a first lieutenant, and the youngest boys looked at all his badges. They elbowed each other so they could get closer to the steps. It was time, the officer was saying. The orders came directly from the city commander, from Oberst Richard Wolf himself, who wanted them to fight for every street. All this waiting and now they were taking the city back. It was only dust and jagged stones, but it was theirs.

The boys up front cheered. They knew no better. They didn't want to go home, not when they could fight, and so they whooped and waved their arms, and there was no lonelier place in the world than here inside this crowd. Soldiers from the 173rd engineering battalion and firemen and small Panzer groups from Erlangen and Bamberg and Grafenwöhr, infantrymen in tunics and boys in sandals and everywhere the old men, those gray heads and stooped shoulders and eyes that watered and had no focus. They stood together and listened, and the sun shone down on them through the broken roof. They were standing together in a temple, this is what they probably thought. They were Romans on the Colosseum, and not boys standing in rubble.

Georg blinked hard and looked to the ground so nobody could see his face. He remembered his Latin for the first time in months. The words from Horace came back to him. *How sweet it was, and right, to die for their country*, his father had waved aside the volunteers and recited the poem himself. He read his favorite passages to the class without looking down once at the page, and his voice dipped and rose with the meter, and Georg was certain he'd find him in the crowd now if he looked carefully enough. His father and young Schneider who was alive again and reaching for his book because the Bannführer was coming. He was at the door already. The wall and the city and all those places in between, they were just the same. Men stood and listened for orders. They filled out their papers and gave them to ladies in hats. They pushed barrows and dug in the dirt and saluted when their commanders passed, and nothing changed for them. They'd fight until the fighting broke them.

The officer waved his arm over the assembled men. He divided them into three groups, and boys came down from the steps and stood in the crowd so the lines between the groups were clear. He left with a flourish. He walked between the divided groups, and Georg saw his face as he went by, how soft it was and hairless. He called out once more to the boys before he went. "It's up to you now," he told them. "Your country lives or dies with you."

"Back to his bunker," an old man said in a low voice after the lieutenant had left. "Back to where it's safe," and someone in the back laughed so hard at that he got the hiccups, but the young boys didn't laugh. Eleven years old, some of them, and they were certain they'd beat the Amis when they came. This was all part of the greater plan.

Little by little it would be revealed. Georg watched them, and he hated how eager they were and how different from Müller.

THE MEN ALL sat in circles that evening and watched for signs in the sky. "I think I see lights," someone said. "Just past the bridge there's something burning." They walked and stretched and tightened their boots. They cleaned their rifles with bootlaces and torn pieces from their shirts because their patches were long gone and it was better to go shirtless than to let their barrels foul. They worked and scared each other with their stories. The Americans made their way through walls. They blew holes in houses, and they set off smoke bombs sometimes and moved quick like ghosts through the vapors they made. Yes, someone said, I've seen the smoke myself, how it floats across the water. There'd be nothing left of the city when the Amis and the Tommies were done. Spiteful as Bolsheviks, that's what they are; they'll burn us in our buildings. Georg didn't want to listen, but he heard the stories anyway. He sat upright. He pulled the laces from his boots. They'd broken in places, and he knotted them so they'd hold a little longer.

A few rows over, an infantryman—an ordinary landser—named Krauss waved down all the talk about the Amis. "Better here than in the East," he said. His face was peeling in spots, and his brows were white from the sun. "Anything is better than the winter over there." Men wrapped their feet and wore two pairs of socks, he told them. They sealed their boot soles with wax, and still the water worked its way inside. Canteens froze and their horses died, and they pulled their own sleds then and cursed at the clouds. "Poor bastards," he said. "They'd trade with us ten times over." Not even a fire to warm them because someone might see. Better here than there. Better the Amis than those

Slavs who shouted like Indians when they attacked. *Urrah*, they called, *urrah*, and other times they went quiet and moved easy as wolves between the trees.

Georg set his boots aside. He came closer so he could hear. "It was only luck that I lived," Krauss was saying. In a single night a dozen others died. They lit a fire when they shouldn't have. They were cold and lit a fire, and the Russians saw. He was grazed across his hands and ribs, and all his things had holes. His canteen was hit, and his jacket and his mess kit and even the heels of both his boots. The only thing that wasn't pocked was his lighter.

"God bless it," he said. "It's my lucky charm. It brought me here and now it's spring and there isn't any snow." He rubbed his chin. The men all laughed at that. A lucky trench lighter, they said, who ever heard of such a thing. They left and came back and left again, drifting around him while he talked. His voice pulled them in. They lay down and listened.

"Do you still have it?" Georg spoke in a low voice because some of the men had fallen asleep. They were curled up on their jackets. "Your lighter, I mean."

Krauss tapped his pocket. "I keep it close," he said. "Even when I'm sleeping I know where to find it." He rolled out his blanket and lay down and he laced his fingers as if to pray, and when Georg spoke again, he didn't answer.

The men slept while they could because any moment now they'd be leaving. They needed to start marching early, before the Amis could cross the river and make their way westward through the city. They'd surprise the Amis at the bank. They'd fan out and defend the broken city. Georg went back to his spot. He rolled to one side and then the other, but he couldn't sleep. He heard Mutti's voice as he lay there. She sat beside him, and a breeze was coming through his open window.

Outside boys were playing. They shouted from the branches. She pulled the chair closer and turned the pages, and he shut his eyes and listened. She kissed his head when the story was done. She laid her hand against his cheek.

## 29

G eorg's group left before dawn. They climbed over broken glass and foundation stones and house timbers blackened from the flames. It took more than an hour to reach the Haug church and its ruined dome because there were no straight lines left in the city. Every street was blocked. The men slid and twisted their ankles and scraped themselves against the rubble, and one boy fell hard and bled from both his palms, but it would be just as bad for the Amis coming from the other direction, and they wouldn't expect resistance, either. They'd be taken by surprise. Krauss was ahead in the line. Even in moonlight Georg saw his white head. He followed it like a lantern. He tripped over a jagged metal pipe and twice he stubbed his foot, and Krauss walked ahead, never bobbing and never swaying, steady as a beacon, and there was a soldierly grace in the way he went between the piles.

The other groups had left from their places, too. They made their way westward toward the river. The middle group went up Ludendorffstrasse, and the third group left from the south railway station and crossed up Edelstrasse. It was only a little ways from there to the Hall of Justice and then to the old crane by the bank, and God help those men, Krauss was saying up front, they have it worst of all. They pulled an unlucky number because their route was the hardest to defend, and nobody knew where the Amis were. The men beside Georg

THE VANISHING SKY          259

shook their heads in sympathy, and still they were grateful they weren't in the southern group.

The sky went gold and then pink and there weren't any clouds. A perfect spring day. Georg's group passed Theaterstrasse, and they could double up in places now because the streets were wider and the Russian prisoners had cleared them out. They came to a stretch where all the streetlamps had bent to the ground like ribs and their canisters had popped and melted. It was stranger than any place he'd read about, stranger even than the planets *Sannah* had visited. He wanted to step aside when he saw them. He wanted to sit for a while and close his eyes, but he held his rifle and kept marching. He followed Krauss and his lucky lighter. They were headed toward the river. They were headed toward the bank where the Amis were crossing. He steadied himself, reaching with his free hand for signposts and fences and broken-down walls.

They came to the small streets, Rittergasse and Reibeltgasse and Holztorgasse, where the houses were built one right next to the other and no cars could pass. Neighbors could stand on their balconies and almost join hands across the street. They could look inside each other's windows and smell the meat cooking in kitchens three doors down. All gone now. Just smoke and stones and dirty lace curtains. The climbing was harder here, and the men slowed. Some knelt behind the piles and rested, but Georg pushed on. He didn't stop because Krauss wasn't stopping. He didn't reach for his canteen or his bread bag or bend down to tighten his laces.

Someone tapped his shoulder and whispered. The other groups hadn't made it to the river. They were stopped down by the Justice Hall, and all their men had scattered. "There's no one to meet us," a fireman said. "We're by ourselves." They had climbed across the city, and the bridge was only a few hundred meters farther, just beyond the alleys and the houses. They had guns but not enough bullets and only a single Panzerfaust for when they got close. An old man stood up and began to wave his arms, and three boys pulled him down and covered him. "Let's go to a cellar," somebody said, "let's get inside, let's turn around before they spot us," but they didn't move. They didn't march forward, and they didn't retreat.

Georg stopped when he heard the news. He knelt behind the nearest pile, and Krauss was there already. He was drawing maps in the ash.

"Here's the bridge," Krauss was saying. "And here's the crane, and this alley here will take us to the water. Every house has cellars on this street, and the primary school still has some walls. For cover," he told them, and all the boys nodded. They listened extra carefully because it was a soldier talking, and he had a plan.

Georg looked at the circles and the squares Krauss drew. He drank from his canteen. He was awake as he'd ever been, and all his aches were gone, the blisters and the cuts, his itching feet and the burning in his eyes. He could see every movement, hear every scrape of boots against the broken stones, and still it was a surprise when the shooting began.

It made him queasy, how loud it was, and he spit up the water he'd swallowed. Men ducked into doorways and dove behind the piles, and there was no order to things. He was flat on his belly. He didn't remember jumping down. Plaster fell over his head, and a piece cut deep into his cheek. He crawled toward the nearest door, and Krauss was inside already. He was always just a little ahead. They were in an empty living room. There were no tables left and no chairs, and the floor was covered with glass and plaster. The Landser behind him wasn't quick enough. He went to his knees and toppled sideways, and his hands were dark from where he held his neck. He cried for the longest while, "Mutti," he kept saying, "Mutti," and Georg pressed his palms against his ears. *Let him stop with his calling, let him go quiet,* and then the soldier lay still.

Krauss touched Georg's shoulder and pointed to the stairwell that led down to the cellar. They were outnumbered here in the alley. They needed to find the others so they could make a plan. They went together down the steps, feeling the wall with their free hands. There was a break in the foundation stones, and Krauss worked it with his hands, pulling out pieces and letting them fall. He huffed from the effort, and Georg came and knelt by the hole, and together they dug through the cracks. The dust stung their eyes and stuck fast to the sweat on their faces. Their fingers bled. They could see the neighboring cellar already. They worked more quickly then and pushed the last pieces through the hole. Krauss went first and Georg pushed him from behind, and then Georg went through, and Krauss pulled his arms. God help us, Georg thought, we're retracing all our steps from inside the houses. We're tunneling like cellar rats.

They worked their way from one cellar to the next, and when they reached the end of the block they waited together and listened. There was no way out from the cellar except up to the first floor of the house, and so they climbed the stairs. Someone was shooting across the way, five shots and then a pause, and eight more came from farther up. German and Ami, five and eight, five and eight, back and forth it went. They stopped only to reload or to run and find a better spot. They were in all the windows. Georg and Krauss hid behind the living room curtains and waited for an opening, and closer still a machine gun fired and rattled the empty window frames. The sound took away all his air. Georg held his rifle against his chest. He grabbed the stock and squeezed.

The shots slowed and then stopped, and the only thing Georg heard was roof tiles falling to the street. Krauss looked from behind the curtains. He signaled to Georg with his pistol. *Time to go. Quick, before they start again.* Krauss climbed through the window frame. Georg waited below the sill. He counted, one, two, and he went on three, jumping down to the stones. The air was thick all around him. Things moved slowly and only he was fast, and he saw things with a peculiar sharpness. Curtains fluttered in the empty frames. They hung like streamers and the doors were open to all the houses and even now a few flowerpots sat on the balconies and their vines had started to turn. He heard shots farther down and shouts from the men, and somewhere on Holztorgasse the tanks began to roll.

He was only ten paces behind Krauss, only eight, and Krauss was shooting at a window. He was weaving as he went, but Georg ran straight. Shots came from the windows across the alley. Three quick shots, then three more. Just before they reached the nearest house, Krauss fell and got back up. His leg was stiff, but he reached the door and rolled inside. He was sitting against the wall when Georg came through. He held his thighs with both his hands and fought back when Georg tried to see. The hole was smaller than one of the Ladies. It was clean and the skin puckered around it was clean, too, and white as candle wax, but the blood that came was a revelation. Georg had never seen so much before. It ran down Krauss's leg and pooled on the rough floor, and there was no end to it.

Georg pulled a curtain from the window and shook the dust from it. He folded the fabric lengthwise and tried to tie it above the wound. Georg wasn't even done yet with the knot when the blood bloomed in the lace and soaked it through.

"Give me my gun." Krauss reached around the floor. Sweat beaded over his lips and the first drops rolled down his forehead.

Georg found it by the door. He set it beside Krauss, who gripped the handle and pulled it to his lap. His fingers were black with blood and powder, and he left marks on the wood. "It doesn't hurt," he said. His head tipped down.

Georg shook him by his shoulders and tugged at both his arms. "Wake up," he said. "Open your eyes and look at me," but Krauss didn't hear. His breathing turned fast and shallow. He began to pant. Georg knelt down and reached inside Krauss's pocket. The trench lighter was where he'd said it would be, where he could always reach it, even in his sleep. It was tiny as a lipstick case, and its metal had no mark, not even a scratch or a dent. Georg lit it and snuffed the flame and set the lighter against Krauss's leg. Dust floated in the rays from the window, and Krauss sat in the sunshine, a perfect square of light, and only his eyes were dark. That was how Georg left him, with his luck charm and his gun.

GEORG WENT DOWN to the cellar of this new house and stepped through the hole to the next cellar and the next one after that. They were all connected by common walls, the houses on these small streets, and their rooms looked just the same. He tunneled through four houses, and sometimes he didn't need to dig because the holes were big as doors. He found an old couple in the third cellar, and they lay together on the dusty floor as if sleeping. Their faces had no marks. He covered his nose and kept on climbing.

The walls in the fifth house were thicker than the rest and the hole was smaller. Georg wiped his forehead, and his hands were still sticky from wrapping Krauss's wound. Krauss might be awake now. He'd be hot in the light from the window. He'd need fresh bandages. Someone to wipe his brow. Georg pulled hard on a rock and fell back when it came loose. He pushed himself through the broken wall and dropped to the floor on the other side. He stopped to catch his breath. A hand reached through the hole. Someone was behind him, following through the cracks. The boy made it look easy, the way he jumped to the floor, his bare legs flashing white. He wiped his hands across the front of his shorts. His knees were knobby, and his clothes hung loose. He carried an old Mauser pistol on his belt.

"We were almost there," he said. He pushed his eyeglasses up with his thumb. One of the lenses had cracked. "All the way to the wooden gate and they tell us to turn around." He shook his head at the shame of it.

Georg set his finger against his lips. Best not to talk, not even in low voices. The Amis might hear. They could be just up the stairs. They could be just outside the cracked cellar walls.

The boy shrugged. He walked across the room and looked through the next hole, stepping high on his toes to see. "Soon as I find my group we'll be coming back. Those Amis don't know what they're in for." He hoisted himself up. He kicked his legs like a swimmer and was gone.

Georg didn't follow him. This hole was too small for him. It needed work before he'd fit, but he stayed where he was and didn't try to make it wider. He couldn't hear anything in the adjoining cellar. The knobby boy had slipped through another hole by now. They were reconstituting themselves, those boys, working their way back to the courtyard so they could begin again. Rolling together like mercury drops, and there was no end to things. The Wehrmacht officers were probably still shouting orders from the steps. They were eating and sitting at their tables and waiting for their men to come back from the center city and the wooden gate. Come back and go out again because there was time still to turn things around. Fight for the streets and the alleys and every last house, fight for the broken stones. They're ours and we'll fight for them, and all the while the Amis were taking the city, winding round it like a rope.

Georg crouched beside the cracked wall that led to the street outside. Krauss must be thirsty by now. Georg wanted to turn around and give him water. He wanted to go back to Ingrid and Irmingard and back to September when the leaves were just beginning to turn. Maus was waiting in her room. The windows were wavy with their old glass, and the sun shone through each afternoon and warmed her spot. They were digging every day and hauling up their buckets, and some days the air was warm as summertime. How good to fill buckets and to sleep at night on straw. How good it had been and he hadn't known. The wall was gone and all the boys and the men who'd been there were gone, too. They planted boys in the stony fields and up along the hills. They planted them, and crosses grew.

HE COULD HEAR voices from the street through the broken cellar wall. Some boys were outside, shouting. This cellar was more elevated than the others and the walls were halfway above the ground. Georg stood on some broken stones and looked out through the biggest crack. The knobby boy was standing in the alley with a taller boy in knee socks. "Drop your guns," one of the Americans said in a funny sort of German. "Hände hoch." The taller boy lifted his rifle. "Verdammt," he said, and he swung it around, but the Amis were too fast for him. They shot from the curb and from windows and somewhere overhead. All his joints went loose. He went to his knees and spread his arms across the rubble. The knobby boy turned around. He ran toward a doorway and raised his pistol, and then he fell, too. He made no sound as he bled out. He lay on the street like somebody sleeping, and there were only old men left, who let their guns drop down. Four came out from one of the houses and then another three. They wanted no trouble, those gray men, they held up their hands and stayed in their places. One of them knew some English.

"Don't shoot," he said. "We have nothing but our helmets." They knelt on the street like penitents and waited for instructions.

Georg stepped back from the wall. The Americans had all the river streets. The fight would move toward the dome now and the center of the city. He could still hear shots outside, but they were farther now and beginning to recede. Boys were dying just beyond the alleys. They were fighting and dying, and their fathers and grandfathers surrendered. They stood in line and held up their hands and lived. They followed the Americans who led them to the bank. Who knew there'd be so many men left in the city, the Amis must be wondering. Where to put them, where to keep them all.

Just a few houses away Krauss was sitting, and he'd be sitting there still when his window went dark. His fingers were probably still wrapped around his gun. All those winters in the field, all his walking from one town to the next, and none of it mattered now. Men had fallen around him and were buried in the snowbanks because there'd be no digging in the ground before April, and he had lived through Finland and Russia and all those strange islands. Men stopped to listen when he talked because he'd seen things that were worth telling. He had lived when his comrades died. He had lived and now he was gone. He was like Müller. He took his stories with him.

Georg paced around the room. His cheek hurt where the plaster had cut him, and his fingertips were scabbed. He lifted his gun and set it back down. He'd gotten one of the nicest ones on the table. The others had been jealous, he'd seen it in their faces, and he knew even then it was wasted on him, this fine Mauser with its wooden stock. He thought of Krauss and his luck charm. Who knew why his luck had changed, why all the things he'd done before had lost their spell.

More voices from the street. It was English that he heard now, only English and no German. He listened and was surprised when he understood. He'd been better at French than English and better still at Latin and at Greek. He'd go farther back if he could, to Sanskrit and Chinese, to the hieroglyphics the Egyptians left on their tombs, with their pictures of stars and birds and strange slanted eyes. How nice it would be to sit beside old Zimmermann's shelves and read all those dusty grammar books. Rules were what he needed, rules and quiet and the chance to close his eyes. There'd be no medals for him, no ribbons or carved crosses. Müller was gone and Krauss with his lighter and the coins fell faceup when he dropped them. He wanted reasons for things. He lived while braver men had died, and he wanted to understand.

He tapped his pocket where the ladies were and went upstairs to the first floor of the house. He took a curtain from the wall. The fabric was yellow with dust. He wrapped it twice around his hand. He climbed through the broken window and held the curtain high over his head. Smoke rose from the dome and down by the south rail station. It softened the light and turned it gold, and all the buildings and the men had a halo around them. He stepped over the stones. He walked between the dead boys who had tried to shoot their guns. The English came back now that he needed it. He remembered all the words.

"Don't shoot me," he said. "I have no gun." The wind caught the curtain, and it flapped in his hand like a banner.

## 30

G eorg went to the river and waited with the old men. There was no cage for them yet, and no one to take their names. He squatted by the bank. Tanks were coming across the bridge. They clustered like beetles by the water, and below on the pontoons more men were crossing. All the hills were green with men and trucks and wagons. The line snaked around the Residenz and the Marienberg Fortress and filled both riverbanks. Men worked on the bridges, stepping from the boats and shouting, and others unloaded crates. He started to count the trucks, twenty, thirty, forty, but he stopped because there were too many. They came from the hills and crossed the bridge, and how foolish the plans seemed now and all the talk from the officer up on the plat-form. He had waved his arms and shouted and all the boys went shivery with excitement, and even then the Americans were rolling toward the city. There was no end to the things they brought.

The old men ignored the trucks and tanks. They were glad to rest. They picked the cigarette butts from the ground and lit them, sucking deep and cupping their hands around their mouths. These taste different, they said, they're not quite right, but they reached for them anyway; they breathed in that sweet smoke. Georg sat apart from them because he didn't want to hear their talk. They knew defeat from years before. They wore it lightly. Soon they'd be home with their wives again, and the Ami tanks would be gone. What kind of God was it who would let them live, what kind of justice. They lived and Müller died and so far away from home.

The sky went dark, and one by one the old men closed their eyes. They lay across the grass and slept. Georg wrapped his jacket tight around his shoulders because the wind was starting to blow. Somewhere down below an Ami soldier shouted. The Amis had set up lights to shine on the water. They were working even at night, strapping the next pontoons together. The stone bridges were gone, and so they made new ones and it didn't take them long. All the planning and all the talk from the German engineers who blew the bridges up, who laid the charges and ran, and it made no difference now because the Amis had brought their bridges with them. All that work and only the beautiful things were gone. The saints on the bridge fell into the water. They were powder now and the steeples were gone, too, and the church bells had melted in their towers. Georg lay down and set his arms behind his head, but he couldn't fall asleep.

AN AMERICAN SOLDIER came by in the morning. He walked through the group, but the old men didn't notice. They were looking along the bank. It was breakfast time, and they were hungry and they needed a good smoke, but who knew what the Amis had for them. They'd be lucky to get stale bread. Bread crumbs and cigarette butts and their water had a funny taste and it was better not to drink it. The American pointed to Georg, who followed him to a quiet spot. Just below, men were still working on the bridges.

The American was thin as a plucked bird, and his Adam's apple moved when he swallowed. His name was Biehler, a good German name, and he offered Georg a cigarette. "How good is your English?"

He squinted at Georg and his eyes were flecked and yellow like a cat's. They were the only thing that was beautiful in his face.

"My French is better." Georg spoke slowly. He was careful with his words. He'd rather say nothing than say it wrong. He took the cigarette and set it behind his ear. It was better than money, a fresh Lucky Strike, and he'd trade it later for something to eat.

"We've got no need for French." Biehler smiled a little. He pulled out another cigarette and lit it for himself. "How old are you?"

"Fifteen." Georg stood as straight as he could. "I'll be sixteen in June."

Biehler looked at all the old men. A single soldier was passing out packages, Georg couldn't see what, and they nudged each other for a place in line. "Another fifty years and you'll fit right in." He stood with Georg a while longer and finished his cigarette. "Best get in line before the food's all gone."

The old men were sitting around the packages when Georg came back. One package for every two of them, and they fought for the chewy bars inside and the chocolate and packages of jam. A few had lemon powder too, and they ate it plain because it was good to taste something sour. Georg sat by himself. He'd missed his chance to share a package and it would be a long wait for lunch. He went through the wrappers when the old men were done, and he found a half-eaten bar and finished it.

Biehler watched him that afternoon. He was standing with three soldiers. One of them wore a single gold bar on his shoulders, which meant he was a lieutenant or maybe a captain. Georg wasn't sure about the pins the Amis wore. Schneider would know. He knew all the insignia and the shoulder tabs of the Americans and the English, and he'd started on the Russians, too, because you never could tell where they might send you. *You've got to know your enemies*, he'd say, as if it mattered what the eagle meant, or the chevron or the star. Biehler pointed toward Georg, and the others looked his way and the man in the middle with the gold bar nodded. And when it was dinnertime the old men had to share again, but Georg had his own packet.

THEY CALLED HIM Fritzi and Klaus and little Adolf. He corrected them, "I'm Georg and not Klaus," but they just laughed and paid him no mind. "Sorry, Fritzi," they'd say, "sorry about that." On the second day they brought him to the Marienberg Fortress, and there were papers on every surface inside the dusty hall. Boxes and bags and journals tied with string, who knew where they all came from. They were stacked on three tables and on the floor, and soldiers stepped over them to bring more inside. "It's schooltime," one of them said, and he gave Georg the nub of a pencil and set him to work. He needed to find the party documents, that was all they told him.

He didn't want to read the papers, but he sat at the table anyway and sorted them into piles. Letters and notebooks and ration cards, they were jumbled all together, and some had been wet and their ink had run and they curled at the edges like leaves. Photographs fell out from envelopes. They were clipped to the letters, and a few were even framed. Wehrmacht soldiers who sat in their tunics and ribbon bars and mothers looking stern and girls who'd curled their hair for the photographer and painted their lips. All these people and the things they wrote. *Your uncle's ulcer is better* and *Your sister is a mother again* and *Little Rudi is walking now. He's making trouble all through the house.* It was strange to read these things. It made him uneasy, and what did these letters matter anyway when the Amis had the city and all the towns?

He wrote a number on each party document and kept a tally on his sheets. He had no idea what the Amis were hoping to find in the jumbled piles. An hour per table is what they told him, and only half in jest. He needed to hurry. He needed to be quick, but he lingered over the letters anyway. He read some of them twice. All the mothers sounded like Mutti. *God keep you*, they wrote, *stay strong for us*, and the words were different, but the longing was just the same. They sat at their kitchen tables and wrote letters to their boys, who carried them around like amulets. He rubbed his eyes and blinked, but the tears came anyway. All that time he had, and he hadn't read her letters. He'd left them by the wall.


THE AMIS SAT in the hallway and told each other jokes Georg didn't understand. One of them had found an old stove in the city and a few coal briquettes, and they were heating water outside and brewing instant coffee. An Ami soldier with red hair took a deck of cards from his pocket and started shuffling. "Hey Houdini," somebody said, "show us something new." The soldier didn't look up. He kept on shuffling, going from an overhand shuffle to a riffle shuffle, and Georg left his table and came close enough to see.

The dealer's name was Green. "What's your serial number?" He pointed to one of the soldiers. "Say it loud so everyone can hear." He gave the deck to a short soldier. "Mix them up, Bliss," he said. "Jumble them as best you can."

The short soldier took the cards, and there was trouble in his eyes. He turned cards upside down, flipped them faceup and others facedown and set them together again. The men all laughed at the mess he'd made. "There's no fixing it now," they said. "You've got a milkshake there."

Green took back the deck, and Georg came closer and stood with the other soldiers now and they didn't seem to notice. Green closed his eyes and shuffled the cards and went through them one by one, sliding each aside until he came to one that sat faceup. "I have an ace here," he said. "Let's see about that second number." He went through the cards, and the next one was a seven. The men leaned in now. It couldn't be. A four came next and then another seven. There were exhalations now. Green went through the rest of the cards. "A three," he said, "I've got a three right here and a two, a nine and a four." He fanned them out like peacock feathers when he was done, and all the men elbowed in to see. It was a marvel what he did. There was no explaining it.

"I want to see the deck," Bliss said.

Green held out his hands. "Take a look. I've got no secrets." His face was round as a farmer's. Only his eyes were sharp.

Bliss spread the cards out and looked at them front and back. He stacked them and examined the edges again. He shook his head. He grumbled. The illusion was an affront, Georg could see it in his face. It was a challenge. It called for answers, and finding none, he went peevish. He waved his arm, dismissing Green and all his cards.

"Where'd you learn it?" Georg should be back at his table. He shouldn't bother the soldiers, but he couldn't step away from Green and his fat magician fingers. "I've read all the books, and I never saw that one before."

"That one's mine," Green said. He put the deck back in its box. "They'll name it after me someday." He took out his lighter and played with it, working the spark wheel with his thumb.

"Is that an eye?" Georg leaned in to see the lighter, but Green snapped it shut and dropped it back into his pocket. He yawned, but Georg stayed there. He didn't go back to his papers.

"How about coins?" Georg was close enough to hear Green breathe. He saw every freckle across the bridge of his wide nose. The ladies felt heavy in his pocket, and he took them out and set them on the table. "Do you ever work with coins?"

Green smiled wide as a criminal. "I'm a card guy. You show me something."

Georg shook his head. He stammered and hesitated, and his face went hot. "I don't know any."

"Sure you do. I saw it right away."

"Book magic is all I do."

"Quit your excuses and show me something."

Georg nodded. He wasn't going to argue with an Ami soldier. He cracked his knuckles and stretched his fingers wide because they were stiff from holding the pencil. He took a lady and worked her around his fingers just as Green had done. How good it felt to work the coins again and to have somebody watch. He felt a fluttering in his belly. They had sat together all those nights, and Müller watched and smiled and shook his head. The hollows below his fine cheeks were black, and he looked cruel as a Slav the way his mouth curved. The smile was his reward. How hard to wait through classes and marches and time in the gym when all he wanted was to come back to the room, to take out his pouch and see that smile.

He closed his eyes and breathed deep. He took a coin between the thumb and index finger of each hand and palmed one tight inside his left. He had no patter in English, no funny things to say, and so he stayed quiet and worked the ladies. They'd talk for him. They crossed just as they were supposed to; they jumped the table. He shook his head when he was done. He blinked as if awoken.

A group had gathered around them. "You need more coins," Green said.

"I've lost one. I used to have five."

"Let me see," Bliss said. He'd worked his way to the front of the group. "What does a Kraut need half dollars for?" he told them. "They were stolen probably. Stolen from the bodies or from soldiers' pockets while they slept." He took all four, and then he looked in Georg's jacket to make sure there weren't any more.

"They're mine," Georg told him. "My uncle sent them. My uncle Fritz who lives in Milwaukee." The soldiers laughed when he said Fritz. They slapped their thighs. "They're mine," Georg said again, holding out his hands, but Bliss walked away with the ladies. He dropped them in his pocket, and nobody stopped him or called him back.

Georg stood beside the chair long after the others had gone back to their Easter cakes and their cigarettes. He reached inside his pocket and felt the spot where the ladies had been. All those nights walking, and they were his company. He'd fought Max for them. He carried them to the school and the wall and worked them at old Frau Focht's table. He kept them hidden because people might take it wrong. They were his secret all this time, and now an American had taken them back. A short American with a weak chin and eyes set too close together. Max would laugh if he knew. *Serves you right,* he'd say. *Don't you worry. There'll be more anyway. The country will be full with their coins and their soldiers and all their strange food. You'll be working for dollars soon enough.*

He went back to work without anyone telling him to. He sat at the table with his pile of letters, but he didn't hurry anymore. He skipped things and changed numbers around and ignored the town council and the HJ papers altogether. He hid them deep inside the piles and didn't number them, and when Green left late in the afternoon he stopped at the table and tapped Georg once on the shoulder. "There's no shame in books." That's what he said. "There's no shame in book magic."

GREEN GATHERED ALL the boys and brought them to the hall. He had pictures he wanted them to see. Horror camps, he called them. The

Soviets had found them and the Americans, too. Nordhausen and Buchenwald, Belsen and Ohrdruf, Green struggled with the names. "Have a good look." He spread the pictures on the table. "Come closer so you can see."

The young boys went first, and then the older ones came a few at a time. They stood behind the table and looked and shook their heads because the pictures weren't real. Those were insects and not people. Bony as crickets and some of the men were sway-backed like women and loose in the joints. The boys laughed at first, and then they were angry. They shouted and swung their fists, and their eyes were hard because they knew the difference between the truth and Ami lies. "You can't fool us," one of them said. He said it loud because his anger made him brave. "We're smarter than you think."

Georg waited by the table. He looked at the pictures for a long while, and then he pushed them away and watched the youngest boys. They were talking about the wonder weapon again. They clustered close together and threw looks at Green and the other American soldiers and called them Jews. Always the same light he saw in their faces. Going to the wall and getting their papers and standing on the steps, waiting for orders and for news and climbing back through the holes only to fight again, and even now the light never dimmed in their eyes.

He went to Green. "It's not true what you're saying," Georg said. "You're making things up."

Green shook his head. "There were only bones in the barracks when they came. Eisenhower saw it himself. With his own eyes he saw it." Only ashes and bones and prisoners half-starved by the gates.

"You're making things up," Georg said again. He looked at the boys shouting in the corner, and he wasn't so sure.

"You'll learn." Green reached for that strange lighter he had. He cupped it in his hand and lit his cigarette, drawing deep just like Müller did. Something softened in his face just then. He looked at Georg. "It's a glass eye," he said. He held the lighter so Georg could see. "My father's an optometrist. If you look real close, you can see the capillaries."

THE AMERICANS LET them go. From one day to the next they opened the doors to all the cages, and the men and the boys walked out free. They signed no papers when they left, and no one checked their pockets. The tanks and the trucks went eastward, and most of the soldiers left, too, marching away from the river toward Neustadt and Ansbach and on through the countryside. Georg wasn't supposed to leave with the other boys. New Amis were coming, and they might need him, too, but Georg left anyway. He left as soon as Green was gone and the others were distracted.

He walked north, away from the fortress and the ruined city. He passed through crowds of people coming the other way. They were coming down from the hills, singly and in groups. They rode on wagons and horses and rusted trucks. They slept in tents by the bank and on the railway platform and in gardening sheds, and without anyone giving orders the work began. The barrows came out and the shovels, and even old people worked on the streets. Mothers swept and watched their children, who played beside the piles. The littlest ones rolled balls and knocked down wooden pins; they kicked stones and flew paper planes, and all the broken buildings and the foul smells of the city left no mark on them. They were children. They wanted to play.

A ball rolled past his feet, and one of the boys called to him. "Mister please. Mister toss it back to me." They addressed him like a soldier and not a boy. He picked up the ball and threw it high in the air. It arced over the pile and all the ladies and the old men digging with their buckets. It cut across the sky, and the boys waved their thanks. He walked past them. He walked along the river, and it had gone to green.

Women were working the fields just outside the city. The lucky ones had an ox or a horse, but most plowed the dirt themselves, and the sun shone down on them. For the first time in months he heard birds in the branches. The boys who'd run back toward the north station were gone now. They regrouped and fought again and were gone, and spring came just the same. The air was thick with the smell of tilled fields and of bulbs coming into bloom. Ladies washed their windows and swept the streets. They called to their children. "It's dinner," they said, "time to come home," and the city lay ruined just beyond the trees.

There were men in front of him and men behind. The roads were full with them. They wore gray tunics and police jackets and a few had only surplus Italian jackets with the tabs and straps cut off, and they all walked together. Their holsters were empty and their rifles gone to the Americans, who had collected them in piles and fought over the nicest ones. They tied their jackets around their waists once the sun was high. Their foreheads shone with sweat. In each town the women came running. "Thank God," they said, "thank God in heaven," and they ran to their husbands and their sons. They sounded like his mutti, the way they called. He could hear her voice already. It was a rope, her voice, and it pulled him toward home.

# ACKNOWLEDGMENTS

Grateful acknowledgment is made to *Rosebud* magazine, in which an excerpt from an earlier version of chapter 23 of this novel previously appeared.

Many thanks to the people who helped me improve this book:

Liese Mayer, Alexis Kirschbaum, Barbara Darko, Miranda Ottewell, Grace McNamee, Emily Fisher, Valentina Rice, Marie Coolman, Laura Keefe, and the whole team at Bloomsbury and Bloomsbury USA;

Claudia Ballard at WME and her assistant, Jessie Chasan-Taber;

Michelle Latiolais;

John Reed and the midnight pirates;

my mother, Helena;

my aunt Ute, who painstakingly transcribed my great-grandfather's journals from the years between the World Wars;

the people and town of Marktheidenfeld, Germany, where my family is from and where I spent my first years as a child. The town of Heidenfeld in this book is based on Marktheidenfeld on the Main River and not on the town of Heidenfeld in the district of Schweinfurt;

Alfons Heck and Solomon Perel, who wrote unflinchingly about their time in the Hitler Youth. For those interested in learning more about the Hitler Youth and the Allied bombing raids on Germany, I've included a list of resources on my website;

and the biggest thanks of all to my husband, David, and daughter, Georgia Lee—you two inspire me every day.

# A NOTE ON THE AUTHOR

L. ANNETTE BINDER was born in Germany and immigrated to the United States as a small child. She holds degrees in classics and law from Harvard, an MA in comparative literature from the University of California at Berkeley, and an MFA from the Programs in Writing at the University of California, Irvine. Her short fiction collection, *Rise*, received the Mary McCarthy Prize in Short Fiction, and her stories have been included in *The Pushcart Prize Anthology* and *The O. Henry Prize Stories* and have been performed on Public Radio's *Selected Shorts*. She lives in New Hampshire.

# The Vanishing Sky

## L. Annette Binder

The following questions are intended to enhance your discussion of L. Annette Binder's *The Vanishing Sky*.

### About this Book

In 1945, as the war in Germany nears its violent end, the Huber family is not yet free of its dangers or its insidious demands. Etta, a mother from a small, rural town, has two sons serving their home country: her elder, Max, on the Eastern front, and her younger, Georg, at a school for Hitler Youth. When Max returns from the front, Etta quickly realizes that something is not right—he is thin, almost ghostly, and behaving very strangely. Etta strives to protect him from the Nazi rule, even as her husband, Josef, becomes more nationalistic and impervious to Max's condition. Meanwhile, miles away, Georg has taken his fate into his own hands, deserting his young class of battle-bound soldiers to set off on a long and perilous journey home.

*The Vanishing Sky* is a story of the irreparable damage of war on the home front, and one family's participation—involuntary, unseen, or direct—in a dangerous regime. Drawing inspiration from her father's own story, L. Annette Binder has crafted a spellbinding novel about the choices we make for country and for family.

**For discussion**

1. Books, magazines, and letters appear in various forms throughout the novel. Sometimes they are hidden away, and other times they themselves become a hiding place for something else. What role does reading and sharing stories play in the novel? How do books, magazines, and letters help bring the characters closer together? In what ways do they create distance between the characters?

2. When Etta remembers Willi, the old man who drowned in the river, she thinks that she and her friends had done a tremendous wrong that day and that this wrong could not "be righted in the telling" (page 122). Do you agree with her conclusion? In what ways could the horror of that day have been mitigated if she or one of the other kids had come forward? In what ways is what happened to Willi and the secrecy afterward similar to what happened during the Holocaust?

3. The Huber men are part of official, or semi-official, war efforts. What's the difference between working as a soldier, a youth trainee, and an elderly volunteer? What obligations do Josef, Max, and Georg feel to the German homeland?

4. How does Josef feel about Max's return home, and how does Etta believe Josef feels about it? What events in Josef's past shed light on his nationalist anger during the Second World War?

5. Eventually, Josef, Max, and Georg leave their posts. Which duties do they uphold, and which do they neglect, after their service is over?

6. With so many men gone to fight, the women who are left must often rely on each other. In which ways do women support each other? In which ways do they undercut each other?

7. How did Max treat Georg when they lived together in Heidenfeld? How do the boys of the Hitler Youth treat Georg? What do these relationships tell us about difference, belonging, and friendship in the novel?

8. An early title for the novel was Mutti, which means "mom" in German. Mothers play a key role in the story, and both Etta and Georg think of returning to their mothers as they navigate the difficult days just before and after the German defeat in the war. What does it mean when Etta returns to her Mutti after the city has been bombed? Why do you think the writer chose to end the scene in this way?

9. "Of all the gifts his uncle had sent, Georg loved the coins the best" (21). What do coin tricks mean to Georg, and how do they connect to his former life in Heidenfeld? How does Georg respond when he loses his coins to the American soldier, after having protected them during his flight from the Westwall?

10. The novel is narrated in the third person, but it begins as if over Etta's shoulder. Which other characters are part of this mode of narration (called "close" or "focalized")? And which are described more distantly, without access to their thoughts? How do these modes of narration affect the telling of the story?

11. Compare and contrast Georg's relationships with Frau Focht and Ingrid. What do they give him, how do they help him, and what dangers do they warn him of? What does Georg feel when he leaves them?

12. What's the role of Roman Catholicism in the novel, and which characters are most observant? What does Georg's conversation

with Father Zimmermann (212–15) tell us about the intertwining of church and state in Nazi Germany?

13. The Americans bring evidence of the Shoah to the captured Germans (275–76). In what ways does the novel refer to the murder of Jews, the Roma, and the disabled? How do Georg and the other boys respond when they learn of these horrors?

## Further Reading

*The Reader*, Bernhard Schlink; *The Boy in the Striped Pyjamas*, John Boyne; *Rise*, L. Annette Binder; *Warlight*, Michael Ondaatje; *The Invisible Bridge*, Julie Orringer; *The Book of Aron*, Jim Shepard; *All the Light We Cannot See*, Anthony Doerr; *My Own Dear Brother*, Holly Müller.

For first-hand accounts of life in the Hitler Youth and the strategic Allied bombings of German cities: http://lannettebinder.com/sources .html